EXPLOSION

Dark Anomaly, book 3

Marina Simcoe

To my husband.
Thank you for being on the same side with me. Always.

Explosion

This book is a work of fiction. Names, characters, places and incidents are a product of the author's imagination. Locales and public names are used for atmospheric purposes. Any resemblance to actual people, living or dead, or to businesses, companies, events, institutions or locales is completely coincidental.

Cover Design by Naomi Lucas and Marina Simcoe

First Edition

Spelling: English (American)

Editing and Proofreading by Cissell Ink

Explosion is a Science-Fiction romance. It contains graphic descriptions of intimacy, violence, and discussion on topics that may be triggering for some. Intended for mature readers.

Chapter 1

The armrest of my seat snapped off, its sharp end jamming into my side. Blinded by pain, I doubled over. The seat belt yanked me back against the seat, jolting my injury. The lightning of agonizing pain shot through my side, making the world around me fall away for a moment.

Blood, warm and sticky, trickled down my skin. The material hadn't been ripped however, so no blood marred the outside of my pale-blue bodysuit covered with holographic patches of sponsor logos.

"Are you okay?" Jose rushed to me to help me out of my seat.

"I'm pretty sure I broke a rib," I groaned, holding onto the side that hurt like hell. What if it was more than just a broken rib? "I'm bleeding."

Lee, our scientist, said something about a medical chamber. Jose checked with the rest of our team of six, making sure no one else had been injured during the landing that felt more like a crash.

Something had happened when Jose was piloting our spaceship in for a landing. The anomaly in space we'd come to hadn't been well explored. We'd expected differentiations from the landings we'd done while in training. As one of the pilots, however, even I couldn't tell exactly what had knocked us off the carefully calculated trajectory. Jose had obviously lost control during the approach. We needed to discuss this in a briefing...

A screeching noise cut through the air.

Were we not done crashing yet?

"Get the suits on, everyone!" Jose shouted. "We have a hull breach."

Lee helped me to the hatch where our spacesuits were kept.

An oval cut-out from the wall of our spaceship fell in, then the interior filled with smoke. I coughed, jolting my wound with mind-blinding pain.

A massive *errock* emerged from the smoke, tossing a lifeless body of one of our engineers to the floor. I hadn't seen the engineer being killed, but I knew the man was dead when his body hit the floor, his limbs dangling like those of a rag doll, his head bent at an unnatural angle.

Without pausing, the *errock* murdered our second engineer by snapping his neck as if it was a twig.

"Oh, my God..." I whimpered. My knees went soft, pain and horror made my head spin. Staggering back to the wall, I slid to the floor.

This must be a nightmare, a hallucination brought on by the pain from my injury and by the loss of blood. It just couldn't be real.

"Run!" Jose shoved Nadia out of the *errock's* way, then grabbed a long tool from the shelf in the suit storage.

Brandishing it over his head as a weapon, he charged the murderer.

The *errock* took the blow on his thick, wide shoulder. Lifting his enormous fist, he smashed it into Jose's arm, against the elbow joint.

With a harrowing crunching sound, my captain's arm overextended and broke. Jose cried out in pain, his weapon dropping to the floor from his weakened fingers.

The *errock* trapped Jose's head between his huge hands and yanked it with a twist.

I watched in horror and disbelief as my captain, my friend, the man I'd hoped would be more than a friend one day was murdered right before my eyes.

And I couldn't take it.

"No..." I tried to crawl to Jose when the killer tossed his limp body on the floor, just a few feet away from me.

My head swam, a bout of dizziness sending me into darkness.

God, please let it all be just a nightmare, or don't let me wake up at all.

WHEN I CAME TO, IT became clear, the nightmare was real.

Another *errock* joined the first one. They now argued over Nadia. Our poor movie producer was lying on the floor, with one of the *errock's* standing over her.

I searched the place for anything I could help her with. The long tool that Jose had dropped was to the right of me, on the floor. If I stretched my arm...

The pain in my side sent me back into the fetal position, both arms pressed to my middle. Hot searing agony spread through my chest. Every breath hurt. I wiped my mouth on my shoulder, it left a red smudge of blood on my suit. The material quickly absorbed it, but it was clear, the injury had caused some internal damage.

A soft noise reached me, like someone was clicking their tongue. It came from the cut-out in the wall. I glanced that way, finding a person standing there, just outside of our spaceship. A *damirian*, I recognized the beige skin and hair of that species.

At first, I thought it might be a hallucination. Tall and lithe, the newcomer wore a serene expression, so out-of-place with the carnage and violence inside the ship. Then I realized, the *damirian* was of the neutral gender, which explained its enviable composure in the middle of hell.

It made another clicking noise with its tongue, gesturing me to get out.

"Kill those who are aggressive," the *errock* standing over Nadia said to the one who'd murdered Jose and the rest of our team. "Let the captain deal with the rest. Those are the rules for each new ship's arrival."

Was he *protecting* Nadia?

I glanced back at her. She looked terrified but alert, watching both *errocks* intently.

A large, three-headed animal leaped in from the opening in the wall. I stifled a scream of horror as it sniffed, turning one of his heads my way. It then, thankfully, headed to the *errocks*. The two didn't pay me any attention, either unaware of my presence or thinking me dead.

The *damirian* at the exit energetically gestured for me to get out.

I had no idea what waited for me outside the ship. *Damirians* were a peaceful nation, though. Their species were born as a neutral gender and became male or female when they met their partner. I'd only ever seen the *damirians* of neutral sex, and even then, only on TV. Those of the neutral gender served in the government and came to Earth with delegations from Ak'ae, their planet.

The one gesturing to me to get the hell out right now was definitely of the neutral gender. Its body lacked the colors that I heard the other genders developed.

Compared to the *errocks* inside the ship, the *damirian* definitely seemed a safer choice.

Gathering my strength, I crawled toward the exit. My arms shook and my knees trembled. Dizziness disoriented me. Consciousness threatened to leave me again, but I kept moving, pulling myself with my elbows toward the table that stood between me and the exit, then over to the wall with the cut-out.

A sound of footsteps came from the outside. Someone was rushing this way.

The *damirian* raised its hand, urging me to stop moving. It then pinched its lips between its thumb and pointer finger, in the universal sign of silence. Clearly, the *damirian* didn't want the attention of the others on me. It wanted me still and silent.

Too hurt and exhausted to figure out its reasons, I simply did what it wanted of me. Muffling a groan of pain, I lay still by the wall next to the cut-out.

"Hey, what's going on here?" A voice sounded from what seemed like right above me.

"Another ship!" someone exclaimed excitedly.

They spoke different languages, but my translator picked up both, flawlessly conveying the meaning to me.

"Holy fuck!" the first one yelled. "Is it a female?"

I drew my head into my shoulders, afraid they'd spotted me.

"Of course, the *errocks* got to her first," he added with disappointment, and I realized he was talking about Nadia.

"The captain's female?" another one asked.

"No, it's a new one. Look, over there."

"The captain's woman went back to her room a while back," a calm voice which I assumed belonged to the *damirian* replied. "This is a new female. Just arrived. Hey," it added casually. "Vrateus still doesn't know about this. Whoever tells him first would most likely get a reward. What do you think, Valmo?"

"A reward?" One of the other aliens sounded intrigued. "Like what?"

"Well, I don't know. Maybe relief from your chores tomorrow. You could sleep in then play cards all day."

"Shit! I'm in!" Valmo hurried away, with the scurrying sound of several sets of feet. Whoever Valmo was, his species must have had a lot of legs.

"How about you, Gahot?" the *damirian* continued. "Don't you want to earn a favor from the captain?"

"Nah," the other male replied. "The *errocks* are about to fight. I want to watch."

I ventured to angle my head a little and saw the pale-blue tentacles slinking over the edge of the cut-out in the wall. Gahot must be a *yourlu*, another alien species of the Federation.

All nations currently in the Federation were civilized and peaceful. Wherever we'd landed, however, I wasn't sure I could trust any of them, not after all the murders I'd witnessed. I probably shouldn't be trusting the *damirian* either. But what choice did I have?

I was about to pass out from pain and exhaustion. I'd rather be away from the murderous *errocks* when that happened.

"Oh look! Who is it there?" the *damirian* said loudly, frantically gesturing to me to climb out at the same time.

"Who?" Gahot asked stupidly, turning to look down the corridor where the *damirian* was now pointing.

Pressing an arm to my side, I awkwardly climbed out through the cut-out and crouched behind the *damirian's* legs. It had its arm wrapped around the *yourlu's* shoulders, directing his attention away from the cut-out and from me.

"Not there." The *damirian* turned the *yourlu* back to the ship. "A fight right there. See?" It pointed inside the ship where the argument had escalated to shouting. Then, the sound of flesh punching flesh came. The fight had started.

"Yeassss!" Gahot released a satisfied hiss. "My bet is on Wyck. He's so damn big!" There was an undisguised appreciation in Gahot's voice, the *yourlu* obviously placed a huge importance on physical size.

Trying to make as little noise as possible, I scurried along the wall in the direction the *damirian* discreetly gestured for me with his hand behind his back.

Outside of the ship, the indoor space had the shape of a long corridor, with uneven floors and dented, mostly white wall panels. There were no windows here. The illumination came solely from the lit cables loosely draped along the ceiling.

How far did the *damirian* want me to go? I had no strength to get up and walk. Crawling over the dips and cracks of the floor aggravated my injury. I pressed my arm to my side, but that didn't stop the warm sticky blood trickling down my side inside the suit. I was losing too much blood for the suit's material to absorb it all.

A sound of thundering footsteps rushed up ahead, coming closer.

Were those made by a friend or a foe?

Most of my crew had been murdered violently. I harboured no illusions and dreaded the worst. Not waiting for them to come closer, I scrambled for a place to hide. There was a set of white doors, shaped like an accordion, on my right. With no time to think, I shoved one half aside and slipped in.

Air, rich with moisture, hit my nostrils on the other side of the doors. The place I found myself in appeared to be a botanical lab or artificial gardens. Raised pots formed passages through the large space, which was illuminated by bright white light. Plants of all shades of green and purple grew in neat rows in the planters. Some were tall enough to form dividers throughout the room, which made it impossible to accurately judge the size of this place.

The sound of the footfalls filtered through the doors to me. Not knowing if the newcomers were on their way to the gardens, I crawled behind the nearest planter, trying to hide out of sight.

Thankfully, there was a small alcove in the wall behind the planter, and I climbed inside it. With my legs drawn up to my chest, my entire body fit inside the alcove.

The effort of crawling through the corridor had drained me of energy completely. Stifling a moan of pain, I leaned against the wall.

The flesh around my ribs throbbed and burned. Gingerly sliding open the front closure of my suit, I examined the injured area. Blood had been collecting inside the suit. It splashed out, leaving a bright red puddle on the floor. How much had I lost so far? My head swam with dizziness, and my limbs felt cold.

The entire left side of my chest and stomach, between my breast and the hipbone was generously smeared with blood. Through the long rip in my skin and muscle, I saw the white of a bone...*my* bone.

The sight made me nauseous.

I threw my head back, leaning it against the wall. My mind teetered on the fringe of consciousness. I clung to the last shreds of my awareness. If I passed out, I would bleed to death, alone.

I thought about Nadia, the last surviving member of my ill-fated crew. What would happen to her, now? With the two brutal *errocks* fighting over her?

The *damirian* had sent someone to get the captain, which sounded like a person of authority. Hopefully, the captain would stop the *errocks* from harming her. Maybe, he'd punish the one who'd killed Jose, Lee, and the others. There must be some kind of order around here, whatever this place was.

Maybe, they could help me then, too?

My hands shook, covered in blood. I touched the wall with my finger, leaving a smear of it on the dirty white surface. No one would see me here, behind the planter if I fainted.

Reaching as high as I could, I wrote, *"Help Me,"* on the wall, using my own blood. I wrote in English which the aliens were unlikely to understand. The only person I trusted not to harm me if they found me unconscious and completely defenceless was Nadia. And I desperately hoped she was safe and sound herself.

For a moment I just sat there, staring at the red letters. I wondered whether it was hope that made me write it or the desire to leave a mark on this world—the last mark before I left it myself.

Then, the swell of dizziness rose higher, shrouding my mind in absolute darkness.

Chapter 2

<u>*VAL*</u>

A song filtered through to my awareness. It had no words, but it had a melody to it—soft humming pleasantly buzzed in my ear.

The pain ebbed and rose with its rhythm. Each wave of agony came slower and smaller than the one before, as if the humming took some of the pain away. I let my mind ride the sound, the darkness inside me growing smaller with each crest of the soothing melody, until it took me away, luring me into a sleep where there was no pain at all.

SOMETHING SMELLED NICE. Like herbs. Italian seasoning? And coriander? Not quite the same, but just as pleasant.

I shifted on my back, turning toward the smell. The movement painfully echoed in my side, but it was no longer the sharp, mind-blinding agony as it used to be.

"Stay still, lest you crack your ribs again and make another hole in your lungs," a calm voice warned.

"Who's there?" I tried to raise my right arm. It worked for a few moments. Then, my muscles trembled and my arm dropped back to my side. "Where am I?" I mumbled, opening my eyes.

"At my place," the same voice replied. "I said don't move," it added sternly. "You don't have the strength for it yet."

I stared straight up above me at a piece of tapestry draped like a canopy over the bed where I lay. Embroidered with weird plants and unfamiliar animals, the tapestry also had garlands of beautiful strange evergreens suspended under it. Their leaves had the shape of snowflakes.

"What is this place?" I winced, trying to remember anything that happened after my journey to what they called the space anomaly GR-A8502.

"Like I said, it's my room." A note of pride slipped into the voice this time. "It's warm, clean, and safe, which is something to be treasured on the Dark Anomaly."

Very carefully, I turned my head toward the voice. The *damirian* sat in a chair at my side in the room with sunny-yellow walls. On the low table next to it, a painted clay pot steamed with something fragrant in it.

The *damirian* took a wide cup in its hand, then spooned some dark liquid into it from the pot.

"How long have I been here?" I asked, trying to collect the broken pieces of my most current memories.

"For sixteen days now. You have no strength left in your muscles. To regain it, you'll need to eat." It leaned closer to me, holding the cup in one hand and lifting my head with the other.

"What is it?"

"Vegetable broth." It brought the cup to my lips.

Pieces of black gelatinous mass floated in the dark liquid, though it smelled rather appetizing.

"What are those?" I wrinkled my nose at the sight of the blobs. "Something is swimming in it."

"Swimming?" The *damirian* tipped the cup its way, taking a look inside. "It's an egg, you dummy. You need protein to recover your muscle strength, and boiled meat stinks too much for me to allow it anywhere near my quarters." It pressed the edge of the cup to my lips. "Drink."

I closed my eyes to get rid of the nauseating visual of the black blobs, and took a sip. The solid pieces of the egg slipped past my lips, making my stomach roil. The delicious taste of the warm, flavorful broth, however, made up for the unpleasant sensation.

"It's...good," I said softly, when the *damirian* lowered my head back to the pillow. I inhaled slowly, as not to aggravate the pain in my side, the tiny effort of taking a drink had exhausted me. "Did you say I've been unconscious for over two weeks?"

"Well, not *entirely* unconscious, but I did keep your mind in a twilight state."

"What exactly does that mean?"

The *damirian* glanced inside the cup with a dissatisfied frown. Clearly, it didn't like how little I'd managed to drink.

"You had some broken ribs," it said. "One of them punctured your lung. You lost a lot of blood. Grave injuries like that are best to treat without the mind's involvement."

"So, you knocked me out?"

"I kept your mind from interfering with the healing process of your body," it corrected tersely. "Your bones and lungs didn't need your brain sabotaging their recovery with grief and mourning."

Grief and mourning...

The pieces of memories suddenly snapped together, forming the horrifying picture of our landing.

"They're dead..." I whispered, closing my eyes again.

Now, I wished so badly to return to that blissfully numb place, with nothing but someone's humming in my brain.

"Yes. They're dead." The *damirian's* voice sounded somber but lacked any true sorrow or compassion. It was like it accepted my grief but couldn't feel it.

Dead...

The pain, a million times greater than any physical injury, crushed my heart. They all had families, friends, loved ones who'd never see them again.

I'd never see Jose...

My eyes burned with unshed tears, and I briefly turned my head away from the *damirian,* needing a minute to collect myself. Its actions toward me had been kind, but I didn't believe it'd done it simply out of the kindness of its heart. I was not going to cry or mourn openly in front of it.

Instead, I swallowed past the tightness in my throat and asked, "And Nadia?"

The *damirian* shot me a glance, its eyes the same beige color as its skin and its long, braided hair. The green and purple vines, the *damirian* had woven in its many braids were the only bright colors on its figure.

"All dead," it reiterated. "Nocc killed them all."

All dead.

The words crushed me, blocking my throat and settling heavily in my chest. I groaned, throwing my arm over my eyes to hide the tears I could no longer hold back.

"I shouldn't have left her there, alone," I wailed, guilt and regret rocking through me.

"Then, you would've been dead, too." The *damirian's* even voice grated on my nerves, even if what it was saying was true.

"What is this place?" I exclaimed. "Is there no order? No justice here?"

"Not much." It shrugged.

I rose on my elbows, grinding my teeth against the renewed pain in my side.

"The murderer must be held accountable. I have to talk to the captain—"

The *damirian* slammed the cup down on the table, its irritatingly perfect composure finally wavering.

"I said you need to stay still," it snapped at me. Pressing both hands on my shoulders, it forced me down on the bed. "No sudden movements, or you'll stay in bed forever. My healing skills aren't limitless, you know. There's only so much I can do if you don't help me by taking care of yourself."

"But I have to—"

It pinned me with its stare.

"There's nothing you can do. Not one damn thing, got it? If you try, you'll die." Its voice was sharp as steel, the serene expression blew away from its face. "I saved your life. Do not throw it away now. No one but me knows you're here. Keep it that way."

"You didn't tell anyone?"

"No, I didn't. And you can't leave here without my permission. If anyone, I mean *anyone* in this place finds out about you..." The *damirian* inhaled deeply then released the air slowly, as if trying to gather its composure once again. "They will kill you," it said in a somewhat calmer voice. "But they'll make you their sex toy first."

"They, what?" I gulped the air in one shaky breath.

The *damirian* leaned over me, keeping its hands on my shoulders.

"There are no women on the Dark Anomaly—"

"How about the captain's woman?" I recalled him mentioning her in his conversation with the two other aliens at the cut-out entrance from my ship.

He blinked, pausing briefly.

"She is dead, too," he said quickly.

"Why?" I gasped.

"Because that's what happens to females around here," he bit out. "Like I said, there're no women on the Dark Anomaly. But there're hundreds of males. Most of them belong to the species that react exclusively to females, which means they can't even have a satisfactory sexual relationship with each other." Its colorless eyes held mine. "Hundreds of males who haven't had sex with a female for decades. How long do you think you'd last?"

I closed my eyes, unable to bear the *damirian's* stare. It couldn't be true what he was saying. People couldn't be this cruel. These things didn't happen anywhere in the world anymore, not on any of the Federation planets.

This wasn't a Federation planet, though. Murders in cold blood didn't happen out there either. Here, however...

No one had known that life existed on the Dark Anomaly before we came here. But now, I knew, and I wasn't going to be silent. I'd report the atrocities that had taken place here, and I'd bring justice to this place myself. I owed that much to the families of my crew.

I had to get well, if only to get out of here.

The new resolve helped smother my grief like a heavy blanket would put out a fire—for now, anyway. I still felt like crawling into a hole somewhere and screaming until my lungs burned and my voice was gone. But in the *damirian's* presence, I wiped my tears away and managed to compose myself.

"For what it's worth, thank you for saving my life," I said, my voice only slightly shaking.

The *damirian* let go of me, sitting back in the chair.

"You're welcome." It accepted my gratitude with a dignified tilt of its head. "What's your name?"

"Valentina." I managed to hold back a sniffle. "My friends and family call me Val or Valya."

Well, my friends stuck to Val. Only my parents and my brother had called me Valya. Both of my parents had been dead for years now. My brother had married and moved to another country. He had two daughters now, my baby nieces. I adored them, though I didn't get to see them nearly as often as I would've liked.

The *damirian's* forehead wrinkled.

"Your friends and family don't like you enough to bother pronouncing all syllables of your name?"

I blinked, wondering if it was its usual sarcasm or just genuine confusion.

"It's a nickname, a form of endearment..." I tried to explain then just waved my hand its way. "It doesn't matter. I really don't care what you'll call me. What's your name, anyway?"

The *damirian* pressed an arm across its chest, inclining its head in a stately, elegant bow.

"I'm Malahki."

"It's nice to meet you, Malahki." I tried a bow, too, which wasn't easy since I was still lying on my back. "It's a pretty name," I said genuinely admiring the sound of it.

Its brow furrowed at my compliment. Had I said something wrong?

"Pretty?" it echoed, a muscle in its jaw ticked.

"Um, I meant it in the nicest way possible," I clarified, wondering if there might be something wrong with the *damirian's* translator.

Its elbows on its knees, Malahki leaned forward, gazing at me intensely.

"Instead of gratitude for saving your life, may I ask you for a favor?" it asked.

"Of course," I nodded. "If there is anything I can do—"

"Can you think of me as a male, please?"

"A male?" I stared at it, confused.

"Yes. I'm a *he*, not an *it*."

I'd never met a *domirian* in person before. I'd only seen them on TV, and I read a little about their technology and their political and social structure. To my knowledge, it was considered insulting in their culture to attribute a person to a wrong physical sex. That included the pronouns.

Did I get Malahki's sex wrong? I'd only ever seen *damirians* of the neutral gender. Maybe the male sex wasn't that different physically as I'd thought?

"A *he?*" I asked again.

As if on its own, my gaze slid down to between its...*his* legs. In Malahki's current position, I had the unobstructed view of his groin. And since he wore no clothes, I could plainly see the smooth surface of his skin between his thighs. A slightly darker, barely visible line marked the vertical seam behind which the base for his reproductive organs lay dormant, completely invisible from the outside.

He was most definitely of the neutral sex.

Malahki followed my gaze with his eyes and cleared his throat. However, he didn't cross his legs, not trying to hide or deny the obvious.

"Will that be difficult for you? To think of me as a man, even if I'm not one, physically?" he asked, the same intense expression on his face.

"No, of course not," I protested. "Back home, people often decide for themselves what gender they belong to. What's between your legs doesn't have to define you," I blurted out, then tried to explain my initial hesitation, "It's just that I thought it was different for *damirians*. Once you choose your identity, the corresponding...um, physical attributes of the sex grow quickly.

His eyes narrowed slightly.

"And who told you that?"

"Well, no one. That's just what I've gathered from some articles I've read. There isn't that much information on your sexual development or customs, to be honest," I admitted.

"No." He pursed his lips, disapprovingly. "We don't advertise our species' gender specifics to everyone. Unlike humans, we don't send pictures of our naked bodies, complete with reproductive organs, all over the galaxy."

"What are you talking about? We don't do that."

He lifted a tablet off the floor and presented me with the picture on its screen.

"This has been sent from your planet, has it not?"

It was a drawing of a human male and female side by side next to the pulsar map.

"Oh," I rubbed my forehead. "That was a part of the message humans sent into interstellar space long ago, before our planet had been discovered by the Federation. Did we have it on the ship along with other historical documents? Why do you even have it?"

"I found it in the library when I searched for information on how best to treat your injuries. This particular picture proved useless for that." He tossed the tablet aside. "You don't even look like this woman."

I followed the tablet with my gaze, looking at the image from his point of view. I definitely didn't have the curvy hips or even the fairly average breasts of the woman in the picture. Mine were much smaller. Visually, I was probably closer to Malahki's body shape than to hers. Taller than average, I'd often been called "sporty" based on my looks. However, I didn't really do that many sports. I liked jogging early in the mornings. And I played beach volleyball with a group of friends, back on Earth.

"I do have long hair like hers," I muttered, dragging my gaze away from the screen. Though, the woman's hair appeared blonde on the drawing. Mine was dark-chestnut, with faint reddish highlights. The length was about the same—somewhere between the shoulders and the waist.

"So do I." He shrugged. "I have long hair, too. That doesn't make *me* a woman."

"True." I shifted on the bed again, very carefully. My side hurt less, but lying in the same position made my back muscles ache.

"Well, whatever you've done worked, I definitely feel better." Physically, at least, I did.

"You have to drink all of this." He lifted the cup of broth again.

Closing my eyes, I did as he said, taking a few big gulps.

As my stomach filled with the warm aromatic broth, my mind kicked into gear. I needed to contact Earth, inspect my ship, find a way to take the bodies of my teammates back home...

"What is the best way to send a message from here?" I asked when Malahki took mercy on me and let me take another break from drinking.

"There *is* no way," he said simply, setting the cup down. Taking a piece of soft cloth from the table, he wiped the corners of my mouth with it.

"Well, maybe I could sneak back on my ship, just to use its communication system, then—"

"You can't." He stopped my attempt to argue with another hard stare of his. "First, communication signals don't go through the Dark Anomaly's force field. Second. Remember what happened on the ship? It's not safe. You can't go there. You can't leave the gardens. In fact, I prefer you didn't leave this room at all."

He leaned over and fluffed the round pillow under my head.

"Malahki," I said quietly, but firmly. "I need to inspect my ship, fix what needs to be fixed, and go back to Earth."

He heaved a sigh, sitting back in the chair.

"This is going to upset you," he muttered under his breath.

"What? What is it?"

He bent over, picking up the tablet again.

"Let me tell you more about this place, Valentina." He changed the slates in the tablet frame then turned the screen with a blueprint on it to me. "We call it the Dark Anomaly. And there is no leaving it."

Chapter 3

I cried. These were the ugly tears I hadn't wanted Malahki to see but now no longer cared about hiding.

It had taken me a while to fully comprehend what Malahki had been saying when he showed me pictures, diagrams, and numbers. Once the meaning of them hit me, it all came crashing down on me at once.

The phenomenon we called "the space anomaly GR-A8502" turned out to be nothing more than a junkyard of crashed ships, smashed together into a disk by an inexplicable force. It was hurtling through space, sucking in all powered objects with the live beings still on board.

It had done it for thousands, millions, or maybe billions of years. Entire lives had been lived here. With no escape.

Time was warped on the Dark Anomaly. In the sixteen days I'd spent recovering, over thirteen years had passed back on Earth. No one had come looking for us. In another month or two, our expedition would live only in history books—just another unsolved mystery of space travel...

Our friends and family had mourned our disappearance and had most likely declared us all dead, including me. They had plenty of time to move on by now—all while I was lying in bed in a semi-conscious state. Even if I had been fully conscious all this time, according to everything Malahki had shown to me, I couldn't have done anything to leave here or even let the Earth know of our fate.

"This can't be true," I sobbed, my arms thrown over my face. My tears kept running from my eyes to be soaked up by the embroidered pillow under my head. "I need to go home."

He stroked my hair soothingly.

"This is your home, now." There was no real emotion in his voice. He wasn't trying to calm me because he cared, but because my crying probably made him feel uncomfortable.

"There has to be a way..." In my mind, the numbers and graphs Malahki had shown to me made sense. In my heart, I just couldn't accept any of it. "There could be a mistake in the calculations."

"The latest data came from one of your own. She—" he cut himself off, as if having said more than he'd intended.

"One of our own? A human, you mean?" I wiped my tears with my hands, peering at him between my fingers. "Who is *she*?"

"She? No." He shook his head quickly. "There is no 'she.' I meant the most accurate data we've collected came from the probes sent here by humans and from your own ship's landing records." He leaned closer, taking my hand in his. The spark of emotion I hadn't seen before flashed through his colorless eyes. "I'm sorry you're hurting, Valentina. But we can't afford to have hope on the Dark Anomaly. I don't want to watch your spirit die slowly over the years to come."

"You'd rather kill all hope in me, now?" I bit off.

He released a long breath, squeezing my hand tighter.

"The sooner you learn to accept your fate, the faster you'll be ready to fight for your survival in this place. Because sooner or later, all of us will have to fight to survive."

"I don't want to fight." I turned my head away from him. At that moment, I wasn't sure if I even wanted to survive.

He sat in silence for a few seconds, drawing small circles on my hand with his thumb.

The sensation grounded me. I focused my mind entirely on that one small movement of the pad of his thumb along my skin, because if I let myself think about anything else, I feared I'd lose my mind.

"Your fate is better than that of many who have come here before you," he said softly. "I've saved you from the worst. Stay with me, and together we may have a chance at surviving what's to come."

I STAYED IN BED FOR a few more days, fully conscious this time and acutely aware of every second passing by. It was exceptionally painful letting the time pass, when each day translated into ten months back on Earth and each moment took me further into oblivion for everyone back home.

Malahki came and went during the day. He said he had chores to do out in the garden. At night, I listened to his even breathing as he slept on the pallet on the floor next to my bed. The purple vines in his hair glowed soft blue in the darkness, and I tried to come to terms with never seeing sunshine or moonlight ever again.

One morning, after breakfast, Malahki came in holding a bowl of water in his hands.

Since the day of our first conversation, he'd started wearing clothes—or something like it. Two long pieces of brown fabric hang off his belt past his knees, covering his front and his back from my view.

"Time to take off the dressing from your wound." He set the bowl on the painted-wood table next to the bed. "Then, you'll have to take a shower."

"Do I stink?" I asked, opening my suit for him mechanically.

"You smell strong enough for *errocks* to catch your scent," he replied.

Opening my suit wider, he exposed me from the waist up, including both of my breasts.

His attention remained firmly on the healing scar on my side, and his gaze didn't stray upward once. The touch of his fingers on my skin was light and efficient as he cleaned off the dark-green paste he'd applied before.

His complete and utter disinterest in me as a woman had made it easy for me to relax under his touch and let him do the job of my nurse that he'd assigned to himself.

He dipped a piece of cloth into the warm water then washed the green residue off around my scar.

"The mark will stay," he observed. "But it'll get smaller and will pale with time."

"I don't care, either way." The emotional scars bothered me so much more than the physical. Only they would take much longer to heal, and I feared I would never be completely whole again.

He pressed his mouth into a tight line of disapproval but continued in a lighter tone, "I'll help you to the shower now. You have to use the berry soap to make sure *errocks* don't smell you."

Errocks...

The image of the two of them towering over poor Nadia on the day of our landing, rose in my mind again.

Malahki had told me about the various species they had here on the Dark Anomaly. He'd told me about Vrateus, their *themul* captain. All of them had been stranded here for years or decades, but had been missing for millennia to the outside world. Just like I would be, too.

"You can't keep thinking about that." Malahki guessed the course of my thoughts. "You'll drive yourself insane, which would kill you more effectively than anything else around here."

"How long have you been here?" I asked, as he started taking off my bodysuit for me.

"Over five years." He helped me free my arms from the sleeves.

"What helped you stay sane?"

"Work." He dragged the suit down past my hips then carefully lifted each of my legs to take it off completely. "I left Ak'ae, my planet, to operate a botanical laboratory in space. As a technician, my job was to maintain the equipment, collect seeds and seedlings, plant them, and record all stages of the plants' life cycle in space. I was on route to Omphi, the large, water world planet in this area, to collect a few oceanic plant species from there when the Dark Anomaly sucked me in."

"Were you alone in your laboratory?"

He nodded.

"That must be hard, to travel through space all by yourself," I said.

The vastness of the interstellar space had often made me feel small and insignificant on our way here. Having my crew helped retain the feeling of normalcy during the two long months of traveling.

"I never minded being alone," Malahki replied. "In fact, the reason I took that job in the first place was to be on my own."

"Why?"

His gaze slid off me, focusing on something only he could see.

"I always liked the peace and quiet of solitude. The clear thinking with the insight that's only possible when one is on their own and their mind is unimpeded by the erratic urges of the body."

"What urges are you talking about?"

"To reproduce, for one," he said, with a grimace of distaste.

"Wait a moment, are you saying you went away because you didn't want having to select another sex eventually?"

I didn't know it was even possible for *damirians* to remain of the neutral gender forever.

"Many of us wish to remain the way we're born," he replied evenly. "The alternative means losing the blissful calm to rage, lust, and other unstable emotions of either males or females."

"Is it even possible for a *damirian* to remain of the neutral sex? For the rest of their live?" I asked.

"It's possible, but the chance of it is slim if one remains in society. Sooner or later, relationships happen and attachments form. The urge to mate triggers the change."

"So, without a potential partner, there is no urge at all?"

"Absolutely none." He gave me a serene smile, helping me off the bed. "The bliss of calm is the hardest to gain and the easiest to lose. I treasured it."

I stood on my own two feet for the first time in weeks. My knees shook and my hands trembled. I would've fallen had Malahki not held me firmly under my arms.

"This way." He led me behind a brocade curtain, through the narrow passage, and into a metallic bathroom. Cold and unadorned, this must be a part from a different ship than the one where Malahki's bedroom was located, but it looked so different from his colorful room that it seemed to be from another world entirely.

Supporting me with one hand, Malahki unclipped his belt, taking off his loincloth and hanging it by the entrance. He then turned on the water from a cone-shaped spout in the ceiling.

"It's cold!" I gasped as the barely lukewarm water hit my skin.

"Energy preservation, on the captain's orders," Malahki replied, calmly. "You only get five minutes a day, so we need to hurry. This is the soap you'll have to use daily." He made me sit on a stool under the stream then lathered my body with the small brick of soap.

He was thorough, washing my hair and lathering every crook and cranny of my body. Just like when removing the dressing from my wound, his movements remained quick and efficient. He made no difference between touching my breasts or my elbows.

"The bliss of calm..." he'd said earlier, and I believed I understood him well.

I'd never been truly in love, but I knew the yearning for love very well. Ever since I met Jose, I wished he'd notice me not just as a friend and colleague but as a woman, too. He never did, which had cost me a lot of sleepless nights of tossing and turning in sweaty sheets—alone.

Maybe having no desire at all would be a blessing as compared to the torture of wanting what one couldn't have?

"I wish it was possible for humans to be of neutral sex, too," I said.

Malahki spread the water rushing from the spout with his hands, rinsing the soap off me.

"I can see the benefits of not suffering from emotions," I added. Sadness and grief had been hanging over me like a dark shroud ever since I'd regained consciousness, making me long for the oblivion of earlier.

The water stopped, and Malahki put a wide, knitted towel around my shoulders, drying me off.

When he helped me up to my feet again, his expression was no longer neutral. A frown settled over his face.

"What is it, Malahki?" I asked.

"There are advantages that other genders have over the neutral sex," he said slowly.

"What are they?"

He'd asked me to think of him as a male, though he didn't have the physical features of that sex. From what I'd gathered about him, Malahki didn't mentally associate with the male gender, either.

"The main advantage of the *damirian* men is their physical strength," he said.

I exhaled a laugh.

"That's it? Brawn is hardly an advantage by itself."

"Around here, that is all that matters," he said firmly.

"Is that why you want to be male?" I guessed.

He flexed his jaw, his mouth settling into a hard line.

"In the world where physical strength can mean the difference between life and death, yes, I've made the decision to become a male."

Holding me by my shoulders, he settled his eyes on mine.

"Sadly, just wishing for it is not enough, Valentina, neither does simply spending time together, I've tried that. It didn't work. I need a partner who is willing to enter into a relationship with me."

"A woman," I said quietly as understanding of his past actions came to me.

"Yes. The partner needs to be of the opposite sex—"

"And as you've said," I added quickly, "there're no females on the Dark Anomaly, but me."

He blinked, momentarily shifting his gaze aside.

"Right. No one but you."

I swallowed hard, my knees shaking.

"Is that why you saved my life?"

"Yes..." His eyebrows twitched, moving closer together. "Well, no. Either way, I couldn't leave you out there to be brutalized by the *errocks*."

"Well, thanks..." I nervously tugged at a strand of my wet hair. "Apparently, you wanted to keep the *brutalizing* part for yourself."

Malahki's "noble" act of saving and keeping me safe somehow no longer seemed that honorable, since he'd had a hidden agenda all along.

He winced.

"I'd prefer not to go about it in any aggressive way. No brutalizing, please," he assured me. "Can't the mating be done in some more civilized manner? I admit I don't know much...or anything about physical relationships, but I have been thinking about a slower, more natural approach."

I gaped at him in disbelief.

"You're honestly planning to mate with me?" A queasy feeling tightened my stomach as I listened to him speak.

"Eventually, yes." He didn't deny it. "As soon as you're feeling well enough, we'll be sharing the bed every night. You'll sleep naked, as will I. You will show me how you like being pleasured, and I will do it regularly."

I might not have known love, but I knew affection—even if unrequited affection—very well. This wasn't it. There was no attraction toward me in Malahki. There'd been more longing in his eyes when he'd spoken about the serenity of working and living alone in space than he had when he looked at me.

"We can start right now, with a kiss." He closed his eyes and lowered his face to mine.

Malahki was generally a good-looking person. His features were symmetrical and straight, his skin smooth and soft to the touch. His long hair, with several long braids and vines of flowers woven through, framed his face, giving him a flare of artful fantasy. I admired his appearance as I would admire a beautiful picture on a wall.

His body had none of the definite male or female features of his species, but that only meant that both men and women would possibly find him physically attractive, in my opinion.

His looks were not what made me recoil from him. His absolute lack of even the slightest spark of attraction for me made his words sound clinically cold, his proposition revolting, and a kiss between us impossible.

"That's not how it works," I said softly.

Twisting out of his grip, I wished I could run away. My weakened legs betrayed me. I only managed one unsteady step to the wall, then had to brace myself with both hands against it.

Malahki didn't seem to be offended by my rejection. Coming closer, he supported me under my arms again.

"We need to start going for walks in the gardens daily, to build up your strength," he observed calmly, leading me back to the bedroom.

Once there, he helped me into the chair by the bed then lowered himself into a crouch in front of me.

"Like I said, I don't know much about relationships, Valentina, but I'm willing to hear any suggestions you may have."

There was no passion in him, not even close. But I sensed genuine desperation in the way he gripped my hands.

"Malahki," I took a long breath. "You are a strong, capable person as you are. More than that, I believe you're happy with who you are, too. Is it really that important to become someone you don't really want to be, for just a little bit more muscle power?"

He briefly closed his eyes. His chest rose as he inhaled deeply. "Have you ever met a *damirian* male, Valentina?"

"No... I'd never met anyone from Ak'ae at all, other than you."

He opened his eyes again.

"Well, trust me then when I say we're not talking about 'just a little bit more' strength and brawn. A *damirian* male is a weapon on his own, which makes our army one of the best in the Federation. But there is a reason why none of our males hold any position of power on Ak'ae, not even in the upper levels of the Military. Their physical power, combined with almost reckless courage and aggression, makes for a dangerously uncontrollable combination when political governance and military strategy require a cool head and calm logic."

He massaged my hands in his as he spoke.

"I used to find physical strength vulgar, Valentina, especially when combined with recklessness. I still do. But here, on the Dark Anomaly that's what rules—the explosive combination of power and aggression. Until now, I've been lucky to survive by what I am here. My neutrality didn't trigger either the aggression or the lust of the males on the Dark Anomaly. So far, they've let me be. But things are changing. The order among us is shaky. It had crumbled before, and I'm afraid it will collapse for good, soon. When it does, it'll be every person for themselves. Even if no one wants to fuck or fight me, many here wouldn't stop to think twice before killing me for food when they get hungry."

"Really? They would?" A breath lodged in my throat at his words. How many horrors could one place hold?

He wrapped his fingers around mine, slightly tugging my hands to him.

"From what I've observed, those who form groups have a better chance at survival here than those who stay on their own. There aren't many people here I would trust, but I've decided to trust you. I figured you are a civilized person. I've studied everything we have at the library on human culture and values, and I believe your gratitude to me for saving your life would facilitate the mutual respect between us." He fixed his imploring gaze on me. "Help me go through the change, Valentina, and I'll be able to protect both of us much better."

I understood what he said, but what he demanded from me still didn't seem possible. This wouldn't even be sex without love. What Malahki wanted was sex without desire. I knew he felt nothing for me in a physical sense.

"That's not how it works, Malahki," I repeated.

His expression hardened with determination.

"Tell me *how*, then?"

How was I supposed to explain this to him?

"You see, you want me to let you touch me, but you have no actual desire to touch me. This may be even worse than demanding sex for money."

He squinted at me.

"You'd prefer to be paid?" he asked, horribly misunderstanding me. "Do you want money for this?"

"What? No! God, no." I shook my head energetically. "That's not what I meant at all. Listen, I thought *damirians'* transformations are triggered by mutual attraction between the couple that develops over some period of time. Not by any amount of regular...pleasuring."

The last word left a bad taste in my mouth. I didn't dislike Malahki. His touch didn't repulse me when he changed the dressing on my wound or helped me in the shower. But I just couldn't imagine him touching me with any passion or intimacy. And without that, how could there be any real pleasure?

He shifted uneasily.

"First of all." His voice held an edge of annoyance, this time. "We may *not* get to have any long 'period of time together.' Time is a luxury on the Dark Anomaly. One has to earn it first. Second, I have tried to simply spend time with a woman before, and it didn't work..."

"You've tried? Who was she?" I remembered now he'd mentioned something about trying to trigger the gender change before.

He waved me off. "It was a long time ago."

"When? Back on Ak'ae?"

"A long time ago," he said firmly, without elaborating any further. "Tell me, Valentina..." He stared at me for a moment, his eyes narrowed with suspicion. "Did you already have a man back home? Is your heart not free? Because I believe that was what impeded my change the last time. The woman was not free."

The memory of Jose tightened painfully in my chest. He'd never been "my man." Though, I always had a place for him in my heart.

"The man..." I started then exhaled, without finishing the sentence. "I don't have a man. My heart is free, but that's not what it's all about, Malahki. I don't know what to say to make you understand. You know what? Come here." I scooted to the edge of the chair, cupping his chin. "I'll show you."

He'd asked for a kiss, back in the bathroom. So, I drew his face to mine and placed my lips on his.

His mouth felt warm and supple. He dutifully parted his lips, allowing me full access, but I didn't take the invitation. The sensations of touching him never went past my skin. There was no warmth in my chest, no butterflies in my stomach, none of the painfully delicious pull of desire in my lower belly, either.

"Do you see now?" I leaned back. "A touch is just a touch. It's the emotions, right here..." I took his hand and placed it on his chest against his heart. "That makes it special. That's where the real pleasure starts."

He moved his gaze from our hands at his chest up to my eyes. His crestfallen expression and disappointment tugged at my compassion. I wanted to help him, I just knew I couldn't.

"I'm speaking as merely a human here, but I believe you have to feel something in your heart first, Malahki."

He appeared to ponder my words.

"Just me? Or both of us have to feel it?" he asked.

"Both would be the best, of course. But mutual attraction has to start somewhere, right? Sometimes, desire can be contagious. If you know the other person likes you, it may ignite an interest on your part in response." I thought back to Jose and me, and finished, a little deflated, "But it doesn't always happen that way, either."

He let go of my hand and swiftly rose to his feet.

"So, you're telling me you've spent all of your life as a woman, and you can't clearly explain to me how the attraction between sexes happens?" The frustration in his voice came from disappointment, but it also sounded like he blamed me.

"Listen," I said. "I wish I could be more helpful here, but nobody really knows exactly how and why people fall in love."

His lips pressed together, turning nearly invisible. He grabbed another loincloth from the chest by the wall and wrapped it around his hips, hiding from view what wasn't there to hide in the first place

He appeared to view his "sexlessness" as a sign of failure to become in form what he had decided to be in his mind. Except that I believed he wanted it for all the wrong reasons. Malahki didn't really wish to be a male. He just wanted to be stronger than he was.

Maybe that was where his failure lay?

Stripping the sheets off the bed, he started changing the bedding.

"Have you ever been in love?" he asked, in a calmer, more usual for him tone.

"No," I replied. "But there was a time when I longed for it."

He paused with his back to me.

"Did you want to have it with Jose?"

Hearing his name out loud twisted the knife of grief lodged in my chest. I inhaled deeply, taking a moment.

"How do you know about Jose?"

"You said his name many times while I was healing you. Was he one of your crew?" He glanced at me over his shoulder.

I nodded, clasping my hands together.

"My captain," I whispered around the tight lump that nearly blocked my throat.

He came closer.

"I'm sorry you lost him in such a brutal way."

I lifted my eyes to his, surprised by the genuine compassion in his voice.

"You can feel emotions?" I blurted out in shock.

He took the towel from me then helped me back to bed, into the fresh sheets.

"Of course I can," he said, indignantly. "I'm a person, not a machine. I have a heart and a brain to feel and understand. What I also have is the ability to process emotions inside gradually, without letting them explode outwardly. The uncontrolled explosion of emotions is dangerous and can be devastating both to you and others."

He tucked the blankets around my naked body then lifted my bodysuit, holding it between two fingers.

"You've had it on for weeks. I'd better soak it overnight."

I smiled as he wrinkled his nose, holding my suit at arm length from him.

"It's fully self-cleaning material," I assured him. "It doesn't need to be washed."

"It doesn't?" He squinted at it suspiciously. "Well, maybe at least air it out a little."

He shook the suit out, then draped it over the brightly painted, wooden trunk by the wall.

"Thank you, Malahki," I said softly. "I really wish I could help you, and I'm very sorry that I cannot. Unlike yours, my emotions are very much out of my control. I know I could never fall in love or even feel an attraction to anyone at will."

He lowered himself in the chair by the bed again. Propping an elbow in the armrest, he placed his chin in his hand.

"You just get well, Valentina," he said after a long sigh. "Two of us are still better than one. We'll manage."

"Can we still try to be friends?" I offered.

He gave me a small but warm smile and nodded.

"If that's all we're destined to be..."

Chapter 4

As of the next day, I started walking regularly. In addition to bathroom trips, I added a few steps around the room at first. Eventually, my walks got longer. With Malahki's help, I soon ventured into the gardens. We started with a trip around a planter, gradually increasing the distance every day.

At the beginning, Malahki almost carried me, my arms draped around his neck. After a few days, however, my body grew stronger under his care. Eventually, he only needed to support me around the waist with one arm, to steady me.

Malahki chose the early morning hours for our walks in the gardens. He said that was when "the others" were still asleep.

The still largely unknown to me world of the Dark Anomaly had been divided in two parts in my mind. One part was the comfortable, colorfully decorated room where I felt safe with Malahki at my side. Beyond it lay the dangerous, colorless space, with dented walls, bent floors, and equally warped people—"the others." I didn't see them, but I sensed their menacing presence out there, beyond the gardens.

One morning, Malahki pointed at the neat rows of shaggy-looking lavender-colored plants. "This here is the *xaevoe*. That's the grains we had for dinner last night."

Despite the relatively limited variety of food, I couldn't complain. Malahki had been using a range of fragrant herbs to flavor the dishes of grain and greens, making our meals not just nutritious but also very tasty. Now and then, he would use black-shelled eggs that came in a cluster, but no meat.

He'd explained that the meat on the Dark Anomaly came from *vasai* centipedes, seven-feet long creatures with a multitude of chitin-covered legs. Their description alone had made me lose appetite even before he added that their meat stunk when cooked.

"*Xaevoe* is much prettier in its plant form," I commented. The grain looked muddy gray when cooked.

"Aren't all plants most beautiful when they're growing, lush and fresh?" he murmured, plucking a yellow flower off the vine from the planter we were passing by. "That's their best stage of life." He tucked the flower in the braid over his ear.

Surrounded by life he'd planted and maintained, he truly appeared to be in his element. Malahki had enough patience to nurture a plant, enough insight to spot any subtle changes in the seedlings, and enough knowledge to intervene when it was necessary. He obviously enjoyed the peace this place offered him in return.

As we rounded a corner of the next planter, his arm around my waist stiffened. I heard the sound of muffled voices coming from the corridor outside the gardens.

"We need to hide, Valentina," Malahki whispered.

The peaceful atmosphere of our walk shattered into pieces by the alarm in his words.

"Where?" I asked quickly, gripping his hand with both of mine.

I wished to be back in the safety of Malahki's room tucked behind a broken piece of paneling far at the back of the gardens. But it was too far for us to get back in time at my current speed. The voices kept coming closer, fast.

"Right here." He stepped between two planters, each holding long vines that climbed up the thick lattices to form walls. Now, I understood the strategic placement of the planters throughout the space. That was how Malahki created hiding places all over the gardens.

"Hey! *Damirian!* Where the fuck are you?" a thick voice bellowed from the entrance to the gardens.

The sound of heavy footsteps followed. Then, a tall, armor-plated figure showed up. A *dimo*, I recognized the species, watching him through the gaps between the leaves. Every part of the *dimo's* gray-brown body was covered in hard plates, reminding me of a rhinoceros.

A group of other aliens followed him into the gardens—a pale-blue *yourlu* with clusters of tentacles for arms and legs, three chitin-covered *kreers* with a bunch of long, segmented tails each, and one of the other species, which took me a while to remember their name as I'd only ever seen them in a picture once—*remoid*. His skin was covered in purple pigment spots, and he had two legs and four arms.

The males fanned out from the entrance. Some plucked and ate seeds and berries off the plants while passing by the planters. Others obviously weren't here to snack. They just uselessly ripped leaves and branches off vines and shrubs.

"Urkril," Malahki whispered. "That's the *dimo's* name. The *yourlu* is Xid. The *remoid* may be Leephron, I'm not sure, I don't know the male that well. And I can't recall the names of these *kreers.*"

"What do they want?" I asked him in a barely-there whisper, too. Some of the group had come closer, and I didn't want to attract their attention by making any noise at all.

"Where is that *thing*?" The *yourlu,* Xid, asked in a whiny voice. "Where did the *damirian* go?"

"Spread out, let's search this place." Urkril ordered.

Malahki squeezed my hand briefly.

"Stay here." He moved to get out from our hiding place, but I wouldn't let go of him.

"No…" I gripped on to his bicep. I wasn't sure if I was scared more for him or myself, but I wanted us to stay together, come what may.

He gently freed his arm from my grip then squeezed my shoulders, looking into my eyes.

"I have to talk to them," he said. "Otherwise, they'll start sniffing all around here. Whatever happens, don't let them see you. Do you hear me?"

I forced down a whimper of protest and nodded instead.

"If they find you, you're dead… Or worse." He frowned, glancing back at the unwelcome visitors.

My hands grabbed on to the empty air as he slipped out of my reach. I bit my bottom lip to stop myself from crying out.

Malahki stepped into the open.

"How may I help you, gentlemen?" he enquired calmly.

"There it is!" the *yourlu* squealed in delight, pointing with all six of his tentacles that his species had for arms—three growing from each shoulder.

"Hey." Urkril strode toward Malahki. "We need *irsen* flowers." He bent over, grabbing a wide silver bucket from under the nearest planter. "As much as you can fit in here." He slammed the bucket into the dirt in the planter, crushing the pale-green herbs that grew there.

Malahki tilted his head, casting but a glance at the ruined sprouts he'd so carefully planted and maintained.

"I can't do that," he said. "Not without personal permission from the captain. You know the rules."

Malahki had told me about the *irsen* flowers. They had some properties that made them useful for medicinal purposes. They also had strong narcotic qualities, which made them addictive and dangerous in large large quantities.

Most of the flowers had been ripped out during the last mutiny by the crew. Since then, Vrateus, the captain, had ordered the planters with the flowers Malahki had re-seeded to be hidden.

The new *irsen* plants had sprouted and bloomed since. Malahki had used them sparingly, for medicinal purposes, including brewing the tea he'd given to me while my injuries healed.

"Fuck the rules!" the *remoid* yelled, swaying on his feet unsteadily. He had to prop two of his four arms on the floor to regain his balance.

"We have the permission," Xid waved him off, shoving aside a *kreer* to get closer to Malahki.

"I need to hear it personally from the captain, then." Malahki crossed his arms over his chest, widening his stance. "Where is he?"

"He's in his fucking room, where else?" a *kreer* snarled, his long, black tails lashing about.

Urkril jabbed him in the ribs with his hard-plated elbow, making the *kreer* whimper and bend over in pain.

"If you don't give us the fucking flowers, we'll get them ourselves," the *dimo* growled, menacingly advancing on Malahki.

"You will never find them on your own," the *damirian* replied evenly.

Compared to the *dimo*, Malahki was so much smaller and leaner. He stood his ground, however, seemingly unafraid.

"...I have emotions. I'm a person, not a machine..."

I recalled his words. Just because he didn't show fear, it didn't mean he wasn't frightened when faced with the massive *dimo* towering over him.

"Where are they?" Urkril roared in Malahki's face.

The deafening sound made me shake behind the planter, yet Malahki didn't waver.

"I said I need the permission—"

Urkril jerked up his elbow, smashing the hard, serrated nob of the joint into Malahki's temple.

I jammed my fist into my mouth to stop myself from screaming in horror as I watched Malahki stagger to the side.

Next, Urkril raised his massive fist then slammed it into Malahki's jaw.

Panic shot through me. I choked on my unreleased scream, shoving my fist so far in my mouth, I could barely breathe.

Malahki's knees gave in and he dropped to the ground.

I hadn't witnessed this kind of cold, brutal, unnecessary violence in my life. Even the murders on board of my ship had been different. Then, I could pretend the *errock* was a deranged man on the loose, who might've been triggered by the fear of the unknown.

Here was an act of deliberate cruelty that had no reason and no purpose other than the demonstration of one's power over a physically weaker being.

"Fucking *it*!" Urkril spat into the bucket he'd failed to fill with what he'd come here for. "No cock, no pussy. Good for nothing."

He spun on his heel, stomping to the exit.

Giving the motionless Malahki a slap with a tentacle, the *yourlu* yanked a vine from the *damirian's* hair. The braid it'd been woven in had come undone, Malahki's long, sandy-colored hair falling over his face.

I wanted to rage, punch, and harm those who'd hurt the person I cared about, my friend—because Malahki had absolutely become my friend. He'd cared for me, talked to me, protected me...for as long as he could.

Suddenly, I understood perfectly clear his desperate desire to change. I, too, wished to be stronger and bigger. I wanted to be ruthless, hurting those who'd hurt us. What could I do, though, if I could barely stand upright, still so weak and sick?

"What are we going to do now?" The *yourlu* hurried after the *dimo*, chewing on the vine he'd plucked out of Malahki's hair. "Nocc said not to come back without the *irsen* flowers..."

The rest of the aliens followed the pair out of the gardens, too.

"Fuck Nocc!" I heard the disgruntled voice of Urkril in the distance.

I didn't wait until the sound of their footfalls and voices had quieted down completely. Ducking behind the plants and containers with dirt, I scurried to Malahki.

He lay on his side, his face turned upwards, his eyes closed.

"Malahki," I called in a loud whisper, taking his face between my hands. "Please, Malahki. Get up. We need to get out of here."

Here on the floor in the fairly open area of the gardens, the danger of being discovered pricked my skin with dread. The fear that he wouldn't get up or even open his eyes overshadowed any concern for myself, though.

"Please, Malahki." I brushed aside the long strands of loose hair from his face.

I would run back to the room to get some water to splash in his face, but I was so scared to leave him lying here alone. What if Urkril came back? I'd recognized the name Nocc, too. That was the *errock* who'd murdered my entire crew.

Malahki's eyelids finally fluttered open.

"Oh, thank God, are you okay?" I kept petting his face, afraid he'd close his eyes on me again.

He grimaced in pain, and my fingers came back smudged with red when their tips brushed by his temple.

"I'm so sorry, Malahki," I gasped, covering my mouth with my hand.

Tears burned in my eyes at the sight of blood where the *dimo's* rugged armor tore through Malahki's skin above his ear. A bright red spot was spreading under his skin along his jawline, where Urkril had punched him. The skin here wasn't broken but a huge bruise was forming already.

"This shouldn't have happened," I sobbed. "They shouldn't get away with this."

"They will," he gritted through his teeth, propping his hands into the floor to sit up. "They always do."

Always?

"Has it happened before?" I asked, feeling hollow in the pit of my stomach.

He looked at me, pausing his eyes on mine for a long moment. A corner of his mouth suddenly rose in a smile.

"Only once or twice." The tone of his voice lifted. "I'm too smart to let it happen too often."

Was he trying to cheer *me* up?

"Oh, Malahki." I grabbed him under his arm, fully intending to help him up.

"No." He freed his arm from me gently. "The last thing we need is you cracking your ribs again. I'm fine."

Gathering his long legs under him, he got up on his own, only slightly swaying on his feet.

"Come. Before any of them return." I took his arm again, tugging him toward our bedroom. The effort cost me my balance, and I steadied myself by grabbing on to one of the containers along our path.

The bright pink and purple plants in it were enclosed under a tall rounded glass dome. My hand slipped down the smooth surface of the cover. The tips of my fingers wedged between it and the edge of the container, sinking into the dirt inside it. I yanked my hand out and moved to wipe them on the side of my suit.

"Wait." Malahki gripped my wrist. "Don't touch anything with this hand."

He produced a spray bottle from under the planter and a clean cloth.

"Why? What are these?" I asked as he sprayed my hand with the liquid from the bottle then whipped my hand dry with the cloth.

"The *fuhnid* mushrooms." He jerked his chin at the wide purple umbrellas with pink fuzzy stripes growing under the dome. "The captain adds their juice to the soap. It makes our scent undetectable to the *errocks'* highly-sensitive sense of smell. But the mushroom juice is also highly toxic."

A faint, pleasant scent wafted around the planter.

"Is it lethal?" I inspected my hand carefully, seeing or feeling nothing out of ordinary. Of course, my fingers hadn't really come into contact with the mushrooms, just with the dirt they grew in.

"If swallowed, even a tiny amount, it's most certainly deadly. But the mushrooms can also kill if they simply come in contact with your mouth or eyes. In other words, don't ever touch them without wearing protective gear. Come now."

He steadied me with his arm on my waist, and I had my arm wrapped around his middle, too. That was how we made it back to the room—two hurt, broken people, supporting each other.

"Sit down." I gestured at the chair when we got inside. "It's my turn to take care of you."

He gave me a sad smile, but didn't argue. His shoulders relaxed, he appeared relieved to be back in the room where we both felt safer.

I filled a cup from the carafe of drinking water Malahki liked having on hand, then took a washcloth from a shelf by the curtain next to the bathroom passage.

"If you tell the captain what happened, would he punish them?" I asked, gently dabbing at the blood on the side of his face.

"Probably."

"Then why don't you tell him?"

"He has other things to worry about." He shrugged.

"He's your captain. Your wellbeing should be on his list of things to worry about."

I rinsed the cloth in the cool water then placed it against the swelling on his jaw, the place where the hard fist of Urkril had planted a blow.

"Valentina, if there is one thing you'll get out of what happened this morning, please, let it be that we're the only ones responsible for our own wellbeing on the Dark Anomaly, no one else." He took the washcloth away from me. "Besides, if Urkril and his thugs get punished because of my complaints, what do you think they'd do to me the next time they visit my gardens?"

I didn't want to think about that, but he stared straight at me, obviously expecting an answer.

"They'd do...something worse than a couple of punches," I muttered.

"That's right." He rose from the chair to get the jar of green substance he'd used to treat my wound. I wondered how many times he'd had to use it on himself before.

"Here." He handed it to me. "I can't see that spot well myself. Would you apply it, please?" He sat back in the chair.

The muscles in my legs started to tremble from the strain of standing for so long, and I lowered myself onto the edge of the bed. He scooted closer with the chair then leaned over the armrest toward me.

I opened the jar, dipped a finger into it then started dabbing with it over the tear in his skin. Setting the jar aside, I took a handful of his hair, holding it back while I worked.

"It's done." I wiped my hand on the cloth he'd handed to me. "How do you feel?"

He beamed an unexpected smile. "Better already."

I personally didn't feel better at all. The hurt and indignation for him burned as painful as ever.

"Why didn't you just give them the damn flowers?" I asked.

Who cared about some stupid rule by the captain who obviously couldn't keep his own people in check.

The smile slipped off his face.

"During the last mutiny, the crew gained access to the *irsen* flowers. Some had too many and died. Others got too aggressive due to the effect of the flowers and started killing each other. I didn't want to be responsible for more carnage," he replied simply.

Whatever his gender, Malahki proved to be a better man than any of the males in this place. He cared about their lives more than they did.

"Why not let them search the gardens like Urkril threatened he would? Chances were they would've never found them, anyway."

I didn't ask that question out loud, because I already knew the answer. If Malahki had let the thugs search, they would've found me. Instead, he distracted them by allowing them to beat him up.

Subdued, I ran my fingers through the locks of his ruined braid. "Do you want me to fix this for you?"

He arched an eyebrow with a glint of interest in his eyes. "You can braid hair?"

"Not as elaborately as you do, of course." I looked closely at his other braids. To replicate their intricate pattern, I'd need some above average weaving skills. "But I could try to do something simple. If you don't mind."

He slid a critical gaze down my messy ponytail. "Only if you allow me to fix that disaster for you."

"A disaster?" I touched my straight, long hair that I'd hastily pulled back into a ponytail. "Is it that bad?"

"No." He shook his head, with another cheerful smile. "I just want to see how a *damirian* hairstyle will look on you."

MALAHKI'S LEAN FIGURE stood by the planter in the garden. There was sky above the lush green-and-purple space he'd created—the real blue sky, with sunshine and clouds. I tilted my head back, letting the sunrays warm my face, and laughed.

A sickening sound of flesh hitting flesh cut my laughter short.

*"You are nothing," a huge dimo roared, grabbing Malahki's head, the same way the errock on the spaceship had with Jose. "Fucking **it!**" he yanked Malahki's head to the side. His braids whipped, and his neck snapped with a cracking sound that I felt all the way through to my bones...*

I sat up on the bed with a gasp.

No, no, no...

Not again.

I breathed hard. Cool perspiration gathered on my forehead and trickled down my spine. Fear shook my body.

Not Malahki, too...

I was in his room. All was quiet. The luminescent garlands under the colorful tapestry over the bed softly glowed blue. Malahki lay right there, on the sleeping pallet by the bed. I'd offered to take the pallet myself before, feeling uneasy about kicking him out of his own bed, but he'd refused. He'd said the mattress was softer and easier for my healing ribs.

"Malahki?" I whispered.

He was so close, all I had to do to touch him was to lean over the edge of the bed and reach down. I patted his shoulder.

"Mmm?" he groaned, sleepily.

"Could you get in bed with me? Please?" I asked tentatively.

Spurred by the fear from the nightmare, I didn't have the time to think it through. The moment my request left my mouth, however, I worried about his potential rejection.

He rubbed his eyes. "What? Why, now?"

His words about us sleeping naked together and his pleasuring me came to mind, warming my cheeks with blush.

"No. I don't mean it like *that*," I mumbled. "I'm wearing my suit, you don't have to touch me." Saying that made my face feel even hotter with mortification. "There is a lot of space here for both of us. It's a big bed..."

Maybe I should've practiced the words first, but I just wanted him next to me, so that if I dreamed about him being killed again, I could feel his heartbeat and hear his breathing the very moment I woke up.

"Oh, all right..." He nodded, and I exhaled in relief.

He climbed from his pallet into my bed. I scooched over to make room for him then drew the blankets over both of us.

"I had a dream about you," I explained as he lay on his side, his eyes wide open, now. "It wasn't good. The *dimo* killed you."

He gave me a small comforting smile, petting my shoulder.

"Don't worry. I've survived this long. I'm not going anywhere."

I longed to believe him, but the unsettling feeling after the nightmare wouldn't leave me.

He lifted a braid he'd made in my hair earlier. It had dark-green leaves of evergreen from his planet, Ak'ae, woven through it. Shaped like snowflakes, they glowed softly in the night.

"This looks even prettier in the dark," he said softly.

I now had the same hair-do as him—five intricately braided pleats on top of my head, two of them framed my face on each side, with the rest of the hair left to fall free under the braids. One of Malahki's braids, the one made by me, was plain and boring compared to the rest. He had insisted on keeping it, anyway.

One arm under his cheek, he blinked lazily, the ghost of a smile lingering on his lips. Then his eyes closed, and his breathing deepened as he fell asleep.

The dark, crusted with blood scar on his temple was clearly visible in the soft glow of the vines in his hair.

I heaved a long, heavy breath at the sight of it. Finding his hand under the blanket, I wrapped my fingers around it.

He didn't need to be big and powerful. He didn't need to be male. Malahki had saved my life, being just the way he was. And he was still finding ways to protect me. Even if it hurt him.

Chapter 5

He woke up with Valentina's leg draped over his middle, her face pressed against his upper arm.

It'd been over two weeks since she'd first invited him to share the bed with her. He was still getting used to waking up with her limbs thrown all over his body, her warmth sending a trickle of perspiration down his back and along his inner thighs.

At first, he'd expected having someone in his sleeping space to be uncomfortable. And physically, it kind of was. He would often wake up when Valentina turned and tossed through the night. Sometimes, she'd groan and mumble things in her sleep. He had woken her up too on a few occasions, by tossing an arm or a leg aside, unaware in his sleep of her presence.

The benefit was that he no longer had to get up to check on her. Whenever he opened his eyes, she was right there, next to him. He could listen to her breathing and see her face, peaceful in the soft light of the glowing plants.

He glanced at the lit dial of the clock on the shelf in the corner. It was time to get up and make breakfast. He had *pherli* leaves soaking in *orkok* juice overnight. When rolled and fried in *gruzo* oil, the leaves became crisp and salty on the outside, but remained soft and mild on the inside. Valentina loved when he made them for breakfast.

He moved to get up, but she shifted closer, throwing her arm over him in addition to the leg and hugging him tighter. She hadn't talked about having bad dreams anymore, but he'd felt her waking up with a start every now and then.

This morning, she was clinging on to him like a lifeline, and he realized he liked the feeling when she held him like that—he felt *needed.*

He'd never cared about being needed by anyone before. In theory, it'd always seemed like a burden to be responsible for anyone other than himself. But Valentina made him feel important, without him having to do anything at all. Just his being there seemed to calm her, bringing back the peace of sleep.

The fresh evergreen in her hair tickled his nose when she put her head on his chest. He felt the sudden urge to kiss her hair, and he didn't fight it. Lifting his head, he buried his lips in the fresh fragrance of her dark hair.

The silky strands tickled his face, making him smile. He felt even hotter with Valentina's entire body now wrapped tightly around him. But the positive sensations of her embrace far outweighed the discomfort of a little perspiration.

"Is it time to get up already?" she muttered sleepily, her lips moving against the bare skin of his chest.

"No. You can sleep for a bit yet." He made a point of keeping a schedule, whether it was on his one-person-crew space lab before or now on the Dark Anomaly. But what would be the harm in letting Valentina stay in bed for a few more minutes if that was what she desired?

"Sleep," he murmured, soothingly gliding his hand up and down her upper arm.

Generally, Malahki preferred the gardens to anywhere else on the Dark Anomaly. Having Valentina here, made any desire to get out into the common areas even smaller. However, he had to keep an eye on what was going on in the rest of the Dark Anomaly.

The last time he'd left the gardens was a few days ago, and he didn't like the mood of the crew then.

He'd overheard that Wyck, the *errock* in charge of the other surviving human woman from Valentina's ship, Nadia, had taken the female all to himself.

In a way, that was what Malahki had done too, with Valentina. Except that Malahki tried to keep her existence a secret, sparing her the disgrace of performing naked in public, when Wyck had to display his woman to the entire crew.

Wyck had come by the gardens, screaming Valentina's name. It terrified Malahki that her presence on the Dark Anomaly might have been discovered. Once, Wyck even brought Nadia with him, as a bait for Valentina, no doubt. Nadia must have been coerced to disclose Valentina's name to Wyck.

Thankfully, Valentina had been too weak back then. She had slept more often than she'd been awake, and she'd missed them coming to the gardens.

After that, Malahki had gone out and listened to the crew talk among themselves. No one else mentioned Valentina's name or even the possibility of a third female on the Dark Anomaly, which had calmed him somewhat. Wyck and Nadia had no way of knowing that Valentina had survived. They must have wondered what had happened to her, but they wouldn't search forever. If they didn't find her, they would eventually give up looking, he hoped.

Of course, he never said anything to Valentina about the others looking for her. Unlike Wyck, Malahki knew he wouldn't be able to physically defend a female from hundreds of males. He had to employ other tactics. He kept her hidden. And if it meant resorting to lies to keep Valentina safe, then so it had to be.

"I'll need to leave the gardens again," he whispered in her ear.

She jerked her head up, alarm flashing through her eyes that were a pretty shade of dark blue like the midnight flower from Ak'ae.

"Why?" She asked.

"I need to see what's going on out there."

He used to get updates from Svetlana, daily. Ever since Valentina had started to recover, however, he'd told Vrateus he no longer needed Svetlana's help in the gardens. The risk of the two women seeing each other would've been just too great.

Malahki had enjoyed spending time with Svetlana while the two of them had worked together. But he didn't trust her not to tell Vrateus if she learned about Valentina. And then, well, Malahki had seen what Vrateus did with Nadia. The captain gave her to Wyck to do whatever the *errock* wanted with her. Malahki had heard that *errocks* had even forced the poor woman to have sex with Wyck in public.

Unlike the captain and the rest of the crew, Malahki arrived on the Dark Anomaly as an adult from more modern times. He understood better than any of them that a woman, regardless of what alien race she belonged to, would not appreciate being turned into a sex toy for hundreds of crude, raunchy males.

As long as he lived, he would not allow such treatment of Valentina.

Now, without Svetlana keeping him up to date, if he needed to know what was going on out there, he had to leave the gardens and go see for himself. Even if Valentina's eyes told him clearly, she wanted him to stay.

"It's important, Valentina." He moved a braid over her shoulder. "We need to know what the others are doing. So we can be better prepared for whatever comes next."

He'd lived through the first mutiny of the crew. He'd witnessed some really disturbing things then. Things that had proven to him how fragile peace and order were on the Dark Anomaly.

Last time, the captain had been poisoned and nearly died. For a while, his power had fallen into the hands of the *errocks*, a brutal group. During those few days, Malahki had seen murder, abuse, and more violence than he'd ever seen in all his life prior.

"When will you leave?" Valentina sat up. Sleep had completely left her eyes, replaced by worry.

"Right after breakfast." The crew would be lingering in the mess hall, chatting while finishing their morning meal—a perfect time to gauge their mood and find out what was brewing in their midst.

"Can I come?" she asked tentatively, not with much hope in her voice.

"Of course not. It's not safe."

"Will it ever be safe?"

What could he tell her? That he sensed the things were actually getting worse? That the safest future he could envision for her on the Dark Anomaly would be her spending the rest of her life right here, in this room, unseen by the others.

He didn't have the heart to tell her that. Instead, he chose to lie. Again.

"One day, things will get better, I'm sure."

They had breakfast mostly in silence. He sensed Valentina's subdued mood. She didn't like being on her own. But he also knew that she worried about him.

She walked him through the gardens, all the way to the last planter with *almai* vines. They rose up to the ceiling then draped down over the pipe up there, creating a safe alcove to hide from the eyes of anyone who might walk into the gardens unexpectedly.

Unlike the captain's, Malahki's safety measures weren't the metal doors and an extensive arsenal of weapons. He used stealth and plenty of hiding places.

"I'll be back before you know it," he told Valentina.

"When?" She gripped his forearms.

"Soon. Before lunch, most likely."

He didn't plan to linger out there. All he wanted to do was a quick reconnaissance.

She raised her face to his. Her eyes glistened, the intensity in them took his breath away. He couldn't physically walk away from her when she was looking at him like that, as if he were the only person in the universe.

Instead, he brought his face closer to hers.

Her eyes flicked to his lips. His mouth felt dry, and he licked his lips.

Her mouth opened, just a little.

He didn't have one single thought in his head when he lowered his face all the way down and touched her lips with his.

With a soft whimper of surprise, she rose on her tiptoes and gripped his head, keeping his mouth on hers. Her kiss felt like her hug, warm and natural.

He'd sensed she needed a stronger form of connection with him before saying goodbye, and he gave it to her.

A warm feeling rose in his chest from the sensation of her soft lips sliding over his. It grew, bubbling and getting warmer. When he felt like his chest was about to explode from that growing heat inside him, he panicked and drew back, breaking the kiss.

Her eyes were open wide, worry floated in them along with fear and something else he couldn't name. Her lips glistened like freshly plucked *lornee* berries.

She kept holding his head between her hands.

"Please, hurry back," she whispered.

THE THOUGHTS OF VALENTINA wouldn't leave him as he walked down the corridor toward the mess hall. The memory of her kiss still tingled on his lips. The odd tightness in his chest wouldn't let go, making him unusually lightheaded.

At the same time, everything around him appeared more acute somehow. The warped panels of the corridor walls seemed whiter than normal. The light from the cables above shone brighter. And the noise of the crowd inside the mess hall as he approached was sharper, each sound separated from the rest.

The morning meal was almost over. Svetlana cooked food once a day in the afternoon. Krakhil and a few others warmed up the dinner leftovers for breakfast.

The gray stew with the foul smelling *vasai* meat had almost been finished by the males. Oddly, Malahki didn't find the smell of meat that disgusting today. It was strong, but not as nauseatingly repulsive as usual.

The crew paid little attention to him, as was the norm. He preferred it that way. Staying close to the walls and away from the groups, he lingered among the males, listening to their conversations and gauging the mood of the crew.

There were the usual complaints about the captain and his rules, which was normal. No matter what Vrateus did, someone was always displeased.

Most of the crew had been on the Dark Anomaly for decades. They'd been sucked in from the outside world millennia ago, back when the interstellar space was a wild place, rife with crime and filled with delinquents.

Even when *he* got here, five years ago—Dark Anomaly time—which roughly translated to about fifteen hundred years in the world out there, one of the popular options to avoid the law of the Federation had been to take off into the dark, unexplored corners of the galaxy. The crew of the Dark Anomaly comprised former criminals, unhappy to live under any rules but their own.

This time, however, there were different notes in the usual disgruntled buzz. Some complaints were new and much more specific.

They got even louder after Vrateus, the captain, came through the mess hall for an inspection accompanied by Wyck, the *errock* from his personal guard.

"They each have a female to fuck whenever they want..." Malahki heard.

"We got nothing..."

"We should've had a fair fight," the dreadfully familiar voice boomed nearby.

Malahki tossed a glance in the direction of the voice, spotting Urkril, the *dimo* he was beginning to hate with the passion he'd never thought himself capable of before.

"A fight! Whoever wins gets the female," the *dimo* roared, surrounded by a group of males charged with anxious energy.

"Or we all could share them," someone else chimed in.

A heavy premonition chilled Malahki's heart when he saw another group enter the mess hall. This one was led by Nocc, the *errock* who'd murdered most of Valentina's crew. Krakhil, another *dimo*, walked shoulder to shoulder with him.

The two groups merged like two dark clouds, and Malahki feared they would create a storm the Dark Anomaly might not weather well.

Ever since the last time, he'd expected another mutiny. The crew had always been volatile. The sudden tossing of the females into their midst could only be the catalyst of an explosion.

Teasing the males with the sight of females then denying them any access to them was a mistake on the part of the captain. It could bring nothing but trouble. Malahki long knew it, but only recently had he begun to understand the captain's actions. As far as Svetlana was concerned, Vrateus obviously hadn't been driven by logic, but by a desperate desire to keep her alive and later to get her away from the others.

Malahki would never let the crew touch Valentina, either. For as long as he lived, he'd do anything to keep her safe.

"How come Wyck ended up with a female all to himself?" someone snarled in the crowd.

"He stole her," Krakhil growled. "From us!"

"Well then maybe we could steal them both back?" Nocc hissed. "You want a fight? We'll force them to fight!"

His words acted like fuel splashed on an open flame. Caught by the crowd, Nocc's call to fight echoed under the ceiling as the crew raged.

Malahki had promised Valentina to be back by lunch, and he wanted nothing more but to rush to her, to touch her hand, to see her smile, to make sure she was still safe and sound, hidden far away from the disaster that was about to happen.

First, he had to try to warn the captain. Vrateus had established control over this mismatched crew of delinquents not once but twice already. If there was anyone who had any chance at stopping the mutiny with its devastating consequences, it would be the captain.

Nocc grabbed a table and slammed it into the floor, smashing it to pieces. The crashing noise drew delighted cheers from the crowd. Wielding the metal leg of the table as a weapon over his head, Nocc stormed out of the mess hall.

A few crew members lingered. Some were still picking pieces of food from the dishes on the tables. Many were so pumped from Nocc's words, they started picking fights with each other.

Carefully avoiding the brawls breaking out all over the room, Malahki slipped out of the mess hall.

Around midday, the captain should be finishing his rounds. Though his schedule often changed, Vrateus would normally be visiting the *vasai* farm early in the afternoon. Malahki turned right from the mess hall, heading to the *vasai* farm first.

Here, large, mismatched cages lined the space. The giant centipedes crawled and screeched in them.

He detested this place probably more than anywhere else on the Dark Anomaly. Poorly lit and noisy, it stunk of *vasai* excrement, no matter how often the captain ordered the cages cleaned. The creatures threw themselves against the bars, their chitin-covered bodies scraping against the metal. Black clusters of eggs were suspended in the corners of some cages. Along with the grains he grew in the gardens, these were the main protein source in his personal diet. He found the food eaten by the rest of the crew repulsive and had long started making his own, using a small flameless stove he'd managed to salvage from his own ship that had crashed here.

Many of the cages remained empty as the centipedes had been needlessly butchered, their meat often getting wasted during the last riot. Because of that, in those terrible days when the *errocks* were in control, food had become scarce. Fights over the remaining supplies broke out, all over the Dark Anomaly. He'd seen the crew attacking and killing each other then devouring the flesh of those who had lost.

He knew that despite his superior intelligence over nearly everyone of the crew, he'd most likely lose a fight against any of them. When it came to physical strength, he'd be the one who'd end up being eaten.

His first thought when he'd seen Valentina back on her ship—the vulnerable, injured woman—was to get her away from the *errocks* fighting over Nadia, the woman he could no longer save. The *errocks* hadn't spotted Valentina yet, and he saw the chance for her escape.

The idea that she might be useful to trigger his change had come to him later, after he'd found her passed out in the gardens.

Obviously, he'd been naïve thinking that simply having a woman in his proximity would get him what he wanted. Valentina had lived with him for almost six weeks now, two of which they had been sharing the bed. Yet the place between his legs looked as smooth as ever.

At the same time, that didn't feel like a complete failure, somehow. There was so much he'd gained since she came into his life. During the past four weeks since she'd been conscious, the two of them had become inseparable. He grew to enjoy having someone to share his meals with, to talk to, and to spend time with.

Not finding the captain anywhere in the farm or in the waste sorting room behind it, Malahki quickly checked the equipment storage room by the airlock next to the farm. It was locked, and no one replied when he knocked.

After that, he headed back to the mess hall. It was almost completely empty now, save for a few males of various species who were passed out on the floor.

The nearly deserted state of this section wasn't unusual for this time of the day. However, Nocc's words from earlier made him worry.

Speeding up his pace, he hurried along the corridor toward the captain's room.

He was still a long way away from the room when a *yourlu* poked his head from a side hallway. Malahki recognized Xid, who'd been there when Urkril had attacked him last time. Normally, Malahki would give him a wide berth. Out of all the species on the Dark Anomaly, *yourlu* were one of the most annoying on the crew.

"Keep moving, *damirian*," Xid hissed, gesturing with all six of his arm tentacles for him to pass.

The air of self-importance that Xid emitted made Malahki pause.

"I said keep going, asshole!" The *yourlu* bounced with the eagerness of someone doing something important.

The insult scraped against Malahki's nerves unexpectedly, causing a flare of irritation.

"What if I don't?" He widened his stance, crossing his arms over his chest.

A new thrill zapped through his muscles. He found himself wishing for the *yourlu* to accept the challenge.

Xid didn't disappoint. Tossing a shifty glance at the door at the end of the side hallway, he moved on to Mahlaki.

"Then, I'll make you. Get out of here!" He lashed out with a tentacle.

Malahki grabbed it, yanking hard.

Obviously not expecting the resistance, Xid staggered on the cluster of tentacles *yourlu* used for legs, losing his balance.

"You fucking *damirian*," Xid cursed under his breath, scrambling to his tentacles. "This time, you're dead!" he yelled, charging Malahki.

Malahki leaped aside, evading the attack.

Avoiding the confrontation didn't feel enough, though. Being "a bigger person" by walking away didn't appeal to him as much as it used to. He craved the satisfaction of a well-placed blow. His fists itched to wipe that arrogant smirk off Xid's face, who expected him to turn his back on him and leave. And normally, he would have.

Not today, though.

Xid whipped around. His bottom tentacles undulated under him, propelling him forward.

Instead of ducking from the incoming blow, Malahki lunged ahead. He grabbed the *yourlu* by his scrawny neck.

"What the f..." Xid croaked.

Startled by Malahki's attack, the *yourlu* hardly offered any resistance. Using the momentum, Malahki threw him backwards and to the floor.

"You've been asking for this for years," Malahki gritted through his teeth.

Blood boiled in his veins. His muscles tingled and ached, begging to be used. He struggled to hold back from punching the life out of Xid.

"Fight me, now!" He gave the stunned *yourlu* a shake.

The air in Xid's throat gurgled as the male strained to pass a word through Malahki's grip. His tentacles lashed around them, whipping Malahki's bare arms and shoulders. The suckers on them attached to his skin, tearing at it, but Malahki barely noticed the pain.

He forced his hand to relax only when the watery eyes of the *yourlu* swelled and bulged out of his skull.

"Let me go..." Xid pleaded, in a voice he'd never used with Malahki before. "I have a job to do. Nocc will be furious—"

He glanced back to the door at the dead end of the hallway and cut himself short, his eyes shifting away again.

"What's behind that door?" Malahki demanded.

"Nothing," Xid replied quickly, way too quickly.

"Is it locked? Where is the key?" Placing his knee onto the *yourlu's* chest, he squeezed his throat once again.

"What key?" Xid croaked, his tentacles tightly wound around Malahki's arms. A couple of them made it for his neck, but Malahki swiped at them. Twisting a bunch of tentacles into a bundle, he shoved them under his other knee.

The *yourlu* whimpered as Malahki put his weight on that knee, pressing down on the pale blue cluster of flesh.

"Key!" he ordered. "Give it to me."

"Fine." A tentacle emerged from the quivering mass of them. On the tip of it, a rectangular piece of metal with bumps and indentations dangled on a ring—the key to the storage room.

"Nocc will kill you both," Xid hissed, each word soaked in undisguised hatred.

"But who will tell him?" Malahki tilted his head, enjoying the flush of terror in the *yourlu's* eyes right before Malahki punched him. He held back, controlling the force of his blow, aiming to neutralize, not to murder.

With a brief, strangled noise, the *yourlu* jerked, his tentacles jolted and twitched. Then his body stilled, his long, twisty limbs spread motionlessly over the floor.

A rush of excitement rolled through Malahki with that blow. He craved to hit again, to feel the flesh give in under his fist. At the same time, the realization that he'd just extinguished the awareness of another being filled him with horror.

Sliding the key off the unconscious *yourlu's* tentacle, he climbed from the male's motionless body.

"Nocc will kill you both."

Malahki wondered what Xid had meant by "both." For a moment he feared that Valentina had been discovered.

When he neared the door, however, he heard a sound of someone moving behind it. Then, a faint scratching noise came through the door panel.

He briefly considered leaving the key and whoever was behind that door to their own devices. He didn't get involved in the crew's scuffles if he could help it. However, he feared that today's conflicts involved more than just isolated fights.

Sliding the flat rectangle into the slot on the door, he unlocked it.

"Malahki?" Vrateus stood on the other side of the door. A laser gun and a long piece that appeared to be a part of one of the shelves in his hands.

A chunk of the door with the lock dropped to the floor with a loud clunk, nearly missing Malahki's foot. The captain had been well on his way to freeing himself.

"Thanks," he said, moving past Malahki and out into the corridor. "Where is that traitor Nocc?"

When Malahki turned around, Xid was no longer there. The *yourlu* must've come to while he wasn't looking then ran away either to hide or to complain to Nocc.

"They all went that way." Malahki gestured down the corridor, in the direction toward the captain's room, the library, and the gardens.

"Who all?" Vrateus tossed aside the long metal piece and made a gun slide out of his sleeve instead.

"Almost the entire crew." Malahki discreetly picked up the discarded piece as Vrateus headed up the corridor. Having any kind of weapon appeared a necessity at this point. "What happened? Why were you in the storage room?"

Vrateus winced, his bronze skin darkened on his cheekbones with obvious embarrassment. His long, furry tail lashed angrily against his boots.

"They attacked Wyck while I was in there, getting supplies. Have you seen Wyck?" Vrateus asked.

"No. But he may be that way, too, because I haven't seen him either in the farm or the mess hall."

Vrateus glanced at Malahki over his shoulder, his expression even more severe than usual.

"Something is brewing, captain. I overheard them talking about taking the women—"

"Svetlana!" Vrateus took off in a mad dash, his weapons at the ready.

Malahki ran after him. He told himself there was no reason for him to worry about Valentina. She would be safe in their bedroom deep inside the gardens. No one usually went to that part of the gardens. He'd arranged the planters around it, in a way that made people pass it by, without noticing. The unpleasant feeling wouldn't leave him, though.

The noise of the crowd reached them as they came closer. The wild rumble reverberated between the warped walls of the corridor. Something was happening up ahead.

They passed by a few crew on the way, all of the males restless and agitated.

As they came around another bend in the corridor, the battle scene opened fully to his view, Wyck and Nocc both falling to the ground. The crew literally crawled over each other to get closer to where the entrance of the human ship was. Laser shots fired, joined by the bullets of the captain's much louder projectile weapons.

Malahki had no time to watch and no desire to linger, worry about Valentina suffocating him.

At the double-doors to the garden, he slowed down.

The anticipation of seeing Valentina rushed over him. He rubbed his chest, trying to ease the growing bubble of heat inside it, but it only seemed to grow bigger, slowly descending down into his belly.

Maybe what he'd wished for and dreaded was about to happen, after all?

Chapter 6

Lunchtime had passed, and Malahki was nowhere in sight. I anxiously paced in circles inside our bedroom, listening to every sound from the gardens.

What if something had happened to him? What if he needed help while I sat here, waiting for him in vain?

I searched the small kitchen area Malahki had set up in a recess in the wall in the bedroom. Grabbing the long, narrow knife he used to peel vegetables, I poked my head from behind the wall paneling that separated our room from the gardens.

Caution warred with the burning desire to find Malahki. I grew up in a crimeless society. Never in a million years would I worry about walking on my own outside of my apartment building back on Earth, no matter the time of day.

I would've never been able to comprehend the extent of danger Malahki had warned me about had I not witnessed the violence of this place with my own eyes. On the Dark Anomaly, I knew I could be attacked without provocation. I could be killed, too.

All seemed to be quiet out in the gardens, though. The irrigation system trickled quietly. The delicate leaves of *almai* vines trembled and rustled as I passed by.

For now, all I wanted to do was to get to the entrance into the main corridor of the Dark Anomaly and take a look in both directions for any sight of Malahki.

I'd never been outside of the gardens, but I knew the layout of the entire place well enough from the maps and charts that Malahki had shown to me.

It was a very simple design, too. The entire habitable sector of the Dark Anomaly consisted of one long corridor that ran along a section of the outer edge of the disk. Smaller hallways and corridors branched out from it, but not too far. Since the gravity created in the centre of the disk compressed the ships crashed on the Dark Anomaly—the closer to the center one went, the higher the pressure. The older ships had been compressed too much for live beings to occupy them. Whatever empty space remained there threatened to collapse under the ever-increasing pressure closer to the center.

I wasn't worried about getting lost if I left the gardens. My biggest concern was being spotted by a member of the crew. Malahki had been adamant, I could not trust anyone here. So far, I'd had every reason to believe him. Going out into the corridor was not my intention.

The noise of footfalls and loud, agitated voices reached me as I made it closer to the entrance. The corridor outside of the gardens seemed to be filled with life today. Could that be what delayed Malahki?

I stilled, holding my knife in a sweaty hand. If I had to use it, I wasn't sure I could. I'd never stabbed a person before, never so much as slapped one even.

"But isn't the *damirian* going to be there?" A voice reached me from the corridor.

I flattened myself against a wall, hiding behind the vines of the nearest planter.

"So?" another voice replied, much closer. "Who cares about the fucking *damirian*. What is it going to do? Run to the captain to complain?"

By the several snorting and snickering sounds, I realized there were significantly more than two males speaking.

Darting my gaze back to the bedroom, I gauged the distance and whether I had enough time to get back. I didn't, as they entered the gardens at that very moment.

There were six of them. Two *yourlu*, two *kreers*, an *ognat,* and an *errock.*

My throat tightened at the sight of the massive *errock.* From the distance, peeking through the vines, I couldn't tell for sure whether it was one of the two I'd seen on my ship. Just the sight of his massive figure, confidently strolling through the place that had been my sanctuary for the past six weeks felt like an invasion. The bounce of energy in his step didn't promise anything good.

"Should I search for the *damirian*, Trox?" one of the *yourlu* asked the *errock.*

"The *damirian* isn't here," the other *yourlu* said, rubbing his neck. "He's with the captain. Busy."

I recognized this one as Xid, the *yourlu* who'd been with Urkril when the *dimo* had assaulted Malahki here, in the gardens.

"How do you know?" the first *yourlu* asked.

"Trust me I do." Xid rubbed his neck with another tentacle.

"The fuck do we need the *damirian* for?" The *errock* spat through his teeth. "Search this place for the *irsen* flowers. Izcigs, you get some of the mushrooms. They could be handy, too."

One of the *kreers* headed for the planter with the pink and purple *fuhnid* mushrooms under the transparent dome. The rest spread through the gardens, shoving aside the planters and knocking on walls.

I crouched in my hiding place, closer to the exit to the corridor than to the bedroom. With the other *kreer* heading in the direction of our room, my not being there, might be a good thing after all.

"Trox! The planter is locked." The *kreer* Trox called Izcigs slammed his fist into the clear dome over the *fuhnid* mushrooms. After the incident when some of the mushrooms had been stolen and their juice had been used to poison the captain, Malahki had put strong hinges and a lock on the dome as a precaution.

"So?" Trox grabbed a metal planter with *xaevoe* grain plants. He lifted the entire thing over his head then tossed it into the glass dome, smashing it to pieces. Most of the mushrooms got crushed, dirt flew out and all over the floor.

"There you go." Trox smirked. "Get them." He gestured at the few pink-and-purple umbrellas of the mushrooms still standing. "Did anyone find the fucking flowers yet?"

"Hey Trox! There's a room here," the other *kreer* yelled from behind the vines that concealed our bedroom.

My heart dropped. Our hiding place had been discovered.

Malahki had done a great job making it look like the gardens ended before it. However, by knocking on walls, the *kreer* found the loose piece of the paneling concealing the entrance to our secret sanctuary.

Both *yourlu* rushed that way, reaching the vine curtain before Trox.

"Ha! That's where the *damirian* sleeps. Look that's his bed," Xid said, followed by the noise of shoved furniture and breaking dishes.

"Not a bad set-up it's got here!" the other *yourlu* exclaimed. "Look at these pretty curtains." He erupted in a loud laughter.

"Well, are the fucking flowers there? Is that where it keeps them?" Trox barged in after them.

The noises of them trashing our living place grew louder.

I sat in my hiding spot, listening as they vandalized the one place on the entire Dark Anomaly where I'd felt relatively safe. The sound of things being broken painfully reverberated through me, making me feel personally violated.

Finally, the nose quieted down.

"They're not here, Trox," Xid stated the obvious.

"Wait, I smell something..." Trox replied.

I stiffened in my crouch, wishing I could make myself completely invisible.

"The *irsen* flowers?" the *kreer* asked with hope.

"No, something else... Much sweeter." The thick glee in Trox's voice made my skin crawl with dread. "Guess what? The fucking *it* isn't living here alone."

A whimper of terror stuck in my throat, and I slammed my hand over my mouth, stopping the whimper from escaping.

"So, who cares—" Xid started.

"Shut up!" Trox snarled. "Did you check all the walls here? Any hiding places?"

"Checked, and no, the walls are solid."

"How about the bathroom?" Trox insisted.

"Nothing."

"She has to be here somewhere."

"She?" several voices exclaimed excitedly.

"Yeah, I smell a female. She must be still around. The *damirian* wouldn't have killed or eaten her. And there is no leaving the Dark Anomaly."

I'd been taking showers with the berry soap daily, like Malahki had instructed me. He'd said the juice of the *fuhnid* mushrooms in the soap neutralized my scent. However, spending as much time as I did in our bedroom must have made the overall concentration of my smell there high enough for the sensitive nostrils of the *errock* to pick up.

Now, that they'd learned about my existence, I had no doubt they wouldn't stop searching until they found me.

My heart thundered in my chest. My hands grew cold as my fingers trembled. I needed to get away from them but where? The commotion outside in the corridor intensified. The sounds coming from there spoke of a real battle taking place, with laser blasts, cries of pain, and shouting.

Here in the gardens, the males rushed out of our bedroom, spreading between the planters in the enthusiastic search for me. Sooner or later, they'd find me.

I was trapped.

Aware of every step taken my way, I kept my gaze at the entrance to the gardens, clutching the kitchen knife in my sweaty hand. If I dashed for it now, I could possibly make it out of here faster than any one of those in the gardens, but then what? With the fighting in the corridor, I risked jumping out of a frying pan and into the fire—getting away from six males only to end up in the middle of a battle of possibly many more.

The heavy stomping of the *errock* closed in on me. I pressed my body into the side of the planter I used for a cover, wishing I could simply become a part of it, invisible, insignificant, and safe.

"Fucking shit! There she is!" Trox bellowed right above me.

A lash of panic spurred me into action. Leaping to my feet, I ducked under his thick arms that reached for me and sprinted for the white folding doors to the corridor.

With no time to think, I took my chances with whatever waited for me out there rather than falling into the clutches of Trox. After the murders of my entire crew by an *errock*, I'd developed a deep ingrained fear of his entire species. And nothing about Trox eased it in me.

My arms pumping, my heart leaping high into my throat, I ran as fast as I could. The doors were almost there, another step or two and I'd be out of here, come what may then.

"Ha!" Trox's burly arms whipped around me, tripping me.

I slammed both hands into the exit doors. So close!

"Nope," he growled into my ear. "You're not going anywhere."

"No!" I panted in terror, my tightened throat hurting with every breath.

"Oh yes." He dragged his tongue along my neck. "Whoever the fuck you are, you're mine for the next little while."

"Hey, Trox! How about us?" the others rushed to us, tripping over their feet, tentacles, and each other.

"I'll hold her for you," the *yourlu* who wasn't Xid eagerly offered, slinking closer. "I know how to open her suit, I did it once on that other female from her ship—"

"Fuck off, Kex!" Holding me with one arm, Trox threw his other fist out, punching the *yourlu* out of the way. "Who cares about the suit? I'll peel the fucking thing off her with my own teeth if I have to."

Holding me from behind, he shoved his big, grabby hand between my legs, squeezing me there so hard I cried out.

"See? She wants it." He ground his crotch against my ass.

Terror choked me, clouding my vision and my mind. Through the fog of panic, the sensation of the hard handle of the kitchen knife still clutched in my hand registered.

My first impulse would be to stab the blade into the rough hands groping me, but I held back, taking a moment to think of a better target. I had but one blow, one chance and I needed it to be effective against the massive *errock*.

At the same time, I couldn't think too long, lest they notice my weapon and take it away. So far, they'd been too excited about finding me to spot it.

"I'm going to fuck you good." Trox flipped me to face him.

There was nothing of a sentient being in his yellow eyes. Unseeing, they seemed to stare past me as he grinded against me forgetting all about getting me out of the suit first.

"No!" I threw my right arm back and up. Swinging my entire body forward, I jammed the long, slim blade of the knife into the *errock's* thick, clay-red neck.

His huge body jerked against mine, his delirious stare jolting back to awareness with a flash of shock.

"What the—"

He loosened his grip on me, and I didn't wait for him to finish the sentence. Yanking my knife out of his neck, I twisted out from his hands. A gush of dark blood shot out of his wound, spraying red over the pale blue of my suit.

"The bitch has a knife!" Xid wailed.

There was no time to run around them and make for the door again. Instead, I dashed between Xid and the *kreers*, heading for the back of the garden. I had no plan other than to put as much distance as possible between us.

I hoped my wounding Trox would delay them. However, all five lunged after me, leaving the *errock* to bleed alone. Falling to his knees, he clutched his neck with both hands in an attempt to stop the blood and life from leaving his body.

"Get back here, you sweet delicious thing," one of the *kreers* hissed, gaining on me. Lashing with one of his long, segmented tails, he swiped me off my feet.

Crashing face first to the floor, I barely managed to break my fall with my arms. Both wrists screamed in pain taking the weight of my body. The knife fell from my fingers.

"Sweet, sweet meat," the *ognat* squawked, using all eight pairs of his skinny limbs to crawl closer to me.

"Hey!" Xid yelled, scurrying over on his lower cluster of tentacles. "No eating her until I fuck her, do you hear me?"

With Trox out of the picture, Xid's confidence grew tenfold.

"Get the knife away from her, first," he ordered to the others.

The *kreer* quickly grabbed my knife off the floor with his black as kohl, skinny fingers.

"As long as we get to fuck her, too." He rolled over to his back, exposing his dirty-white belly. A slit opened in the pouch in his crotch and a cluster of black, wiggly appendages unfurled from it. Glistening with slime, they swarmed, straining toward me.

My stomach roiled with revulsion and horror. I clawed at the hard, metal floor, trying to crawl away from all of them, but the *kreer's* tail held my legs firmly like a rope wound around my ankles.

"Me first!" Xid announced, spreading his leg tentacles in a circle to reveal a thin, undulating one in the middle.

A long, strangled growl rolled through the gardens, then a strong arm hooked around the *yourlu's* scrawny neck.

"I should've killed you before," Malahki gritted through his teeth.

Xid's expression turned to an intense mix of hatred and terror, but he didn't get a chance to say a word. Yanking *yourlu's* head aside, Malahki stabbed a long metal piece into his neck.

Kex, the second *yourlu* jumped on Malahki's back, wrapping him in his tentacles.

I grabbed a handful of the wiggling mess of the *kreer's* genitalia. The slime coated my hand, seeping between my fingers as I squeezed and twisted my fist.

Tossing his head back, the *kreer* squealed as if being murdered. The noose of his tail finally loosened around my ankles. Kicking my feet, I tossed it off and crawled backward.

Malahki reached back and grabbed the head of the *yourlu* attacking him. Throwing him over his shoulder, he snapped Kex's back over his knee.

I couldn't even begin to process the horrors of everything that was happening. My concentration narrowed. Every single male in the gardens beside Malahki was a threat to him and me. And my entire being focused on eliminating the threat.

As the *ognat* and the second *kreer* closed in on Malahki, I lunged for the knife in the first *kreer's* hand.

"You nasty female!" he cursed, yanking it away from me. "I'll chew your head off while I fuck you, like the *ognats* do!"

The pouch low on his belly closed, however, hiding his genital cluster from view. When he lunged after me again, there was more murder than lust in his black as bullet hole eyes.

I crab-walked away from him, struggling to get up. He wouldn't let me regain my footing, grabbing my right leg with his hand, all of his tails curling around my left one again.

My shoulder hit a planter behind me, and I reached for the edge of it to haul myself up. Straining the muscles in my arm so hard they hurt, I tried to get up to give myself a fighting chance with the male.

"Let's see how you taste." He slashed at my calf with the knife. The suit fabric held, protecting my skin, though it didn't make the blow of the blade much less painful.

I groaned, trying to kick my feet free. My fingers sunk into the dirt in the planter as I gripped its edge.

"Valentina!" Malahki punched the *ognat* away, on his way to me. However, the second *kreer* had his tails wound tightly around Malahki's chest and waist. One of them inching dangerously close to his neck.

Sharp pain cut through my finger as I dug my hand into the dirt. Glancing back, I realized this was the planter with *fuhnid* mushrooms. A shard of glass from the dome destroyed by Trox sliced through my skin.

Grabbing one of the surviving mushrooms, I squished the delicate umbrella in my hand. The deadly juice beaded bright between my fingers.

"Eat this!" I shoved the whole thing into the *kreer's* half-open mouth.

He choked, spitting it out. But I jabbed my juice-soaked fingers into his eye sockets. He bellowed in pain, recoiling from me.

I ripped another mushroom from the planter, shoving my knee into the *kreer's* belly. He swayed on his feet. Losing his balance, he crashed backwards. I quickly jumped on his chest, not giving him a chance to recover. Though, judging by his bulging eyes and puffed up skin around them, his recovery was questionable at best.

"You want to eat me?" I growled wildly, not recognizing my own voice. "How do you like this?" I shoved the mushroom into his mouth, cutting off his screams of pain.

My hands shook. Everything inside me vibrated with terror and adrenaline. I had no coherent thoughts, no other emotions but aggression and fear—aggression against those who wanted to hurt me, fear that I might prove weaker than them.

Wet, garbled noises bubbled up from the *kreer's* mouth, muffled by the crushed mushroom gag I'd stuffed in it. His body arched and stiffened under me. All eight pairs of limbs scraping against the floor in agony.

Then, he stilled.

I darted a glance at Malahki. Baring his teeth and straining his muscles, he ripped to pieces the tails restraining him. The second *kreer* screeched as green blood sprayed from the remnants of his tails.

The *ognat* was already lying on the ground, his head smashed in, his black-and-beige body convulsing with its last tremors.

The knife dropped by the *kreer* I'd just killed lay on the floor at my boot. I kicked it Malahki's way. He grabbed it and slit the last *kreer's* throat, giving him a quick death.

Still sitting on top of the male I'd killed, I leaned back against the planter.

The feverish energy that had been fueling me during the fight was draining now, but no relief came. Only emptiness moved in on me.

"Valentina." Malahki rushed to me. "Are you hurt anywhere?"

Taking my chin in his hand, he peered at me intently. Red, orange, and purple swirls swam in his eyes, beautiful and bizarre.

I lifted my hand, and he caught my wrist.

"Wait. Don't touch anything yet." He grabbed the familiar spray bottle from under the planter.

I hissed when the liquid hit the cut on my finger, the cut left by the shard of glass.

"Is your skin broken anywhere?" Concern rang in his voice as he turned my hand over.

The small cut on the inside of my ring finger was bloated and angry red. The skin around it swelled and turned purple.

"It acts fast," I mumbled, my tongue barely moving as my mouth turned dry.

"No. Hold on. Valentina. Please." Malahki hurriedly sprayed my other hand then wiped them both, using the cloth from under the planter. "Don't close your eyes," he pleaded, lifting me in his arms. "Talk to me. Say something, anything."

I threw my arm over his shoulder as he carried me between the planters to our ransacked bedroom. His familiar scent and warmth of his body pressed to mine made everything right with the world, even if just for one moment.

"I'm...so glad..."

I wanted to say I was glad he'd returned. I wanted to tell him how I waited for him to come back, how much I missed him and worried about him. But my tongue refused to obey me.

My thoughts scattered. Then my mind drifted away someplace much darker than even the Dark Anomaly.

Chapter 7

Valentina muttered something in her sleep, and he placed a cool, wet cloth on her hot forehead.

He'd made the decision to give her some tea with just a drop of the *irsen* juice again, to make her sleep while her body fought the poison of the *fuhnid* mushrooms and its aftereffects.

And she fought hard. It'd been a week now. Her skin still flushed with heat, delusions bothered her judging by her screams, but her breathing was strong, and her heartbeat stable.

She remained alive.

For the tenth time that morning, he said thanks to the higher spirits for helping him heal her again. Taking her unbandaged hand in both of his, he pressed her palm to his face, breathing in her familiar delicate scent.

"One more day," he whispered against her skin. "Tomorrow will be the time to wake you."

Bursts of excitement pulsed in his chest. He'd spent most of his life alone, feeling no need for a companion. Now, he couldn't wait to see Valentina open her eyes and to hear her voice again. The anticipation warmed his heart, making it so full, he thought it might explode.

"Soon," he murmured as a promise, kissing her hand.

A tinkle of a tiny bell alerted him of someone entering the gardens. He'd installed a simple mechanical system of ropes and springs recently. It triggered the bell in the bedroom when the doors to the gardens were opened—a warning system that alerted of the intruders.

With a last quick kiss, he let go of Valentina's hand. Taking the two biggest knives he had, he slid one in the sheath at his belt that he'd made, keeping the other one ready in his hand.

He'd heard that Nocc was killed on the day of the last unrest, along with many others. The population of the Dark Anomaly had been steadily shrinking due to fights even before that.

There had been over seven hundred of the crew just a few months ago. After the two mutinies that had taken place since, no one bothered to count the number of survivors. By Malahki's estimate, there were just over half left, and that number kept going down daily. Those alive, however, remained dangerous.

As he had dreaded before, order on the Dark Anomaly had been weakening. Malahki hadn't seen the captain doing his rounds anymore. Neither did Svetlana come to the main kitchen to cook the crew's meals as she used to.

He believed Vrateus had retreated into hiding with her, possibly locking themselves in his room. The captain had given up on his treacherous crew, choosing to protect what was most important to him—Svetlana. And Malahki had done the same, keeping safe at all cost the one person in the world who'd become more precious to him than any other—his Valentina.

As noiselessly as possible, he stepped to the entrance from the room to see who had come to the gardens this time. The place had been raided a few times in the past two weeks. As the order crumbled, hunger had raged among the crew. Though most of them preferred eating meat, they'd been coming here to comb through the planters for anything edible at all.

Peeking from behind the remaining vines, Malahki saw an *errock* come in. He was alone, which was good. Malahki could fight him if needed. Lately, the possibility of a fight didn't disgust him as much as it used to. He found himself wishing for it, even with someone as huge and intimidating as the *errock*.

As the male circled the gardens, Malahki recognized Wyck, the one who got the human woman Nadia in his charge. Malahki's fists itched even more for a fight now.

The *errock* had come here before, looking for Valentina, but as long as Malahki was alive, he wasn't going to get her.

Adjusting the grip on his knife, he quietly followed Wyck. The *errock* collected some of the leftover plants and fruit, then stopped at a planter by the exit.

Malahki froze, motionless. He wouldn't shy away from a fight, but the caution dictated it was best not to pick one either.

Finally, the *errock* headed out the door.

Malahki creeped after him into the corridor, too, then followed him as Wyck turned right. There was nothing at that end but the crashed human ship. The cut-out that served as the entrance to the ship was now blocked with a piece of metal. The dead bodies left behind after the last mutiny and the battle that had taken place here had been moved away or eaten by now. Everything dead served as food lately.

Wyck stopped in front of the blocked entrance to the human ship and tilted his head back. The metal part slid aside, letting Wyck in. From his vantage point, Malahki couldn't see the person who opened the door, but it most likely was another *errock*. The *errocks* always stuck together on the Dark Anomaly. The entrance then closed again, followed by several hard clicks, which must be the sounds of the locks sliding back in place.

All surviving *errocks* must be behind that door with Wyck. Knowing that, Malahki made a metal note to stay away from this part of the corridor.

Chapter 8

VAL

"Wake up, Valya," a familiar voice said softly.

Latching on to it, I followed the voice out of the darkness.

"There you are." Malahki smiled when I opened my eyes. He lightly stroked my forehead. "The fever is finally down. How are you feeling?"

I blinked in the soft light of the vines under the ceiling. The beautiful canopy that used to hang over the bed before was now gone.

"I'm good," I croaked, my voice low and rough.

"Here." He shifted closer, holding a small cup of tea to my lips. "Drink this."

I did as he said. The warm, slightly sweetened tea refreshed my mouth, making my tongue easier to move.

"Here we go again." I gave Malahki a weak smile. "You keep nursing me back to health, and I can't stop getting hurt."

He placed the cup back on the upturned plastic crate nearby but didn't release me from the half-hug he had me in. His arm around my shoulders, he sat on the bed next to me.

I leaned my head against him, my neck too weak to hold it up for too long.

He stroked my hair. "I need to do a much better job at keeping you from harm in the first place."

I lifted my right hand up. My ring finger was tightly bandaged with a piece of yellow cloth. The skin on my hand had a light bluish tint. My finger felt warm and tingly under the bandage but there was no pain.

"How long have I been under, this time?" I asked.

"Today is day eight."

Another week had passed by. But did time really matter anymore?

"And how have *you* been all this time?" I shifted to see his face better and paused.

He looked hardly like the Malahki I knew. I leaned further back, taking in his appearance.

His features seemed harder and more angular somehow. His eyebrows thickened and darkened from their previous sand-blond to the current sable-brown. Thick strands of the same darker color were sprinkled through his hair, too.

"You're changing." I frowned, cupping his face. Unsure of the reasons for the changes, I couldn't tell whether they were good or bad, which worried me.

"Am I?" He rolled his shoulders uneasily, glancing aside. I suspected he might not be comfortable with the changes.

"How are you feeling?" I stroked one of his sharpened cheekbones. His jawline seemed harder and more prominent, now. The vines in his hair had withered, most of their leaves gone. He hadn't replaced them in days. "Malahki, are you okay?" I turned his face to me, forcing him to look me in the eye.

The swirls of vivid color I'd noticed in his irises the day of the last attack were no longer there, though his eyes weren't their former serene beige either. Uneven splashes of brown and burgundy spread through them like ink spots.

"I'm fine." His words were clipped. He pressed his lips together as he often used to do before. Except it looked different now, on his barely familiar face.

"Were you hurt? That day?" I asked, concerned.

"No. Nothing like what you got." He took my bandaged hand in his and started unwrapping the yellow strip of fabric.

My mind went back to the day I got attacked, to the massacre in the gardens, and to the people I'd killed.

"Did all six of them die?"

He nodded, understanding what I was talking about without questions.

"What happened to the dead bodies?" I had to know.

"Gone."

"How?"

He spoke, without looking at me, "I loaded them into a wagon I use to transport the garden waste that's too large for the garbage chute and took them down to be incinerated."

"Were there any questions? Did someone come looking for them? I'm so sorry you had to deal with all of that on your own." I sighed.

He removed the bandage from my finger, revealing the dark purple powder caked over the cut.

"There is no one to look for the dead, Valya," Malahki replied somberly. "Those still alive are busy killing each other."

The new, steel-cold expression made him even less familiar—almost a stranger.

Unable to bear the look in his eyes, I dropped my gaze down to his lap, noting that he was wearing a pair of black pants. A little loose around his trim waist, the pants were held up by a wide leather belt with handmade sheaths that held knives. The pants weren't his. I saw them last on Trox. Malahki had stripped the dead body before disposing of it.

"What are you saying, Malahki?" I kept staring at the pants of the dead *errock*. "What's going on out there, outside of the gardens?"

"The captain abandoned the crew after they almost killed him—again. There's no order, now. We're on our own."

"On our own..." I echoed, staring straight ahead and afraid to think what exactly that meant.

"We're fine here. For now, anyway," Malahki added in a softer voice, as if sensing my dread and wanting to reassure me. "I have some food collected. And I replanted the *xaevoe* grains. The crops will be ready in a few weeks."

He gestured at the long narrow planters hanging on the wall in rows, right here, in the room. I swept the place with my gaze, taking in other changes. The colorful rugs and tapestries were gone. The painted ceramic dishes had been replaced by a few metal containers. Malahki's artfully decorated trunk, where he used to store clothes and bedding, was also no longer there. The room appeared harsher and more utilitarian, very much like its owner looked now, too.

I remembered the intruders trashing this place. Malahki either hadn't been able to replace all the beautiful things they'd broken or simply didn't care about replacing them.

"I killed two people," I said, my voice hollow just like everything inside me at that moment.

"One," Malahki corrected. "The *errock* was still alive when I got here. I finished him for you."

I darted a glance to his face, but his focus was on cleaning and re-bandaging my finger.

"I'm sorry I had to kill, but I don't regret it," I said, to eradicate any doubts he or I might have on the subject. "If someone, anyone comes back here with the intention to harm you or me, I won't hesitate doing it again."

Kill or be killed. Never before had the meaning of this phrase been this clear to me.

"I don't judge you for murders," I continued, wondering if guilt or trauma of what we'd done might be the reason for the hard expression in his eyes. "I hope you're not judging me, either. We did what we had to do. It didn't mean we enjoyed the murder or wished for it to happen in the first place."

He settled his heavy stare on me, the weight of it pressing down on my chest.

"Except that I did, Valentina." Each word of his came out as if laden with lead.

"What do you mean?" I swallowed hard.

"Fighting them thrilled me. I reveled in watching life leave them. I did enjoy the murder." He spoke in short clipped sentences, like flipping a play card with each one to reveal what he'd been hiding all this time.

Had he always been this cold-blooded and ruthless? Did the changes to his body bring it up? The change of our circumstance, maybe? Or both?

I thought I'd gotten to know Malahki well during all the time we'd spent in close proximity. Now, he seemed a complete stranger to me, and it was not just his altered appearance. I felt I had to start getting to know him anew, and I feared what kind of a person I might discover.

He turned his back to me, lowering his feet to the floor. Placing his elbows on his knees, he rested his forehead on his hands, his fingers spearing through his hair.

"What is happening to me, Valya?" he exhaled.

Air rushed out of me in a breath. Compassion squeezed my heart so hard, I could cry. I was merely watching him change. What was it like for him, having to go through it all?

"Oh, Malahki..." I walked on my knees to him and hugged him from behind as he sat on the edge of the bed. "It's happening, isn't it? That's what you wanted. You wanted this change."

To be bigger, stronger, ferocious. To be able to defend himself and to protect me better.

"I know I did. But it's like having everything that I am—everything I've ever been—slowly slip away. And I'm not sure I like the pieces that are left behind."

"Don't say that." I kissed his cheek then buried my face in the side of his neck, my chest pressed to his back.

Whoever he had become, whoever he was still becoming, I could never abandon him. I was with him in it to the very end.

"We'll figure it out somehow. Okay?" I said. "We will find a way to put all your pieces back together again. You and I."

Chapter 9

"This is just…" My sentence broke off as I was unable to put into words the devastation that lay in front of me.

The seeds that Malahki had carefully planted and scrupulously nurtured into plants had been ripped out, their fruit destroyed before it had a chance to ripen. Most of the planters had been moved around or upturned. Their careful order dismantled, dirt spilled everywhere.

"We have to fix this," I said resolutely. It would take a long time for just the two of us, but we could restore the gardens if we worked hard every day.

To my surprise, Malahki shook his head.

"We'd be only wasting our time. The gardens will get raided, again and again. We'll never get a chance even to finish planting anything."

"Is that why you've moved the little we have left to the bedroom?"

He nodded. "The smaller the area, the easier it is to hide and protect."

I glanced around the destroyed gardens again, seeing them in the new light. Some plants had withered and all but died. Others, on the contrary, took off, sprawling out of their planters in a wild unkempt fashion.

The entrance to our bedroom had been camouflaged with dead vines then hidden behind the wild, overgrown bushes. There was a purpose in all this chaos, I realized. Others might have destroyed the gardens, but Malahki had directed the destruction in the way that suited him—us.

"You've watered some and let others die, haven't you?"

He nodded again.

"The dense shrubs deter most from getting too close to our room. The dead vines behind them tell those who make it past the bush that there is nothing to look at there. So, they wouldn't go through the effort of searching closely, hopefully."

The six aliens who had seen me were now dead. My existence on the Dark Anomaly remained a secret. All because of Malahki.

"Thank you," I said. "Thank you for saving me—again—and for keeping me safe."

He took my hand in his silently. Despite everything that had happened, stubborn hope clung to my heart that together, we may still make it here, no matter what.

INSTEAD OF TRYING TO fix what would be inevitably broken again sooner or later, Malahki and I focused our energy on our personal survival.

With my hand healed fully in the next few days, he taught me how to dry and preserve the plants, berries, and vegetables we still had. For days, we'd dried, pickled, and salted, accumulating food to sustain us for even harder times that Malahki was convinced lay ahead.

I helped him to hide our preserves around the gardens, in places that only he and I knew about. A few containers, Malahki took out of the gardens and hid them elsewhere on the Dark Anomaly, just in case we might be driven out of this place.

I dreaded to think about a situation that might force us to abandon this piece of the Dark Anomaly—even destroyed, the gardens had been our safe haven.

Between all the food preservation activities, we worked on a plan. A part of it was to create as many hiding places as possible throughout the gardens. After having been caught by the *errock* once, I made sure each of our small hiding spots had at least two escape routes—one had to be a direct path back to the bedroom; the other one, a way to get to the exit from the gardens. Preferably both of those routes had to be concealed from view, too, so that we could sneak away undetected.

One morning, after breakfast, Malahki helped me move yet another planter to the spot I thought would be a good hiding place. One of the handmade knife sheaths I had strapped to each of my thighs caught on a branch.

"Do you think we should start stockpiling some weapons, too?" I asked, freeing the strap from the bush.

"That wouldn't hurt," Malahki replied calmly. In addition to a knife at his hip, he had several smaller ones on the belt he'd made to carry over his shoulder and across his chest.

Danger had been hanging in the air so thick, I could never dismiss it or even forget about it for a moment anymore.

"I'll see if there is anything left in the storage rooms that we could sharpen to use as blades," he said.

To raid the storage room, Malahki would have to go out again. He refused to let me accompany him whenever he went out. And I agreed to remain behind only because he said I would attract attention and bring danger on both of us if spotted. It was safer for him to get around on his own.

Instead, I stayed behind, worried sick whenever he was out, and counted seconds until his return.

He frowned in thought.

"I'll see if I can repurpose—"

The loud thumping and screeching noise cut him off mid-sentence. I whipped around, frantically searching where the noise was coming from. Malahki grabbed me with his left arm around my middle. His other hand went to the largest of his knives, the one he carried on his right hip.

"Up there!" I yelled, realizing the sounds were coming from the ceiling. The height of it was at least thirty feet in this section of the gardens.

"Watch out!" Malahki leaped away with me in his arms as something dark and large dropped from an air vent high above.

It hit the ground next to the planter we had just moved.

"What is this?" I gaped at the creature wiggling on the floor.

At least six or seven feet long, it had a cylindrical body, with numerous skinny legs along each side. Its round, multifaceted eyes bulging out, it kept snapping its mandibles with a clunking noise.

"It's a *vasai* centipede." Malahki held me closer to him. "The crew used to breed them in cages, in the farm close to the kitchen. The farm has been ransacked with all of the *vasai* now gone. This one must be a wild one. There're a few of them around."

He and I had eaten *vasai* eggs often before the farm got destroyed, but I certainly had never seen a live centipede before.

"Do they just drop down like that?" I asked, snuggling closer into the safety of his body.

The creature had stopped screeching when it fell. Its movements now turned to erratic convulsions.

"Never," Malahki said. "This is the first time I've seen this happen."

Moving me to the side and behind him, he stepped toward the centipede.

"Careful." I touched his arm.

But he sheathed his knife and crouched at the centipede's side. The poor thing looked like it was dying.

"It's no longer dangerous," he assured me, though his dark eyebrows moved together into a frown.

"It must have hurt or broke something on impact," I offered a possible explanation.

Carefully avoiding the sharp mandibles that could cause damage even through the last contractions of the creature's muscles, Malahki took the *vasai's* head in his hands then turned it, inspecting. The light in the gardens broke up into rainbows in the thousands of facets of the centipede's large, round eyes.

"I think it was unwell before it hit the ground," he said. "That's why it fell out of the vent in the first place."

The long body stopped contracting, the dozens of skinny legs curled and stilled. I ventured to come closer, too.

"How did it get up there?"

"There're a number of wild *vasai* around here. A load of them was on a ship that crashed here a while back. Most were captured and farmed. But some managed to hide in the many tunnels and openings of the Dark Anomaly and survived on their own."

"How?"

He shrugged.

"By eating scraps, each other's eggs or the garden waste. I run into them every now and then in the garbage disposal chutes when I climb in to maintain the conveyor belts or clean a blockage. They're vicious and energetic, always alert and ready to attack. Not like this one." He dropped the creature's head, getting up to his feet.

"What do you want to do with it?" I asked.

He eyed it critically, from a distance.

"We can't eat it." He touched one of its legs with the toe of his boot. Ever since I woke up from my last injury, Malahki had been wearing black leather boots along with the dead *errock's* pants. "We don't know what it died of. Its meat could be contaminated."

The Malahki I knew from before would've never even considered eating meat, contaminated or not.

"If we leave it here, the scavengers will find it," I noted.

We'd been getting visits every now and then. The crew came, combing through the gardens in search of food, even as there was nothing left to take. I had no doubts, most of them would grab the dead centipede for meat. If the *vasai* died from a disease, they might get ill, too.

He nodded.

"The scavengers will find it, no matter where we put it. But we have to get rid of it before it starts to rot." He bent over, grabbing the centipede by its head. "Can you get its tail, please?"

I lifted the bottom end of the *vasai* by the last pair of its legs. Hard and shiny, they proved to be also smooth and slippery, making carrying it a difficult task.

Together, Malahki and I managed to get the body to the nearest garbage chute. As I held the panel over the opening up, he shoved the long body of the *vasai* through, bit by bit. The moment the textured conveyor belt connected with it, it dragged the rest of it through and out of sight.

A heavy feeling pressed on my chest. The unexplained death of the creature bothered me, adding to the general anxiety of day-to-day life on the Dark Anomaly.

Malahki squeezed my shoulder, and I leaned into his body, seeking the comfort I always got from our contact.

Lately, however, things had been different. We continued to share the bed, and he would hold me in his arms as I fell asleep. But when I woke up, he always lay away from me, with as much distance between us as the size of the bed allowed.

After that kiss on the morning of the latest mutiny of the crew, there hadn't been any more kisses. He never even fully hugged me anymore, giving me instead just a one-armed half-hug every now and then, like the one he was giving to me now.

I missed the easy camaraderie we'd achieved earlier and somehow had lost now. I wouldn't even mind his former snappy attitude, if only the gloomy cloud that seemed to perpetually hang over him would disappear.

"We should get back in for lunch," he said, taking his hand off me, and I immediately missed the contact, leaning after him.

We had barely made a few steps across the gardens on our way back to our room when the crashing noise of the entrance doors made me jump. Malahki stiffened at my side, his knives in his hands again.

I didn't even realize how my knives ended up in my grip as well. Living constantly on edge, I acted automatically. I jerked my head his way, and he pinched his lips between his fingers in a call to silence. He noiselessly stepped behind a planter with an outgrown shrub, taking me with him.

Growling and scraping noises came from the entrance. They grew louder, increasing in numbers, not just volume.

I moved a branch aside, peeking through the bush in that direction.

At first, it appeared to me a large group of animals crashed into the gardens from the outside corridor. Wild beasts I'd never seen before. Peering closely, I realized these were some of the crew of the Dark Anomaly.

Dozens of them crawled in, mostly *kreers*, with a few *ognats* and some other species in between. They didn't walk or run. They *crawled*. They scurried on all their limbs, low to the floor, like a dark, glistening mass, tails lashing, teeth snapping at each other.

A *kreer* whipped one of his tails around the neck of another one, closest to him. The second *kreer* screeched, sinking his sharp teeth into the segmented tail around his neck. Dark green blood burst in a spray from the wound, dripping between his teeth. The first *kreer* snarled, lunging on the one biting him. Blood stained them both from the bites and scratches they shelled out to each other.

The rest of the group crawled over the two on their way further into the gardens. Some lingered to take a bite from either one of the fighters. Both were eventually trampled and consumed by the crowd.

My stomach churned, bile rising high in my throat. Despite the loud screeching, growls, and yelps, not a single discernible word came from the advancing mass. It was as if they had lost either the physical ability to speak or the mental ability to form the words. Just like they had obviously given up walking upright.

Afraid to make a sound, I glanced at Malahki. His expression was as confused as mine. Taking my hand, he backed away from the half-beasts that were invading the gardens.

My confusion was quickly replaced by horror as the snarling crawling creatures spread through the gardens. They tipped over planters, chewed on the vines and dried branches, and dug through the dirt.

Every now and then, a fight would break out. With both opponents ending up injured, the rest would then move in to gnaw on what was left of them.

The horror of the scene choked me. The knives squeezed in my hands, I crossed my arms over my chest, afraid I'd scream or vomit.

A tug on my shoulder almost sent me into a panic attack before I realized it was Malahki, silently urging me to retreat toward the wall with the chute, away from the crowd spreading through the gardens like vermin.

To move away, however, meant to abandon our cover. It wouldn't serve as such for long, anyway. The *kreers* and the *ognats* swiftly moved through the space, upturning and sniffing everything. By staying in our hiding spot, we risked being discovered and surrounded, cut off from every escape route.

A loud screech slashed through the air, assaulting my hearing. One of the *kreers* had spotted us. Scurrying over the others, he climbed over the planters, upturned and upright, on his way to us.

"Run!" Malahki turned to the wall with the chute, shoving me ahead of him on our dash to escape.

Afraid to look back, I sprinted through the open space. An ear-splitting squeal behind me, forced me to glance back in concern for Malahki.

He slashed with his knife, cutting across the face of the *kreer* pursuing us. The male whimpered in pain, falling back. Several others swarmed him quickly. The green blood splashed on the floor as his body was ripped to pieces, the crew feasting on the flesh of one of their own.

Others moved in our direction.

"Valya, fast!" Malahki yanked me to the garbage chute. "Go first," he ordered.

With dozens of the wild things swiftly approaching and even more of them pouring into the gardens, there was no time to argue or debate.

Shoving my knives back in their holders, I broke off the panel that covered the entrance to the tunnel as Malahki slashed and sliced the *kreers* chasing us.

I gripped the edge of the opening, swinging both legs in and onto the conveyor belt. It caught grip on my boots, tugging me further in. The slope of the tunnel made it easy for me to let go and slide in, but I propped my boots into the walls slowing down my progress.

"Malahki!" I screamed over my shoulder.

There was no way in hell I'd leave him to fight the horde of feral *kreers* on his own. I'd find a way to climb back up and out if I had to.

"I'm here!" He slid into the tunnel behind me, and I let go of the walls traveling further down to give him space.

His shoulders must have gotten wider since the last time he'd come into the tunnels to fix the belt. They spanned across the entire width of the tunnel, wedging him in place.

"You don't fit," I breathed in horror, slowing down my descent again to grab on to his boot. The belt screeched, scraping against both of us.

With a grunt, Malahki shifted to the side, curling his shoulders to make himself smaller. The belt jerked again then moved, dragging both of us along.

The screeching of the *kreers* echoed through the tunnels. They were way too big to fit through to follow us. They fought at the entrance of the chute, shoving each other away until I lost them from view with a bend of the tunnel.

"Valya, listen." Malahki's voice sounded strained and urging, not allowing me to relax even for a second. "There is an opening coming up on your left. Try to feel for it with your hand. A piece of loose paneling. That'd be the exit into the corridor, roughly across from the captain's room. I want you to try to stop. Can you?"

"Okay." I let go of his boot reluctantly, feeling the wall with my hand on my way down.

When the piece of the panel clapped under my hand, I braced my boots into the walls, slowing down. I wasn't fast enough, however. The opening slid past me. I grabbed onto Malahki's boot again as he curled his fingers around the edge of the opening, forcing both of us to stop.

"Here," he said confidently.

Muffled growls and shuffling filtered through the wall.

"Careful," I half-whispered, holding my breath as he lifted the panel to peek into the corridor.

A pale-blue tentacle lashed through the narrow slit. Malahki shrank back with a startled sound. Growls and screeching grew louder, reaching a deafening volume. A black segmented tail of a *kreer* whipped around the *yourlu's* tentacle, yanking it back into the corridor. Blood sprayed into the tunnel, staining Malahki's shoulder with the dark red blood of the *yourlu*, not the green of the *kreers*.

"Keep going." Malahki let go of the opening, letting us continue to slide downwards, along the slope of the garbage chute.

Mayhem appeared to be taking place all over the Dark Anomaly.

"Where exactly will this tunnel take us?" I asked, shaking from fear and adrenaline.

What was happening out there? A massacre? The crew, deranged and unhinged, were brutally murdering each other.

My chest tightened, making it hard to breathe.

"The chute will take us to the waste disposal room," Malahki said. His voice sounded deceptively calm, but I knew he must be freaking out, too. He just didn't want to scare me any more than I already was. "There is always a pile of debris on the floor under the drop-off. The crew never managed to clean it off in time even when the captain was there to make them do it regularly. You'll land in it. Watch out for anyone who might be there. The room is next to the *vasai* farm. The cages may be empty now, but the crew are hungry. Someone may still be lurking around."

The crew were hungry. And we were nothing but food for them. Not unlike the centipedes.

Cold fear gripped me as I bent my head, staring ahead while we kept moving. My breathing grew heavier. Every drag of air required an effort.

When a pale light showed up at the end of the tunnel, I slid one of my knives out again, keeping the other hand free to guide and brace myself if needed on the way out.

The tunnel slope tilted more sharply down, speeding up our descent.

The fall wasn't as high as I'd expected. I hit something soft before Malahki rolled out of the tunnel and on top of me.

The air reeked of rotting meat. The hand I used to break my fall with slipped in something.

"Watch out!" Malahki warned, leaping off me.

Slipping and sliding, I managed to sit up and look around. I was sitting on top of a pile of...dead bodies. I screamed, scrambling off it. These weren't even whole bodies—pieces of decomposing flesh and half-eaten carcasses littered the small room. They were piled up high in the middle, judging by the condition of the rotting flesh, no one bothered to bring anything fresh here for days. Or maybe anything fresh was simply eaten out there, without ever making it here anymore.

Disgust racked me. Revulsion brought up the remnants of my breakfast. I vomited at the bottom of the grisly pile of rotting flesh.

The sounds of a fight with grunts, screeching of teeth, and flesh hitting flesh brought me back to my senses. Spurred into action, I climbed over the bones and rotten meat around the pile, finding Malahki on the other side of it.

He hadn't had a chance to draw his knives. His fist covered in green blood, he pummeled a *kreer* in the head. Another one lay dead on the ground already, next to the body of the dead centipede Malahki and I had dumped down the chute just a little while earlier. Two more *kreers* were feasting on the flesh of both the centipede and their dead comrade.

I could throw up again or simply faint from it all, only worry for Malahki kept me upright. With a knife in my hand, I lumbered through the mess on the floor to him.

He smashed through the head of the *kreer* he was fighting, killing him instantly. Without so much as taking a fresh breath, he grabbed one of the two who were eating and punched him in the face, too.

The *kreer* hissed, baring his sharp teeth and slinking his long black tongue out. Grabbing the *kreer's* head with both hands, Malahki twisted it, ripping it off the males's shoulders.

I gasped, pressing my hand to my chest as the green blood gushed from torn vessels.

He tossed the head aside and kicked the lifeless body out of the way, before going after the last remaining *kreer*.

"Malahki," I said softly, hardly recognizing *my* Malahki in this person who hit and murdered relentlessly, without stopping.

He killed the last *kreer* with a punch in the head then kept on punching again and again, spraying the blood in green bursts all over the corpses and himself.

"Malahki," I called louder, as he didn't seem to hear me, lost to the no longer needed violence. "He's dead...Stop it."

He wouldn't listen, pummeling the body of the *kreer* into a bloody mess.

"Malahki!" I yelled. "Stop it!"

He stilled, as if suddenly deprived of the energy to make another move.

"Stop it," I said softly, tentatively touching his back.

His muscles stiffened under my hand. A long shudder rolled through his tense body, his hands still fisted at his sides.

"We need to think about what to do next." I carefully dragged my hand down, stroking his back.

His shoulders lifted with a deep breath.

"Right." He stepped over the dead *kreer*. Shaking out his hands, he finally unclenched his fists.

I was afraid to look him in the eye, but I had to see his expression. It wasn't as easy for me to read him now as it used to be.

Glancing up, I caught his eyes in my gaze. The remnants of bloodlust still glowed in them, swirling red, orange, and purple in his irises. Eerie and terrifying.

I removed my hand from him, taking a step back. Pure aggression radiated from him, barely contained.

Yet when he reached for me, offering me his hand, I took it, sticky and covered in blood as it was.

"That's the farm." He pointed with his chin at the only entrance from the gory waste disposal room to our left. "There may be more of them out there. Stay close."

Chapter 10

<u>VAL</u>

"Stay behind me," Malahki instructed, punching the code into the lock panel to the storage room, located not too far from the airlock. He'd said the crew kept the space suits collected over time from the crashed ships here.

We'd gone through the farm and the nearby section of the corridor, finding the same devastation everywhere. Remains of *vasai* centipedes littered the floors, mixed with bones and body parts of the sentient beings who once populated the Dark Anomaly. The stench was unbearable, forcing me to cover my nose and mouth with my elbow. Thankfully, there was a bathroom in the farm. So, we'd been able at least to wash the gore and blood off our hands and faces.

The storage room was the last place at this end of the habitable sector that we hadn't checked yet. Malahki hadn't explicitly stated so, but I knew what he was looking for—survivors.

Something horrible had been happening on the Dark Anomaly while the two of us huddled in the relative safety of the gardens. The crew's self-extermination and the cannibalism were a part of it. Or maybe the consequence.

Like Malahki, I wanted to get answers, hoping to find someone who could still speak.

The door to the storage room screeched, shifting off its hinges when Malahki opened it. The room had been raided. Most shelves here were empty. Some of their contents had been swept to the floor. Five or six spacesuits remained upright, attached to the walls, the rest had been knocked over.

Two large figures lay on the floor on their sides.

"*Akuks,*" Malahki said.

I recognized this lesser-known species, visually at least. I knew little about them, despite having studied everything I could get my hands on about the species of the Federation while getting ready for our expedition to the Dark Anomaly. Their lower bodies reminded me of giant black caterpillars, complete with dozens of small skinny legs. Their heads, arms, and torsos appeared more humanoid, the black blotches on their backs turning to bright yellow on their bellies.

"They don't look like they were murdered," I pointed out, covering my mouth with my arm again. The air inside the storage room was stifling, the stench of decomposing bodies unbearable.

I stepped back, closer to the exit.

"No one has eaten them, either." Placing his hand over his mouth and nose, too, Malahki crouched by one of the bodies.

The *akuks* had no visible wounds. They lay in natural poses as if having fallen asleep.

Malahki got up to his feet again. Tilting his head back, he surveyed the vents positioned around the room, under the ceiling.

"Is it me or is it exceptionally hard to breathe in here?"

"It stinks." I pointed at the bodies.

"Not just that." He heaved a breath. "The air seems to be low on oxygen."

Now that he'd said it, I had a hard time getting enough oxygen into my lungs. My breathing was deep and fast, yet I felt suffocated.

"Let's get out of here." I tugged at Malahki's arm. Quickly checking the corridor first, I hurried out of the storage room.

Malahki followed me. He leaned the broken door against the entrance to the room, not quite closing it completely since it was now partially off its hinges.

I kept thinking about the two *akuks*, who appeared to have lain down for a nap to never wake again.

"Do you think someone killed them by cutting off the oxygen to the room?" I asked Malahki as we carefully moved along the corridor back to the farm.

He shook his head.

"The door can be unlocked and opened from the inside. They would've had no trouble getting out."

"Why didn't they, then?"

"They didn't know they were in danger of suffocating. They just went to sleep."

"And never woke up," I finished for him. Silent invisible death was hanging over this place, making my skin crawl.

"Did you notice the air was thin in the garbage chute as well?" Malahki asked unexpectedly.

"I thought I couldn't breathe because of fear and worry, but now that you mention it..." I let my voice trail off, pondering his words for a moment. "Is something wrong with the air supply system?"

Dread slithered cold down my spine. If the oxygen production system had failed, there was no hope for any of us.

Malahki knew it, too. He drew in a long breath as if savoring the fact he still could.

"If the central system's air supply drops, the oxygen levels would be reduced in the harder to access places first, those that do not have the direct vents to it, such as the garbage chute, and any other areas of space trapped between the walls and ceilings of the ships. The centipede of this morning must've fallen out of such a place, not out of an air vent."

"You think it was suffocating when it fell."

"Possibly. That would explain why it fell in the first place. *Vasai* are good climbers otherwise."

I considered that for a moment.

"The storage room has vents, though," I said.

Malahki rubbed his forehead.

"The supply to it might've been cut off, intentionally by someone or accidentally, due to poor maintenance. No one has been looking after the system for weeks, now."

He stopped in his tracks abruptly. The sound of scuffling and grunting came from up ahead in the corridor.

"Come here." He hurriedly ushered me into the closest room, which was the farm again.

All cages stood empty. The doors on many of them were missing. A thick layer of dried blood of various colors and the content of broken eggs covered the floor.

Malahki took me behind the cages, along the wall to the left from the entrance and out of sight from anyone entering.

Emitting short, panicky screams, a *yourlu* rushed in, the lower cluster of his tentacles practically vibrating from the effort to move fast. It wasn't fast enough as a *kreer* scurried after him. With a loud screech, the *kreer* lunged on top of the *yourlu*.

The sharp teeth of the *kreer* closed over the *yourlu's* head. The *yourlu's* tuft of bright purple hair disappeared in the *kreer's* mouth, red blood dripping down his face as the *kreer* sunk his teeth into the *yourlu's* skull, crushing it.

I whimpered, covering my mouth with both hands. Wrapping his arm around me, Malahki dragged me down to the floor to hide behind the cages.

My back pressed into the wall, and the wall gave in. Losing my balance, I would have fallen through it backwards, had it not been for Malahki's arm. He pulled me to him.

The *kreer* must have noticed the commotion. Letting the dead *yourlu's* head drop out of his mouth, he peered our way intently.

My heart dropped into the pit of my stomach in horror as the *kreer* shifted off the dead body, visibly getting ready to head in our direction.

"Stay here," Malahki whispered, getting a knife out.

Before he had a chance to make a move, however, something launched from the entrance. Long and shiny, it speared through the *kreer's* head, dropping him dead.

"Got him!" a deep voice exclaimed with glee.

I grabbed on to Malahki's wrist, silently urging him to stay in place, hidden with me.

A large *errock* entered.

"Gler," Malahki exhaled, barely audibly.

I understood Gler was the *errock's* name. Dressed in a dark pair of pants, similar to the ones Malahki himself was now wearing, Gler headed for the *kreer* he'd just killed by hurling the metal rode at his head.

"I'll take this one," he said to the *akuk* who followed him in.

"The *akuk's* name is Ivall," Malahki said softly.

Gler heaved the dead *kreer* up and draped his long body over his shoulder.

"You get the other one," he said to Ivall, tipping his head at the body of the *yourlu*. "Let's go back to the ship." He then turned to leave. "We'll have enough to eat for a few days, now. As the only *errock* on the ship, I'll get the first pick of the piece of meat I want."

"*Meat.*"

The *yourlu* and the *kreer* were on the same crew as the *errock* and the *akuk*. All used to live and work together. Chances were Gler knew their names. Yet all they were to him now was "meat."

I hugged myself watching the two haul their "kill" away.

"What 'ship' did they go to, you think?" Malahki said with a thoughtful expression on his face. Unlike me, he managed to focus on practical parts among the horror of the chaos.

"A spaceship?" I offered.

"Yes, but which one?" he asked, rubbing his chin.

Obviously, I couldn't give him an answer to that. Besides, my attention honed in on something else.

"Gler spoke," I said, the full significance of the fact dawning on me. "The rest of them look like they've lost their minds, but he acted normal. Well, normal for an *errock*."

The *akuk* hadn't said anything, but he hadn't behaved crazy or deranged, either.

Malahki nodded, thinking out loud, "The air on the Dark Anomaly is supplied through a combination of a central system and individual ones of the ships that have them. Gler and Ivall must have moved to one of the ships with its own autonomous air supply. That's why they weren't affected by the malfunctions of the central system."

"The malfunction might've affected different species differently, too," I added. "Do the gardens have their own system as well?" I felt grateful that Malahki and I had escaped the fate of the *kreers* and *yourlu*—so far, anyway.

"The gardens have both. I found the central air supply inadequate from the very beginning and incorporated an axillary system in their design, for the improved air flow for the plants."

I drew in a lungful of air. The stench of death was a little less here than in the waste processing room. There were no decomposing bodies in the farm, and the layer of grime on the floor was old and had crusted over.

"The air appears okay in here," I said tentatively.

Malahki's chest rose with a deep breath, too.

"It does, doesn't it?" he agreed. "I wonder if the malfunction was temporary, or if it just affected certain areas."

It could have been both. It also didn't mean that there wouldn't be more malfunctions, and not just with the air supply system. No one had maintained anything around here for weeks.

"Did the crew all just go crazy simply from the lack of oxygen, then?" I speculated.

"I don't know how the lack of oxygen affects each species, but there might be more than that involved. I wish we could talk to someone who was here when things started to change."

"Someone who could still speak at all," I added, fighting a heavy feeling in my chest. I couldn't detect any unusual smells in the air. But the stench of decay had penetrated these walls so thoroughly, it was hard to smell anything beyond that. "Can we find the problem and fix the system?"

Malahki blew out a breath.

"I'm afraid there might've been more problems than one. And more may still happen as the system is deteriorating. In any case, we don't have something like a central control room here. The things have been created over many years. New parts have been added as new ships crashed. We'd have to thoroughly inspect the entire system, vent by vent, pipe by pipe to find what is wrong. That would take time."

The time we didn't have, surrounded by deranged crew and those who might still have their mental capacity intact but chose to use it for murder.

Malahki let go of me, getting up.

"Come." He offered me his hand. "I have some pickled *caur* hidden in the ceiling near the kitchen."

"You do?" Despite our bleak situation, I couldn't hold back a smile at his resourcefulness.

He grinned, too, wiggling his eyebrows.

"You know I'm good at finding hiding places. I've stuffed food all over the Dark Anomaly. We'll eat, then figure out whether to try making it back to the gardens or find a safe place here, instead."

"Are there any safe places left on this smashed tin can in space?" I muttered under my breath. Today was the first time I'd ever left the destroyed, ravaged gardens and so far, everything else I'd seen of the Dark Anomaly had been even worse.

I leaned back, ready to get up to my feet, too. My shoulder blades pressed against the wall panel again, and it gave in behind me. With a strangled cry of surprise, I grabbed on to Malahki's hand.

"What's back there?" He crouched next to me.

"A loose panel. I nearly fell in twice already," I explained, feeling silly for forgetting about it.

"Let me see." He peeked in the gap between two panels. "There's light," he said softly.

"What?" I brought my face next to his, trying to get a look, too.

"Stay back," he warned, lifting a knife and getting ready to strike if attacked.

Bending back the loose panel, he revealed a dark open space behind it. It could barely be called a room, more like a large closet with a prolapsed ceiling. A pale reflection of shimmering, undulating light filtered from the narrow opening on the opposite wall, which appeared to lead to an adjacent room.

"There is no one here," I said, in a whisper for whatever reason.

"You don't know for sure." Malahki fitted his shoulders between the panels. Holding his knife in his hand, he crawled in.

He couldn't stand up all the way, the ceiling was too low for him. In a crouch, he approached the opening to the tunnel on the opposite wall and carefully looked inside it.

"There is another room here, with a window." He gestured for me to follow him as I still sat outside in the farm.

Glancing around the farm to make sure no one had seen us, I slipped into the closet-room with him.

He poked his head into the faintly illuminated tunnel. His shoulders bumped into the edge of the opening on each side. He swore under his breath.

"I can't fit through here," he said. "Not anymore."

"Not anymore."

I took a closer look at him. Malahki's proportions had changed. I wasn't sure how long it had been happening. The physical changes didn't seem to happen smoothly or gradually. Or maybe they had been so slow that I didn't always notice them right away. His shoulders indeed appeared significantly wider now. He was taller too, I could tell as he bent over next to me to avoid hitting the ceiling with his head.

"Let me try." I crouched down by the opening.

"Be careful." He grabbed my hand.

I nodded, taking out one of my knives. From here, the room on the other end of the tunnel appeared empty. I saw or heard nothing. But one could never be too cautious on the Dark Anomaly. Holding the hand with the knife ahead of me, I moved in.

My head and shoulders went through without problems, the rest of my body followed in.

The new room was even smaller than the one I'd just crawled from. But there was a window here—the round porthole with the view of the spectacular lights of the Dark Anomaly.

"Wow," I whispered in awe, unable to take my eyes off the magnificent colorful tendrils of light that curled and undulated, following the pattern of some invisible power. "This is...mesmerising."

"Don't stare at the lights for too long," Malahki warned from the other end of the tunnel. "They say it'll drive you mad."

"Apparently, you don't need the lights to go crazy on the Dark Anomaly." I sighed, thinking about the madness that took over so many of the crew, bringing them a tragic end.

"True," he agreed. "There're many ways to lose one's mind and life around here. How is the air in there?"

I drew in a breath. It wasn't any harder to do than breathing in the *vasai* farm. The air felt even cleaner, since the stench didn't reach in here as much.

"Good," I said, turning away from the window, ready to go back to him.

"Stay there," he stopped me. "If I can't fit through, no other male can. You'll be safe there while I go get the food."

I exhaled a brief laugh, peeking at him through the tunnel.

"I hate to break it to you, Malahki, but you're no longer the smallest man on the Dark Anomaly. Have you looked at yourself lately?"

His dark eyebrows twitched as he rolled back his shoulders.

"I did get bigger," he muttered under his breath, rubbing his upper arm, which I'd just noticed also had significantly bulked up.

"That said," I continued. "I believe you're right, I barely squeezed through myself, so no one else around here would probably make it."

I reached for him through the tunnel, and he grabbed my hand in his.

"Please be careful," I begged, my worry for him never left me. I hated parting from him even for a little bit. Would there ever be a time when the two of us could walk freely everywhere together?

"I won't be long." He squeezed my hand tightly. "Please stay there."

Then he was gone.

I stood on my knees in the tiny room with the low ceiling and with the dancing lights behind the window. I hated watching Malahki go, hated waiting for him alone while I measured the time with my heartbeats until his return. I worried for him every second of every minute he was out there on his own.

On the other hand, I understood that if I went with him, my presence would be like an open invitation for an attack. Malahki might be turning into someone more dangerous and even lethal, but he was not invincible. I didn't want to make this trip any more dangerous for him.

I had no way to tell how long it had been since he left. Every moment without him seemed like an eternity.

When the panel cracked and the rustling noise of someone crawling through reached me, I felt more excited than scared. It could be a mad *kreer* coming for me. But my heart leaped with anticipation, making me lean closer into the tunnel.

"It's me," Malahki's voice sounded from the other room.

Not losing a second, I quickly slinked through the tunnel to his side.

"I got some food and water." He chuckled as I covered his face with kisses. He had to hunch over under the low ceiling, which made his head easier for me to reach. Hugging his neck, I placed one last kiss on the edge of his jaw, before finally letting go of him.

"Here." He sat down on the floor, placing two containers between us.

"How did it go?" I asked, sitting next to him. "Is it quiet out there?"

"Mostly," he replied evasively, wiping a green smudge off his right hand on his pants. A *kreer's* blood? I didn't want to know. "I had the *caur* in double containers, to better conceal their smell from the others. I filled the second container with water from the tap in the bathroom here. Thirsty?"

I nodded. "Did you have some?"

"I did." He opened the smaller container with the dark green leaves of the *caur* plant. Like round, chubby cactus, the leaves had soaked up the marinade we'd preserved them in, tasting juicy and simply delicious to me right now. After all the horrors of today, I hadn't even realized how hungry I was.

"Thank you," I said, stuffing my face with the *caur* and washing it down with the water he'd brought.

Malahki ate a few, too. His eyes seemed even darker in the dim lighting of the room. His hair had turned to dark-brown with streaks of ink-black through it and with no beige left at all.

"How are you feeling?" I studied his body for more changes that seemed to happen all the time now.

He brought his gaze to my eyes, and I knew he understood exactly what I meant.

"Different," he said softly.

"In a good way?" I asked, hopefully.

He stretched his neck awkwardly, breaking our eye contact.

"I'm not sure yet," was all he said.

He obviously didn't want to discuss the changes he was going through.

"I'm here whenever you want to talk," I said softly. If he needed some time, I just wanted him to know that I had enough patience to wait until he was ready.

"I know. Thank you." Stretching his long legs, he bumped his boot into a long, silver canister I'd just noticed by the exit to the farm.

"What's that?" I asked, changing the subject.

"Oxygen tank," he replied, visibly relieved to be talking about something else. "With two masks. I found them in the spacesuit storage."

The one with the two dead akuks, echoed in my brain.

"We'll stay here for now," Malahki continued. "There're still some crew scavenging in the corridor around the kitchen and the mess hall."

"How long do you think we should stay here? Is there no other way to the gardens other than the main corridor?"

He shook his head, his expression contemplative.

"You could try to climb up the garbage chute. It'd be more difficult than going down, though. I'll have to cut the belt, to stop it from pulling you in the wrong direction."

"*Me?* But how about you?"

He laughed.

"I doubt I'll fit in the tunnel, Valya. I'd need to use my arms and legs to climb up, but there's just not enough space for me to do that."

He appeared to have grown bigger even since the last time I saw him. His shoulders now were much wider than that morning. I didn't think he'd fit in the garbage chute tunnel at all.

"Then, I don't want to go that way, either," I said.

"I don't want to send you up there alone." He wrapped his arm around my shoulders, drawing me closer to him.

I leaned my head against his upper arm.

"Is that what we're doing then? Trying to get back in the gardens?" I asked.

He tugged at the braid that fell across his chest, looking lost in thought for a moment.

"That's the place we both know best," he finally said. "We have the most food stored there. And now that we know what we're up against, we'll take the necessary precautions to make our life there safer."

"Like reinforcing the entrance doors?" I took another chubby *caur* leaf out of the container.

"I'm thinking about blocking them permanently. Shutting them closed, barricading and reinforcing them so that no one from the corridor could ever open them again."

That would isolate us from the rest of the Dark Anomaly and any other survivors for good. A lifetime spent with only Malahki for company was not the worst thing in the world. Never seeing another enraged *kreer* again seemed appealing.

I heaved a sigh.

"We could replant the gardens, then, without the threat of them being ruined over and over again. But we'll need to do something about the air supply, to make it completely independent from the central system, which will probably completely fail soon, anyway," I thought out loud. "I'll help you with that. I'm pretty good with tools and stuff."

"We'll need to have our own oxygen production, just for us," Malahki agreed. "The same goes for water and light."

"It'll take time to get it all done."

"Yes, but we'll have to hurry before things start falling apart."

I chewed on the *caur* leaf, which had lost its taste to me as I tried to imagine the future we faced. With the doors shut and blocked, we'd be completely isolated from the rest of the Dark Anomaly. A world within a world. There'd be a lot of hard work to make it happen, and that would be if we didn't get killed or eaten first...

We were already isolated from the rest of the world here. However, further sealing ourselves away in the gardens felt even more extreme, like walling in during the medieval times.

"Are you absolutely sure no one else has survived this?" I asked softly. "No one else worth rescuing, I mean?"

Malahki bit his lip, looking as if considering something.

"We'll need to stop by the captain's room on the way back to the gardens," he said, with not much hope in his voice. "Vrateus is the one who I hope has managed to survive. Though, he's always been the first target of the crew during every mutiny."

I drew in a long breath, thinking I should consider myself lucky that I could even breathe still. I'd survived the crash, the murders of my entire crew, the many attacks by those who craved to hurt me. I was with the person who cared for and protected me. That was so much more than anyone who'd come to the Dark Anomaly with me got.

As if sensing my troubled thoughts, Malahki drew me even closer into his side, kissing my hair.

"We're safe here for now," he said firmly. "We'll make it, Valya. You and I. We'll keep on surviving."

Chapter 11

Valya danced in the clearing of the purple forest on Ak'ae, his home planet.

The soft grass of the clearing shone pink in the bright morning light of the large, orange sun. She twirled, throwing her arms open wide. And she laughed, tilting her head back and turning her face up to the light.

She was naked, no suit, no boots. Nothing. Only garlands of bright red and purple flowers woven through her straight, dark-brown hair.

Smiling, she faced him as he approached.

"You've changed, Malahki," she said. Her slim, black eyebrows twisted into a frown, and her blue eyes darkened to violet.

He slid his gaze down her body, taking in the small perky breasts with dark nipples, the expanse of her pale skin, the triangle of dark hair between her thighs.

The sight of her made his own body buzz with something he couldn't name and had never experienced before. Heat coursed from his chest down through his stomach, pooling and throbbing in that one spot low in his belly.

"I can't even recognize you anymore," she said wistfully and lightly touched his chest.

The contact of her fingers sent a rush of thrill along his skin. The hot mound between his legs swelled so much, it ached. It was an unfamiliar, tingling kind of pain that begged to be touched, stroked, rubbed...something.

She turned around, getting ready to leave.

He couldn't have that.

"Come back." He grabbed her shoulders, but it wasn't enough. He needed to touch more of her. Sliding his hands down, he found her breasts. They filled his hands perfectly, the nipples turning hard as he pinched them between his fingers.

She gasped—a breathy sound between a moan and a cry of surprise.

He pressed himself to her, needing to feel her body with every inch of his. Still it wasn't enough. He needed to get closer, to crawl inside her, to make her a part of him.

Desperately, he ground his pelvis—the part where the bulge between his legs grew and throbbed—against her ass. The stronger he pressed, the more contact he craved. The harder he rubbed, the faster and harder he needed it to be.

"No..." she pleaded as he used her body, unable to satisfy the need that consumed him and deprived him of any sense or thought. "No!" She fought against him, trying to pry his hands off her.

Yet he couldn't stop, he couldn't even slow down.

He couldn't...

He woke up with a start. The air swooshed out of his chest as the forest of Ak'ae vanished, the metal and plastic of the worn walls came into view. In the faint reflection of the multi-colored lights of the Dark Anomaly, he remembered where he was, in the small room behind the wall of the *vasai* farm.

The rest of his dream remained. Valentina was here with him. Her back turned to him, she curled into a ball in her sleep, breathing softly. He had his hands on her hips, his fingers digging into the fabric of her suit, his pelvis still grinding against her ass.

Mimicking the lights outside, the skin on his hands glowed with red and purple swirls. The colors pulsed, echoing the throbbing pain in his groin.

He grunted in mortification, forcing his fingers to uncurl and release her.

"Malahki?" she murmured in her sleep, making a move to turn around.

Spirits, he couldn't face her! Not after waking her up like that. Not while he yearned to ravage her with each cell of his body and every fibre of his soul.

Scrambling away from her, he crawled out into the farm.

His hands shook, swirls of red burning his skin. The pain between his legs spread through the rest of his body, making him shake as he stumbled between the cages, unseeing. Every step made it worse, yet he couldn't stop.

His muscles tingled and ached. His bones groaned. He had to stop this madness, but he didn't know how.

Passing by a cage, he slammed his fist into the bars, bending them. His knuckles hurt, but it diverted his mind from the longing in his chest and the burning between his thighs.

His shoulder bumped into the door frame on his way out of the farm. He looked at it with surprise. When did his body become not his own? So much larger than it used to be, it felt like borrowed clothes or the living quarters he occupied but did not own.

His new body demanded a price. His hands fisting tight, he needed to do something or he'd go mad. He'd crawl on all fours back to Valya, begging her to either fuck him or slit his throat with her knife.

The corridor was disappointingly empty, but there were noises coming out of the kitchen. Loud clanking of pots. Whoever made the noise obviously believed they had no reason to be afraid of attracting anyone's attention. Well, now they attracted *his*.

He stomped into the kitchen, finding a *dimo* in front of the flameless stove. A large pot of water boiled on it, with a pile of butchered meat on the floor.

The *dimo* lifted his head as Malahki approached.

"Who the fuck are you?" he snarled.

The male didn't recognize him, but he knew exactly who the *dimo* was.

Urkril.

"You've tormented me enough times to remember who I am," Malahki gritted through his teeth, stalking closer.

"*Damirian?* What the fuck has happened to you?" Urkril gaped at him with disgust and some trepidation.

"The question is what is going to happen to *you,* now." Malahki growled.

With a sweep of an arm, he swiped the boiling pot off the stove. The hot metal singed his arm, but he hardly noticed the pain. The boiling hot water splashed over the butchered meat, steam rising into the air in a cloud of stench.

"Hey!" Urkril roared, infuriated. "Fuck off! Or I'll cook you with them!" He jerked his chin at the steaming pile of meat.

Malahki silently fisted his hands. Blood pumped through his muscles with a tingle of energy and strength.

Grabbing the empty pot off the floor, the *dimo* heaved it over his head, charging at him.

Malahki blocked the blow with his forearm, the hard metal of the pot painfully bruising against his bone. The pain rushed through his body in ripples of aftershock, agonizing and energizing.

"Yesss," he hissed, riding the wave of thrill as he slammed his fist into Urkril's plated face. The hard shells cracked, the ragged edges tearing the tissue underneath and bursting the *dimo's* blood vessels.

The sensation of the warm blood misting Malahki's fist made his head spin.

Urkril staggered back with a roar of pain.

The sound pushed Malahki's bloodthirst surge higher. He threw another punch then another. The *dimo* crashed to his knees first, then slumped to the floor into a motionless heap. Still Malahki couldn't stop punching.

Blow by blow, he turned the *dimo's* head into a bloody mess, and still it was not enough. Growling like a beast possessed, he clawed and tore at the hard plates on the *dimo's* chest. Ripping them off, he tore through the sinew and tissue underneath, broke and wrenched out bones until he made it to the warm heart of Urkril.

Insatiable hunger rolled through him—the hunger that no plants could satisfy. With a triumphant roar, he ripped the still quivering organ out of the *dimo's* chest then sank his teeth into it.

As the warm blood trickled down his neck and chest, a faint thought fluttered in his mind like a fragile moth in the night.

"What have I become?"

The answer came unbidden but clear—a monster.

Chapter 12

"Malahki?" I patted the empty space around me.

I could have sworn he was just here. He'd held me as I fell asleep. And he was still holding me tight just a little while back. I faintly remembered feeling him move. And now, he was gone.

We'd slept fully clothed. I'd just removed the knife sheaths from around my thighs before going to sleep. Taking a knife out of its sheath now, I crawled to the exit and peeked out into the farm.

All seemed the same out there. The broken, rusty cages arranged haphazardly throughout the space, with not a movement in sight.

I ventured to stick my head out, carefully surveying the entire room, wall to wall. Still nothing.

Where did he go? To get more food? We had enough left for breakfast. The water container was also still half-full.

Worry that something might have happened to him slithered into my heart.

Afraid to attract unwanted attention, I didn't call out his name, carefully moving along the wall toward the exit to the corridor. I had no intention of strolling along the corridor on my own. I wanted to simply take a look in both directions as far as I could see to orientate myself. If he wasn't there, I'd go back to the room and wait for him. Again.

The heavy stomping of feet made me freeze in my tracks. Someone was coming, and they didn't care about being stealthy.

If they weren't afraid of anyone, chances were I had to be afraid of them.

I started backing along the wall to return to the room where we'd spent the night.

Someone walked in, and I stared at him in shock, my feet refusing to move.

My heart knew it was Malahki, but my eyes could hardly recognize him. He'd grown even more, being at least a head and a half taller than me now. His shoulders all but blocked the doorway. His long hair had fallen out of the braids. Ink-black now, straight, and glossy, it streamed down his shoulders, reaching his waist.

Bright red, glowing swirls of color curled and curved along the skin of his bare arms and torso, reaching his face, too. They blended with the thick layer of blood that covered his entire front from the lower part of his face all the way down his pants. His arms looked like he had dipped them up to his elbows in blood.

It must be someone else's blood, since he didn't appear to be injured, though there was suffering in his gaze. His eyes shone as he slowly moved them across the room, stopping on me.

Breath caught in my throat, I was unable to stir a muscle, caught in his stare like a fly.

With a low growl, he lunged my way.

There was so much power and menace in his large figure charging at me, I screamed, terrified. At that moment, there was nothing of Malahki that I recognized.

Spinning on my heel, I dashed back to the room. If I could make it through the narrow tunnel, he wouldn't be able to get to me.

I weaved between the cages and the wall, running as fast as I could. Afraid to look back over my shoulder, I heard the slamming and crashing noise of the cages being shoved out of his way.

Reaching the crack between the panels, I dropped to my knees to crawl in, to safety.

A heavy hand landed on my shoulder, hauling me up to my feet, instead. Afraid to face him, I kept my face to the wall.

Slamming his hands in the wall above my head, he caged me in with his massive body, pressing his pelvis to my back. Something throbbed and bulged between his legs, something that wasn't there before.

"What's the matter, Valentina? Why are you running *away* from me not *to* me this time?" The bitter sarcasm in his voice as well as the use of my long, formal name brought the memory of the old Malahki back. The one who saved my life and cared for me. I'd never been afraid of him.

Did I have any reason to be afraid of him, now?

His entire body was pressed against me, his breathing ragged and heavy, but he didn't touch me anywhere otherwise.

I panted hard, struggling to catch my breath after running. My heart still pounded fast in my chest. The heat of his body surrounding me seeped into my muscles.

"Do you no longer want to see me?" he growled, nuzzling the side of my face.

His familiar scent enveloped me, putting me more at ease. Ever since our one and only real kiss, I craved being closer with him. But he'd been keeping me at arm's length ever since, caring for me and protecting me, but nothing more.

"Does the look of me disgust you, now?" Hand on my shoulder, he flipped me around to face him.

I sucked in a breath and held it, staring at him smeared with blood, the bright swirls of color blending and curling all along his skin and in his eyes.

"Malahki..." I exhaled, tripping over his name as all other words deserted me.

He leaned closer, reaching for a kiss, but I turned my face away from his blood-stained lips.

"What's the matter?" He rasped in my ear. "You no longer want my kisses?"

"I do," I whispered, so quiet, I could barely hear it myself.

I missed his kisses so much it hurt. I wanted Malahki's arms around me, his lips on me. I just didn't know who exactly this wild beast of a man in front of me was. His behaviour sent chills of trepidation down my arms. I was afraid to breathe, to move, to speak, but I was *not* afraid for my life with him. Whoever he was, whatever he had turned into, I just didn't believe Malahki would ever hurt me.

Slowly, I raised my gaze to his, meeting his terrifying eyes. Terrifying, but also beautiful, I found. The bright colors swam in his irises, spreading and disappearing like drops of paint in water. Mesmerising.

The wild desire—so new and exciting—in his gaze sent another charge of heat down my body. At the same time, something sad and broken deep inside his eyes made my heart ache.

Lifting my hand to his face, I gently wiped the blood off his lips.

"I always want your kisses, Malahki," I said, louder. I just needed a moment to gather my courage to receive them. Some strength to return them. I heaved another breath, placing my hands flat to the wall behind me, willing the cool surface to help me control the feverish heat coming awake in my body.

Instead of being relieved, however, he seemed to get angry.

"You do?" He shoved away from the wall and from me. "Do you want *this*?"

He unclipped his belt, yanking his pants down.

A cry of shock lodged in my throat as I gaped at the place where there had been absolutely nothing when we met. His genital slit was now wide open, turned inside out. A massive, fully erect penis sprouted from the center. Tapered at the end, with a pointy head, it looked thicker than my wrist at the base. Pulsing red, it seemed to glow from strain and heat.

Instead of hair, a cluster of thin, flexible antennae circled it. A little shorter than his shaft, they were almost as thick as a pencil each.

Also erect and bright red in color, they vibrated as if charged with electrical current.

"Is that what you want?" he asked again, with a bitter note.

"I..." I swallowed hard. The thought about how that amazing cluster of his would possibly feel between my legs made me squirm.

So much about this barely familiar man felt strange and intimidating. Yet... I'd craved intimacy with Malahki for some time now. It'd been a soft desire that had glowed gently under my skin, keeping me warm in this cold hostile place. I'd always doubted he'd ever want me back, though.

There were no doubts any longer. He practically shook with need, devouring me with his stare.

"Desire can be contagious," I once told him.

And in our case, it proved true. My body caught his fever, fueled by nothing but his hungry stare. My breathing grew shallow. My suit that I'd barely ever noticed before now chafed against my flushed skin. My breasts tingled. The nipples pebbled, pushing hard against the thin fabric.

His hands propped into the wall next to my head, he leaned his forehead to mine.

"I'm a true monster now, Valya."

Lifting a trembling hand to the suit's closure at my neck, I slid it all the way down in silent invitation for him.

"Be *my* monster, then," I said softly.

His wide chest expanded with a deep breath as he stepped back. Sliding a long, heated stare down my body, he lowered his head, reminding me of a bull about to attack. Without another word, he grabbed the edges of my suit and yanked it off my shoulders.

Dropping to his knees, he kept peeling the suit off me. I swayed on my feet, freeing my arms from the sleeves, as he licked and nibbled my skin down my belly, shoving my suit all the way down to my ankles.

His nose pressed to my skin, he inhaled deeply then sprang to his feet.

"Is that what you want?" he repeated, sounding delirious.

Spinning me around, he kicked my legs open with his knee.

"You want to be fucked?" Curling his arm around my hip, he dipped his hand between my legs, pressing my ass to his hard, pulsing length.

Biting down on my shoulder to keep me in place, he slid his fingers between my folds, already slick for him.

"Fuck." He sounded shocked. "You do want this."

My entire body trembled, and I no longer knew whether from trepidation or need.

His mouth firmly latched to that place where my neck met my shoulder. He found my breast with his other hand, pinching my nipple. I whimpered, grinding my hips against the fingers that kept moving between my thighs.

"You want me to fuck you," he growled against my skin.

He thrust forward, sliding inside me. The tapered tip of his shaft entered me smoothly. The base stretched me wider and wider for him as he thrust deeper.

The little antennae—or feelers or whatever blessed things they were—trembled all around the place where our bodies connected, charging my every nerve with thrill.

"Oh yes, Malakhi..." I panted, bending over to take him even deeper.

One arm around my middle, he gripped my hip with the other hand, slamming hard inside me again.

I braced myself on the wall with both arms as he rutted in me from behind.

With a loud roar, he came, but hardly slowed down. Taking a long breath, he kept going, frantically thrusting inside me.

Another climax rocked his large body. Sliding out of me, he turned me over to face him.

I threw my arms over his shoulders to support myself as my legs shook and my knees threatened to give out. Where my bare arms touched his skin, more colors flared to life. Deep purple, magenta, and iridescent green joined the red and orange swirls. They spread in tendrils along the dips and valleys of his muscular arms and torso like spilled paint.

"Beautiful," I breathed out, tracing the colorful swirls with the tips of my fingers, which appeared to create more and more tendrils.

"You like that?" he grunted, shoving his hard length inside me again.

How was he hard again already?

I got no time to ponder that. At this angle, his body hit my sensitive spot as he started to move. The tender, flexible antennae caressed between my thighs, like fingers.

My entire body pulsed with heat, in rhythm with his swirling colors. Pressure built inside me, teasing me with the approaching orgasm. With another hard thrust from him, pleasure exploded through me. I threw my head back, ready to scream, unable to keep it all in.

He caught my mouth in a kiss, swallowing my screams of pleasure while pumping his third climax into me.

Breaking the kiss, he curled his body around mine, spent. We stood like that for a few moments. Being pinned between Malahki and the wall was the only reason I remained upright at all.

"*You like it,*" he'd said. And I still had no idea what I'd reply to that.

No one had ever taken me like this, fully and completely before, with so much need and desperation. I felt both used and thoroughly loved.

Every muscle in my body vibrated with the aftershocks of the most intense orgasm I'd ever had. I realized I would not want to go on without this anymore. Anything I'd had before with anyone else paled in comparison with what we'd just had.

"I did like it, Malahki," I murmured, pressing my lips to his shoulder in a kiss.

"You did," he said, a note of wonder in his voice. "You. A human."

"I'm a woman first, I guess." I shrugged.

And as a woman, I felt very satisfied at the moment.

Letting go of me, he leaned with his back to the wall then slid down to sit on the floor. Without his support, I lowered to the floor too. My body felt boneless, my trembling muscles too weak to keep me upright.

Placing his forearms on his bent knees, he flexed his fingers, staring at his blood-stained hands. I slid a glance down my naked body, there were plenty of red smears on my skin, too.

"Whose blood is it?" I asked, relieved it didn't appear to be his.

"Urkril's." His voice sounded hollow.

"Is he..."

"Dead." He nodded, running his hand over his face.

"Serves him right," I said firmly, remembering Urkril's senseless beating of Malahki many weeks ago.

He slid me a curious look, as if seeing me for the first time.

"What? I'm not going to feel sorry for that one." I pulled up my suit, threading my arms into its sleeves.

He glanced back at his blood-covered hands then stared at me again.

"Did you really like what I just did to you?" he asked.

I shifted on the floor, tugging the two sides of my suit together over my chest.

"I enjoyed it. Physically. It was different." I was not going to apologize or feel bad about how I felt. Not about Urkril, not about the sex.

"How do you feel about me?" His frown deepened as he awaited my answer, but there was a faint glow of hope in his expression, too.

"I've always liked you, Malahki." I took his hand in mine, wiping the blood off it with my sleeve.

His skin returned to its previous color—smooth beige, like the color of prairie sand or unbleached canvas. When I stroked his hand with a finger, however, the multi-colored swirls came back to life in its wake. They spread along his hand, fading away and disappearing the moment I removed my finger from him.

"You like the monster I've become?" he insisted, gazing at me intently.

"Did you really change that much?" I met his eyes, the colorful storm in them slowed down, settling into a pretty pattern of brown, purple, and red.

He huffed a bitter laugh, dropping his head between his shoulders. His pose reminded me of the one he had when I'd woken up after being poisoned by the *fuhnid* mushrooms. Back then he asked me what was happening to him.

Just like then, I couldn't even pretend to understand what it would be like to have one's identity completely changed like that, mentally and physically. But when I thought about that now, I wondered if the change had been as drastic as he feared.

"Malahki," I started, squeezing his hand in both of mine. "You're still you. It's not like you disappeared anywhere. There have been certain…um, additions to you, physically and mentally, but do you feel like anything has been taken away? Do you have a feeling of loss? Or do you think you've lost more than you've gained?"

He stroked my knuckles with his thumb, staring at the floor straight ahead of him.

"Well, I've gained you." He moved his gaze to me and paused as if giving me a chance to argue or disagree, though he looked like he hoped I'd confirm.

I smiled.

"You've always had me. Only now, you can have me in some *other* ways, too."

His frown eased a little. I studied him carefully—all the new things about him. His increased height and width. The bulky muscles on his arms and thighs.

His hair was so glossy and black, it even seemed heavier now. His high cheekbones looked as if carved from a stone—hard and sharp. The thick black eyebrows furrowed over his bright eyes. The serene beige didn't return to his irises, and I didn't think it ever would again.

There were many changes, but I spotted the old and familiar pieces of him, too. They were mostly in the intonations of his voice, his expression, and his body posture.

"There are changes, for sure," I said. "But fundamentally, I don't feel like I lost you. You're still there, despite all the muscles and that, um...spectacular thing you grew between your legs."

I moved my gaze aside, determined not to stare at the bulge between his thighs. He'd yanked his pants back up, but his belt was still undone.

"I'll need to learn how to walk again," he said suddenly.

A laugh burst out of me. "Does *it* get in the way?"

"No!" He laughed, too. "Well, a little. But I mean I'll have to get used to my bigger size, overall. I keep bumping into things." He rolled back his shoulders, demonstrating how massive they'd grown.

I loved hearing him laugh again.

Now, that the frenzy of sex had calmed down, however, anxiety returned to me. The constant feeling of danger surrounding us urged me to nervously scan both the entrance to the waste processing room and the exit to the corridor on the opposite end of the farm.

"We should probably get back in, to hide." I gestured at the crack in the wall. "Someone might come."

Malahki just shrugged.

"Let them come." He jumped to his feet, fastening his pants. "No more hiding."

"What? You just want to walk around? In the open?"

His sudden carelessness puzzled and worried me.

"Let's have a shower," he said.

When we used the bathroom yesterday, we'd done it quickly, looking over our shoulders all the time. Now, Malahki scanned both entrances to the farm calmly, looking ready to fight, not to run.

"Come." He gave me a hand, helping me up. "I made a mess." He rubbed at the smudge of blood on my chest in the opening of my suit. "Let me clean you up."

"But what if someone sees us?" I asked nervously.

"Who?"

"Well—"

"I'm bigger than anyone of the crew, now, Valya. Gler said he was the only *errock* left, and I can fight him with one arm tied behind my back."

For as long as I knew him, Malahki had always been confident. When he was smaller and weaker, he had a cooler, more calculating type of confidence. Now, it was hot and careless, bordering on arrogance.

"It's not just about the size, or strength, or even the weapons, Malahki. A little bit of caution never hurt," I objected.

"All right." He headed for the bathroom with an easy swagger. "Let's be cautious. We'll close the door to the bathroom when we shower. I'll even lock it, okay?"

Chapter 13

In the bathroom, he fucked me again. Because of the five-minute shower limit, we hadn't even turned on the water until Malahki had come twice.

Washing off the blood and the evidence of sex from me, he caressed my body with his hands under the stream of the shower.

"I dreamed about this so often." He bent his knees and lowered his head to lick a drop of water off my nipple. "I feel so sorry about all the showers I've wasted on just washing you, instead of doing this."

He sucked the tip of my breast in his mouth, twirling his tongue around it.

I wouldn't call any of our time together as being "wasted." Every moment I'd spent with him, we learned more about each other. Because of all that time before, I knew now that I could trust him completely. With him, I felt safe, even when he fucked me hard, like the monster he thought he'd become.

He seemed calmer now, his caresses decadently slow. Slipping his hand between my legs, he circled my opening, my flesh still highly sensitive from his earlier touch.

I moaned, leaning back against the wall for support. He dropped to his knees, draping my leg over his shoulder.

Burying my hands in his thick, silky hair, I rode his face as he nibbled and sucked. The water had long stopped running, yet he wouldn't let go of me until the orgasm hit me. A shuddered moan escaped my lips as my hips jerked against his mouth.

When my tremors finally subsided, he kissed his way up my body back to my lips.

"Showers are definitely much more fun, now." He beamed at me before kissing my mouth again.

"SO, YOU JUST WANT TO go back to the gardens in the open?" I asked, needing him to confirm it again. After weeks of striving to be invisible to everyone on the Dark Anomaly, I couldn't fathom just strolling down its main corridor in plain view of whoever might come along.

"That'd be the easiest." Already fully dressed after the shower, Malahki wrung the water out of my hair, divided it into sections, then deftly braided it as I pulled up the closure of my suit.

"How about something less dangerous?" I argued.

"Like what?" He shook his hair out then braided it into one thick plait that almost reached his waist.

My thoughts flickered to the garbage chute again. The cover it provided appealed to my sense of caution. Malahki wouldn't fit in the tunnel, being nearly twice his initial size now. My taking it would mean I'd have to separate from him, but I didn't want to let him out of my sight ever again, no matter how terrifying walking out in the open felt.

Sensing my hesitation, he placed his hands on my shoulders.

"There's hardly anyone left around here, Valya," he said softly. Hearing the name my parents and my brother called me felt comforting. He rubbed my shoulders gently. "The survivors are holed up in their ships. There might be some deranged males scurrying in the corners, but I'll deal with them if they decide to attack. All right? Don't be scared. I'll protect you."

I'd trusted him to protect me before, and I nodded now.

We took the canister and the oxygen masks with us. As we passed through the farm, Malahki grabbed the dangling door of one of the cages and wrenched it off its hinges.

"Here," he yanked out one of the thick bars and wielded it like a spear over his head. "See? A weapon." He grinned at me. "We're even better armed, now. Do you feel safer?"

I gave him a tight smile in reply. Seeing him break the thick metal bar out of the door frame was reassuring. It was also a shocking demonstration of the pure physical strength that Malahki now possessed.

He strolled out of the farm in long, confident strides as I slid my knives out of their sheaths, constantly scanning the space around us.

"How many survivors are left, do you think?" I asked.

"No idea. It really depends on how many ships we still have with fully functioning air supply systems."

"My ship would be one," I said. "As far as I know the air system still worked when we landed. You said someone occupied it already."

"The *errocks*." He winced, with dislike.

I grimaced, too, sharing his resentment for that particular group on the Dark Anomaly. His frown was suddenly misplaced by a calculating expression.

"What is it, Malahki?" I wondered.

He blinked. "Gler said he was the only *errock* on the ship."

"Yes, but the *akuk* was with him. There may be other males, too." He waved me off.

"The others don't matter. I can take them all. I can fight the *errock*, too. If there were more than one that might be a problem, but if he's the only one."

Malahki walked with an added bounce to his step, as if eager for the fight.

"How do you even know what ship he was talking about?" I asked.

"Yours."

"Why?"

He turned to me.

"I saw Wyck, another *errock* enter it a few days back."

"So? Gler may be on another ship, with another group—"

"No." He shook his head resolutely. "*Errocks* always stick together. If Wyck was on that ship, the rest also would be there. If Gler was the only one left, then the rest are all dead."

I pondered his words for a moment.

"Gler didn't look that upset about losing his entire tribe."

"The *errocks* on the Dark Anomaly are...*were* a brutal bunch. They called themselves a family, but I always had a feeling they'd end each other over a piece of meat if it came down to it. They stuck together for power and intimidation, not for any real attachment or affection for each other."

Two sets of pewter double doors came on our left. One had been welded shut and sealed. The other, not far from the first, was partially open.

"Wait." Malahki touched my arm.

I stopped in my tracks, nearly tripping over my feet. Being on edge made me jumpy. My heart leaped to my throat.

"What is it?" I looked around wildly.

"The captain's room." Malahki moved to the partially open doors, gesturing to me to fall back behind him for safety.

I noted he stepped lightly. The sense of caution hadn't completely deserted him. He glanced inside then slid his hand along the edge of one of the doors. It appeared to be stuck half-open. It wouldn't budge either way even under Malahki's newly-found incredible strength.

The edge of the door was jagged and chipped. As if something sharp had been used to open it in the first place.

"Is anyone there?" I asked. "The captain?"

"No." He shook his head with a gloomy expression. "The room is empty."

"Do you think he's survived?" I came a little closer.

Malahki threw a glance in both directions along the corridor, then squeezed his large body between the doors, gesturing for me to follow. I slid into the room after him.

The room was made entirely out of glass. The bright lights of the Dark Anomaly moved outside of it in their eternal dance.

"It's gorgeous." I wondered what it would be like to live in a room like that. Mesmerising at first, but it would probably cost me my mind at the end.

"The lights will drive you mad," Malahki had said.

For me, the most infuriating would be looking *outside,* while knowing I could never get there. All of us were trapped in this place. At least when I was in the gardens, I could fool myself that they were my "outside," with all the plant life, greenery, and space.

Malahki inspected the room. Aside from a narrow metal cot and a few pieces of broken plastic that littered the floor, the space was completely empty. Unlike so many other places on the Dark Anomaly, there weren't any decaying body parts in here, no signs of blood, either.

"He could be hiding elsewhere," I offered, knowing that despite his strong disdain for the crew, Malahki held a true respect for his captain.

"Maybe," he said, slowly circling the room. "If he is dead, he wasn't killed here."

After leaving the glass room, we continued down the corridor toward the gardens. When we reached the white doors of the gardens, however, Malahki paused, not entering.

I wondered if he was thinking about the *kreers* and the others who had driven us away from the gardens yesterday. The fine hairs on the back of my neck stood up when I thought about those creatures.

Behaving worse than wild animals, they couldn't even be called sentient beings, anymore.

"Do you think they're still there?" I asked, shifting closer to him.

"Maybe." He shrugged.

Malahki certainly didn't look scared, but his thoughts appeared to be elsewhere.

"What are you thinking about?"

"I'm not afraid of the crew," he said. "Especially of those who can no longer even think for themselves. What worries me is that the central air supply system is unreliable. It can fail at any time. What if the supplementary system proves inadequate?"

"We have the masks." I touched the device strapped around my neck.

"We can't wear them forever. What if the system fails when we're asleep? Or anything else fails without us knowing? Whatever happened to the crew may happen to us, too."

I released a sigh, thinking about the dead *akuks* in the storage room. It could have been us, had the malfunction happened in the gardens. Expanding the auxiliary system would take time, each minute of which would be like sitting on a timebomb, dreading another breakdown that could happen any time. Malahki was right, other life-support systems could fail, too.

"We need a safe place to stay while we modify the air supply in the gardens and get ready to seal them off," Malahki concluded. "Your ship is right up ahead." He headed in that direction.

"But you said the *errocks* are there." I hurried after him, a heavy feeling pressing on my chest.

"*One* errock." He kept going.

"And who knows how many others!" I didn't necessarily disagree with his idea, but I wished he would think it through first, instead of barging head first into the danger.

I grabbed his arm, forcing him to stop.

He could have shaken me off like a fly, but he faced me. Drawing in a long breath, he patiently explained, "You said your ship has a functioning air production and filtration system. It must be true since the *errocks* have been living there, obviously unaffected by the malfunctions of the central system—you saw Gler, he functions well. You and I will need a safe place to live while we're working on fixing and improving the gardens. Your ship is safe. So, we will go and get it."

"What makes you think they will just let us take it?" I propped my hands on my hips.

He gave me another one of his nonchalant shrugs.

"I won't ask. I'll just take it from them."

"And if they fight back?"

"Then, I'll kill them," he said simply.

"What if they kill you?"

He lifted an eyebrow, giving me a lopsided grin.

"Malahki," I exhaled, worry shooting through me, sharp and painful. "Please, think about it first. There're others there, not just the *errock*. We have no idea how many—"

"Couldn't be that many, after all the fighting that has happened here lately." He proceeded up the corridor again, leaving me no choice but to follow.

I hadn't been in this section since the day of the crash. As if on their own, my feet slowed down as the memories rose in my mind. Last time I'd been here, I'd crawled, stricken by panic and grief. Had it not been for Malahki, I had no doubt I wouldn't be here today.

He took my hand in his, pulling me to a stop at his side. The opening that the *errock* had made in the wall to get on our ship had now been solidly blocked.

"I want you to stand over there," Malahki said in my ear softly, pointing at the wall opposite from the entrance.

"Me? Why?"

"There is a camera right above the door, I want them to see you."

"You what?" I tripped over the words. After doing everything possible to keep me out of sight before, he was willing to display me for the others to see, now. "You want to use me as a bait." It dawned on me.

"Yes," he said, with an easy smile. "Don't worry," he added quickly as I just stood there, gaping at him. "I'll never let any harm come to you. I need them to open the door. Once they see you on the camera, they'll come out to try to catch you.

"You think?" I huffed a nervous laugh.

"That's when I'll get them." He adjusted his grip on the makeshift spear in his hand.

A spark of anticipation flashed in his eye. A muscle moved in his jaw as he shifted his weight to the other foot, impatiently.

Not only was he not afraid, he yearned for the fight.

"Have you ever seen a damirian male?" he'd asked me long ago.

Now, I completely understood his earlier reservations and concerns. Malahki had known all along what would happen. He knew *what* he would become, from the beginning. For someone inherently detesting any kind of violence, it must've been especially disturbing to know he'd crave it one day.

"Okay," I said softly. "I trust you."

"Oh, Valya," he murmured. Coming closer, he lowered his head to me, shielding me from the world with his wide shoulders. "Don't worry, please. No one will get close enough to touch you. I won't let that happen."

I nodded, drawing in a bracing breath.

"I know, honey. I trust you."

He brushed my lips with his in a soft, comforting kiss.

"Let's do it." I marched over to the entrance, not waiting for my courage to waver.

Coming to the metal piece that had been fitted over the cut-out in leu of the door, I firmly slammed my fist into it a few times. Clutching a knife in my other hand, I hid it behind my back.

"Hey, boys!" I yelled, lifting my face to the camera. "Come and get me."

I had no doubt they'd bite. From what I'd learned about them, the crew of the Dark Anomaly rarely exercised caution or even common sense, letting their instincts guide them more often than their brains.

Sure enough, it took but a second before the sounds of clunking and clicking of what must be locks and chains came through the door.

My heart leaped high with trepidation. I didn't have Malahki's reckless bravery or even any affinity for confrontation. Backing all the way to the wall, I forced myself to stare straight ahead. Even the quickest glance in Malahki's direction would be risking giving away his presence prematurely.

The door slid open.

"Val!" A familiar feminine voice exclaimed, rendering me speechless.

A woman?

Nadia!

She rushed to me from the opening.

And Malahki struck.

Chapter 14

MALAHKI

He didn't waste time to see who it was. The person moved toward Valya, and he charged at them. Considerably smaller than an *errock*, or any male for that matter, they didn't present much of a challenge, crashing to the floor the moment his chest collided with their body.

A whimper, followed by a small cry of pain, made him take a closer look at whom he'd tackled. Green human eyes, open wide in terror, met his gaze. The feminine scent and feel of her small body under him doused his urge to fight, like a rain putting out a wildfire.

"Nadia!" Valya rushed to her friend.

"Um..." He tried to scramble off the woman without causing her any more damage with his weight or weapons.

"Get off her!" Someone bellowed, before attacking him.

The impact felt as if a spaceship crashed into him or he had gotten into the path of a humongous meteorite.

His new opponent was definitely an *errock*. Malahki's bones groaned from the shattering blows of the male's hard knuckles. The two of them rolled away from the females, the *errock* furiously pummeling his face and shoulders.

Malahki's blood boiled. His insides heated. His muscles swelled with energy. The thrill of the fight bubbled in his chest with effervescence, causing him to feel drunk on violence.

He laughed with joy, though the sound came out more like a threatening snarl. Ducking from another blow of the *errock's* massive fist, Malahki landed one straight into the male's temple.

The *errock* grunted, his eyes growing glossy. Malahki shoved the male's heavy body off his.

"Wyck!" the female, Nadia, cried out.

Malahki made a move to get up, but the *errock* grabbed him around the middle, tossing him back on the floor.

"Malahki! Stop it!" Valya's voice broke through the fog of excitement and violence.

"That's enough!" Vrateus shouted.

What was the captain doing here? The question flickered through his mind faintly as his fists pounded Wyck's hard, muscular chest. The *errock* unfailingly returned his punches, matching them blow by blow, neither of them willing or able to stop.

Ice-cold water suddenly crashed over Wyck and him. The deluge rushed over his face, flooding his mouth and nose. He splattered and choked, his thirst for fight immediately quenched for the time being.

"What on earth is going on here?" Svetlana glared at the *errock* and him, an empty bucket in her hands.

Lesh, Wyck's three-headed monster pet, hissed, letting go of his ankle. Malahki hadn't even realized when Lesh appeared. Absorbed by the fight, he didn't even feel his boot had been trapped in the animal's jaws.

"Get up, Malahki," Valya said softly, casting a cautious glance at Lesh as Wyck called his pet off. "These are friends." She glanced at Nadia, and the other woman nodded.

"Malahki?" Svetlana's eyes opened wider. "Is that really you?"

She came closer as he climbed to his feet. Svetlana and he used to be almost the same height a few weeks ago. Now, her face was somewhere around his chest area.

She tilted her head back to look him in the eye, then took in the rest of his face carefully.

"I'm so happy you're alive, Malahki. But I can't believe how much you've changed." She shook her head.

"Nice to see you again, Svetlana," he said. "Captain." He inclined his head in greeting of Vrateus.

Svetlana's presence brought the memories of the calm times when working in the gardens with her, further helping him regain control of his bloodthirst. He moved his gaze from her to Vrateus then back again, his heart swelling with gratitude at finding both seemingly well and alive. He had no idea how the two of them ended up here, in the company of an *errock* and the human woman who Malahki believed would've been long dead, but he was really happy to see them unharmed.

"Wow!" Svetlana gasped, walking around him in awe, as if he were a rare exhibit. "You look so different. I wouldn't have recognized you if I didn't hear your name."

For someone who had only seen him as neutral gender, the physical changes in him would be sudden and dramatic.

He was at least a head and a half taller and probably twice as broad as before. The pants he'd taken off Trox a while back—the ones that used to be so loose on him, he'd needed a belt to hold them up—now felt almost too tight around his buttocks and thighs.

He knew his facial features had hardened and sharpened. His hair, eyelashes, and brows had turned completely black.

And his eyes...

He'd had no chance to examine his eyes lately, but he suspected they'd be even brighter than his skin, which was still flaming hot with the battle colors of red, orange, and pink.

"What happened to you, Malahki?" Svetlana asked. "Are you okay?"

"I changed." He spread his arms aside.

His attention then snapped to Valya, who regarded the two of them with a confused frown.

"You know each other?" she said, and his heart dropped into the empty abyss of his stomach. "You said there were no other women on the Dark Anomaly, but you knew Svetlana Kostyk was here. Alive."

STAYING OUT IN THE open while having an emotionally charged discussion was never a good idea on the Dark Anomaly. Once all six of them got inside the human spaceship and locked the doors behind them securely, Nadia hugged Valya tightly.

"We've been looking for you. Everywhere. We thought you were dead," she sobbed.

Valya turned an accusing stare at him, and he couldn't hold it. He knew they'd been searching for her–Wyck was. But Malahki had been convinced the *errock* was abusing Nadia. And, spirits may damn him, but Malahki would've never let Wyck know about Valya. He still was shocked that Nadia turned out to be alive and appeared well after what he'd heard the *errocks* of the Dark Anomaly had done to females in the past.

The hurt expression on Valya's sweet face floored him.

"You lied to me?" she said softly.

"Valya, please." He forced himself to remain in place, even as everything inside him screamed to grab her in his arms and kiss her until she forgave him everything.

"You told me there were no other women on the Dark Anomaly. You said *all* of my crew were dead." She breathed rapidly.

Grabbing a chair from the table in the middle of the large open area of the spacecraft, Nadia put it behind Valya. As if her knees wouldn't hold her, she plopped onto it. Her dark-blue eyes remained on him, accusations floating in them, demanding an explanation.

How could he explain what he'd done? He'd been led mostly by fear—fear that if Valya knew about Nadia or Svetlana, she would try to make contact with them, likely revealing her presence to the crew in the process.

Until recently, stealth had been his most effective weapon against the brutalities of this place. He stayed out of sight of others to avoid conflicts with them. He kept Valya away from everyone, too, for the same purpose.

"I didn't want any harm to come to you," he said, trying to keep his voice even, though his heart pummeled so hard, his chest felt like one huge bruise inside.

"They wouldn't harm me!" She gestured wildly at the four people surrounding them.

Rubbing her forehead, Svetlana swiftly walked over to a raised panel with a screen on the wall. She filled a metal cup with water then brought it over to Valya. With a deep breath, Vrateus went to the front of the ship and took a seat in one of the crew chairs by the control panel.

"Maybe they wouldn't." Malahki measured with his gaze each of the four people who watched them carefully. "But they wouldn't do much to protect you, either."

"That's not true!" Nadia bristled.

Wyck stepped closer to Nadia's side in silent support. Malahki had no time to ponder why the *errock* was here and not with Gler and the likes of him.

"Isn't it?" Malahki addressed Nadia. "How much have any of the crew protected you? Tell Valentina what the captain made you do. Tell her what the *errocks* did to you."

Valya shot a questioning look at her friend, but Nadia didn't meet her eye. Blinking rapidly, the woman turned away, blush spreading thickly over her face.

"Leave her alone!" Wyck boomed, stepping forward.

"I need Valya to know what fate she's escaped by staying with *me*, not with *her*." He gestured at Nadia, who lowered herself into another chair by the table, wrapping her arms around her.

"What are you talking about?" Valya moved her gaze from him to Nadia then to the *errock*.

"Tell her, Nadia, how he paraded you naked in front of everyone!" Malahki pointed an accusing finger at Wyck. The indignity of what had been done to the woman he'd hardly knew spurred another wave of aggression to rise to the surface. "Her too!" He pointed at Svetlana who quietly stepped aside.

Vrateus leaped out of his seat. "I had reasons—"

"Reasons!" Malahki scoffed, outrage bursting from him. "Hear that, my sweet Valya? If you stayed with them, he'd find *reasons* to make you undress for the crew, too."

Her eyes open wide, Valya sank her fingers in her hair, wildly shifting her eyes from one person in the room to another. "Is that really what's happening here?"

"No—" Svetlana stirred, but he wouldn't let her speak.

"Then, he'd force you to touch yourself in front of everyone, and if you refused, he'd get someone to do it for you, so they all could jerk off while watching you. Now tell her, everyone, that's not what happened here. Tell her I'm lying!" he demanded, moving his gaze from one face to the next, daring them contradict his words.

Valya had paled so much, she almost looked blue, like her suit.

"Nadia?" she half-whispered, her eyes pleading with her friend to reassure her.

Nadia hid her face from her, shaking her head with a quiet sob. Wyck placed his hand on her shoulder, hurling a glare at him, sharp like a dagger.

Malahki was beyond any warnings, however.

"The captain would've made you have sex with someone like *this one* here," he moved his finger to the *errock*.

"Fuck you!" Wyck took a step forward, swinging his fist at him.

Malahki ducked, evading the blow then shoved the *errock* aside.

"I protected you, Valya," he kept talking, with the desperate hope she'd understand and forgive. "None of them would've protected you from that."

Without any further warning, the *errock* turned on his heel and punched Malahki in the back of his head. His teeth clanked from the blow. The echo of it reverberated inside his skull.

The captain leaped to them, rushing to break up the fight. Malahki swung his fist, without looking, knocking Vrateus in the face. The captain staggered on his feet, then drew out a gun and punched Malahki in the jaw with its handle.

Aggression took over again. He growled, trying to hold back. His aim was to clear a path to Valya, not to kill anyone.

"That's it!" Giving the three men an assessing look, Svetlana hurried to Valya. "Come, you can stay in our room until these hot heads cool off."

Valya still looked shocked from his revelations. Sadly, he couldn't tell what she thought about him from her stunned expression. Svetlana helped her get up then led her to the open door in the wall to the right.

Wyck twisted Malahki's arm, making him bend over. His attention fully on Valya, he didn't fight back.

"Where are you taking her?" Alarm shot through his system.

Nadia joined the two women, opening a second door next to the first. "Her bed and her things are here, Svetlana. Val, I put the divider up in your area. No one has been there since."

The women were ignoring him, taking Valya away from him.

"Valya, wait!" The aggression sharply shifted into rage. Punching the men who tried to stop him out of the way, he lumbered after her.

She turned in the threshold to the room.

"You have to calm down, Malahki, and let me think. Please," she said softly, her voice trembling, her eyes glistening with unshed tears.

Nadia ushered her through the door, and the panel slid closed, separating him from his woman. Svetlana stayed on this side of the door. She quickly jumped aside as Malahki charged the wall.

"No! Valya!" He slammed into the panel at full force.

"Fucking *damirian!*" the *errock* growled, getting to his feet after the last blow of Malahki had sent him to the floor. Grabbing the closest chair, he smashed it over Malahki's head. "I think I liked you better when you were beige."

Malahki staggered on his feet, his vision momentarily cloudy.

"Stop it. Now." Vrateus's voice was cold like metal. Something hard pressed to the back of Malaki's head—a gun. "Or I'll shoot."

He swayed, his head swimming from the impact with the chair.

"Do you think these may be the effects of the *kronite* leak into the air supply system?" Svetlana asked, keeping a safe distance from the men.

"Maybe," Vrateus replied grimly. "If so, then it would be best if I shot him sooner rather than later."

Taking a leather belt from around her waist, she handed it to Wyck. "Let's just tie him up for now."

"Is Val all right?" Vrateus asked, moving to Malahki's side. The cold barrel of the gun now pressed hard at the side of his neck.

Svetlana nodded. "She's safe."

Valya was safe with *him*, no one else. He'd kept her well and alive all these weeks on his own.

"Let me go to her," he gritted through his teeth, forcing himself to remain still to prove to the captain that he was not a threat and didn't need to be shot. He even let the *errock* bind his wrists with Svetlana's belt, every muscle in his body vibrating with strain and the need to fight.

Svetlana ignored him, talking to Vrateus. "I'll have to examine Val to confirm she's okay, but if they didn't spend every day together, he might've gotten a dose while she didn't."

What were they talking about? He couldn't focus on anything else but the horrible fact that Valya had been taken out of his sight, that she willingly walked away from him.

"Take me to her," he growled, lowering his head and squaring his shoulders. He could hold back for just so long, though. His body felt tight like a wound spring, ready to unfurl to bring menace and devastation.

As if sensing the threat, Vrateus pressed the gun more firmly to Malahki's neck.

"This may be just the way he is," the captain said, his expression contemplative. "The *kronite* leak may have nothing to do with this. I read *damirians* turn vicious when they change to males."

"His transformation is incredible. But I hope it didn't change his mind or his personality too drastically." Svetlana heaved a sigh, giving him a compassionate glance. "You'll have to calm down and get some rest, Malahki, so I can test you for *kronite* exposure later."

He couldn't stand it any longer.

"Valya!" he bellowed, tossing his head back.

The captain jammed the gun hard into his skull. "That's the opposite of calming down, my friend."

Friend? A friend wouldn't keep him away from the only person he needed to be with right now.

"Where is Valya?" He shoved his shoulder into the *errock* who held his arms, then launched for the door again.

"Fuck." Wyck jumped on his back, knocking him down.

With his hands tied, he crashed to the ground like a cut down tree.

Vrateus stood over him with a gun at the ready. "I'm locking you up. Until you calm the fuck down!"

"We could put him in the escape capsule, maybe?" Svetlana suggested, rushing to him with a small cylinder in her hand. "I'm so sorry, Malahki," she said softly. Then a cool mist with a sharp chemical smell hit his face.

He gasped, drawing a lungful of mist-rich air. The walls around him seemed to liquify, the edges of the paneling softening and curving. The floor and the ceiling wavered, with dips and swells. The faces of the people surrounding him distorted into soft, fuzzy circles.

Then, everything disappeared.

"Valya!" was the last thought echoing through the vast, dark emptiness of his mind.

WHEN HE CAME TO, HE was lying in a reclined seat inside what appeared to be a small spacecraft. The lights had been dimmed, and one of the six seats had been converted into a bed for him.

Valya wasn't there.

Svetlana had sprayed him with a sedative, he guessed. Then the rest of them had hauled him in here.

He jumped to his feet. Too fast. The aftereffects of the spray made his head spin, sending him down again. He missed the chair, landing on the floor. Scrambling up again and holding on to the backs of the seats on the way, he made it to the round door at the back.

It was closed and locked.

He slammed his fists into the door, clawing at the plastic and metal and calling her name until his throat hurt and his voice turned to croak. Until his muscles ached, and despair and exhaustion descended on him.

It'd been a while since the last time he'd slept alone. He'd had Valya next to him every single night lately, and he couldn't rest until he got her back. She had to be with him, *needed* to be where he was.

His swollen cock throbbed painfully. The feelers vibrated from strain. Back on Ak'ae, his home world, the newly mated couple would stay in their bedroom for days after the transformation. They would take short breaks for food only, spending the rest of the time satisfying their new burning need for each other.

Here, he was alone. And it wasn't just his body that craved her, his heart twisted in agony at the thought she might never again want to share his bed or his life with him. He'd lied to her. She had every reason to hate him.

Gathering whatever strength he had left, he slammed into the door separating her from him.

"Valya!"

He needed her more than food, air, or water. He had to get back to her.

Chapter 15

VAL

The clock above my bed told me it was morning. Most of the night I'd spent tossing and turning, worrying about Malahki.

Svetlana and Nadia had come to my area after dinner. They'd talked to me a little about how they survived and about the last attack of the crew, when Wyck had been nearly killed. The four of them had gone into full lockdown mode on the ship after that.

It was surreal to find Svetlana Kostyk, the scientist who'd been missing for decades, alive and physically unchanged. But then again, more than five decades had passed since our expedition left Earth for the Dark Anomaly, when it'd been just barely over two months for me here. All of us were now trapped in the bubble of warped time, forgotten by the rest of the galaxy.

I'd cried and kept hugging Nadia. Seeing her well and alive was like having her come back from the dead. I was so grateful that she'd survived, unharmed.

To my shock, she'd said she was in love with Wyck, and that they were expecting a baby. I had a hard time wrapping my mind around that after viewing all *errocks* of the Dark Anomaly as brutal and heartless. Though, I had to admit that Wyck treated Nadia with nothing but love and adoration in my presence.

Nadia's eyes shone with excitement when she'd told me about her pregnancy. However, I'd spotted worry deep inside them, too. There were many reasons to worry. I'd never heard about a naturally conceived *errock*-human baby. Besides, life on the Dark Anomaly had been all about survival. What parent wouldn't be extremely worried about bringing a baby into this harsh and unforgiving world?

After Nadia and Svetlana had left, I'd lain in bed, thinking about everything that had happened.

Finding more survivors made me feel optimistic—we were not entirely alone in this godforsaken place. At the same time, spending the night on my own, made me exceptionally lonely. My thoughts kept drifting to Malahki.

Svetlana had said he was staying in the escape capsule tonight. I knew it was best for both of us to spend some time apart. Ever since we'd met, we'd been inseparable, and I needed to step back to sort out my feelings for him. Maybe he needed to do the same, too.

He'd lied to me. I'd asked him, and he'd said to my face that all my crew was dead. He'd told me there were no other women around, that I had to stay hidden because the crew wanted me and they would kill me in some brutal way if they found me. They would've done worse things before killing me, too.

Stunned and angry after discovering his lies, I'd spent the evening talking to Nadia and Svetlana to discover the truth on my own.

I understood that some of what he'd told me was true. Had I known about Nadia or Svetlana, I would've certainly wanted to get in touch with them. But I wouldn't necessarily run out there recklessly, putting myself in danger. There had been other ways for us to reconnect, but I had to know that they were alive.

The problem was that Malahki didn't trust any of the men on the Dark Anomaly. He might have respect for the captain, but he didn't trust even him with my safety.

Malahki knew he could only protect me if I remained hidden. I hated that he resorted to lying to me instead of talking to me, but I realized that my ability to fully comprehend the danger in this place, so different to what I was used to, might've been limited back then—because he, Malahki, had sheltered me from the worst.

My head full of worrisome thoughts and my heart heavy, I sat up in bed.

"Knock, knock." Nadia poked her head behind the partition separating my personal area from the rest of our room. "Are you up? I brought you breakfast."

She slipped onto my side of the partition with a tray in her hands.

"Hungry?" She put the tray with a mug and a plate on my work desk that also served as a night table. "Sorry, it's nothing fancy. We've been rationing food," she said, gesturing at the plain toast and a cup of coffee.

"No, it's great. Thank you." I took the cup from the tray.

"Are you okay? Did you sleep well?" Nadia took a seat next to me on the bed.

"Yes, I... How is Malahki?"

Nadia bit her lip. "Still locked up."

"Locked up?" I stared at her.

Nadia's gaze flicked aside.

"Well... He gave Wyck and Vrateus some trouble last night."

"What do you mean?" Setting the cup aside, I rose to my feet. "What kind of trouble?"

"He was difficult to talk to. So, they locked him in the escape capsule to give him some time to cool off." She shifted uneasily before adding, "I have it recorded if you want to see it, with his permission of course."

"Recorded?" I echoed numbly. While I slept in my comfy bed, Malahki had spent the night locked up, like a prisoner?

Nadia blew out a breath, twisting the end of her light-brown ponytail between her fingers.

"I should've told you last night, but there was so much to talk about. Remember the cameras I had installed around the living area? I have them working again."

"Why?"

"I'm not sure." She shrugged with a sigh. "This was my one purpose on this expedition, you know, to make a movie..."

I snapped my gaze to hers.

"Nadia," I said somewhat harshly. "There is no expedition anymore. No one out there cares about us any longer. No one will ever see your movie."

She dropped her gaze down, twisting her fingers in her lap.

"I know..." she said softly. "It just gives me something to do, takes my mind off things."

I couldn't stand her defeated expression. My heart twisted and ached. Who was I to tell her how best to deal with what all of us had been going through? I shifted closer to her and hugged her so tight she squeaked.

"Do it if it helps, then," I said softly, kissing the hair over her temple. "Do whatever helps, Nadia."

She patted my hand.

"Do you want to see the recording of last night?" she asked.

"No." I released her from our embrace and headed to the partition. "I need to see him."

Nadia made a move to stop me. "Val. What if he attacks you? Svetlana wants to test him for *kronite* exposure."

"For what?" I paused.

"*Kronite*, the toxic gas that leaked into the air supply in the mess hall a few days ago. Most of the crew had a terrible reaction to it. Wyck and Vrateus were attacked when they went out to the supply room after that."

"Is that what she tested me for last night?" We were in the middle of the conversation when she'd asked me to breathe in some tube.

I'd been too distracted by so many other things to ask for details at that point.

That was what had caused the crew to lose their minds—*kronite*.

Nadia nodded. "Yours came back negative, but if Malahki was in the mess hall when the leak happened—"

"No." I shook my head resolutely. Malahki was nothing like the beast-like creatures who'd attacked us. "He is not like them. He will never hurt me."

He might've called himself a monster after his transformation, but even when he fucked me, delirious with lust, I knew I could make him stop any minute if I wished. I just happened *not* to want to stop him. Malahki's way of "lovemaking" was not something I would ever consider before, but I had enjoyed being with him. I craved it even.

Maybe whatever changes Malahki had been going through somehow had affected me, too. My feelings and emotions had synched with his so easily. We ended up resonating in love as well as we had in friendship before.

I missed him.

"Nadia, I need to see him. Now." I stepped behind the partition, heading for the door out of our room.

She caught up with me, taking my hand in hers.

"You have every right to be angry with Malahki," she said, misunderstanding my intentions. "He lied, and he kept you away from us all this time. But things really could've been worse if you stayed on the ship with me the day of the crash. Other than Vrateus and Wyck, there was really no one else. Vrateus did what he could to keep the crew under control. Wyck had to fight them off me. If there were two of us to protect, I'm not even sure if anyone could stop the males if they rushed us in a free-for-all stampede. And then...who knows where we would be."

Dread slithered cold down my spine at the thought of how much worse things could've been for both of us.

I drew her into another hug.

"I'm so, so sorry about what happened to you, Nadia."

She hugged me too, patting my back soothingly.

"I'm lucky, I got my Wyck out of this," she said, with a sigh. "But I'm glad you avoided facing the crew altogether. Don't be too harsh on Malahki. Okay?"

"I won't," I promised as she released me from our embrace.

She nodded with a smile. "Let's go see if he's tame enough this morning to have visitors."

Svetlana was having breakfast in the main living area of the ship, along with Wyck and Vrateus.

"Morning." She waved her hand, smiling.

Both men nodded in greeting.

"Morning." I gave them all a smile in return. It was nice to have people around—people who wouldn't try to bite your head off, literally.

Each of the three had a cup and a plate in front of them. A tray with tea and toast stood on the side of the table, untouched.

"Is that for Malahki?" I asked.

Wyck grunted, stretching his neck. "I'll take it to him." He made a move to get up.

"I can do it." I stopped him.

He gave me an incredulous look.

"He'll rip you apart," he warned me. "He tossed a cup at Vrateus's head and punched me in the face when we tried to deliver his dinner last night." He rubbed his jaw where Malahki's last blow must've landed. "Svetlana still didn't get a chance to test him for *kronite* exposure, but if you ask me, he must've taken a huge gulp of it."

"He didn't. He's spent almost all of his time with me." Other than a few trips to hide food, Malahki hadn't left the gardens before our trip down the garbage chute. The last part of his transformation, including the sudden surge of aggression, happened just yesterday, after the leak. "I'm so sorry, guys." I scraped a hand over my face, feeling guilty for leaving them to deal with the enraged *damirian*. "Malahki... Well, he's just been a little unstable after his change."

"A little?" Wyck scoffed, still rubbing his jaw.

"It's the transformation," Vrateus agreed with me, taking a sip from the mug in his hands. "I've read about *damirian* men. They're unstoppable in battle. In the early days of interplanetary conflicts, other nations always sought an alliance with Ak'ae, to have the *damirian* army on their side."

"If that's what he wanted to be, I'm happy it worked. But a part of me will always miss the old Malahki," Svetlana said wistfully. "I liked working in the gardens with him. His unaffected calm had always been so soothing in this crazy place."

Her words felt like a knife through my heart. Was Svetlana right, though? Were some parts of Malahki gone for good? Irrecoverably lost? I loved all his pieces, every single one—from the inferno of his passion to the serenity of his calm.

"No. He is still there," I protested, clasping my hands so tight, my fingers ached. "Malahki is...well, Malahki. He hasn't changed. He's just...evolved. All of him is still there, old and new. I—" I picked up the tray from the table. "I'll have to go to him."

"I'll come with you." Wyck grabbed a metal rod from a shelf in the corner.

I glared at him. "That won't be necessary—"

"Go with her, Wyck," Vrateus cut me off. "Make sure he's stable."

Wyck took the tray from me, heading to the escape capsule door. I had no choice but to follow. The door appeared as if it had been cut through before and then fixed after. Wyck shifted the metal rod under his other arm then turned the handle.

I touched his arm quickly, begging, "Please don't hurt Malahki."

He glowered. "Let's hope he won't give me any reasons."

I tripped over Malahki when Wyck opened the door. My *damirian* lay on the floor in the threshold.

"Valya," he croaked, catching me in his arms before I could hit the floor.

Tension that had been seizing me since our separation drained from my muscles the moment his arms wrapped around me.

"Hey! Watch it." Wyck deposited the tray on one of the seats and moved to my "rescue," wielding the rod over his head.

"No, Wyck." I shielded Malahki with both arms. "I'm fine."

"Get out, Wyck," Malahki growled menacingly, pressing me to his chest like the most cherished treasure.

Wyck took a wider stance, crossing his arms over his chest, demonstrating he wasn't going anywhere without making sure I was safe.

"Are you sure, Val?" he asked.

"I'm good, Wyck. Honestly." Malahki's burly arms crushed me to him without leaving a sliver of space to move, but he was careful not to squeeze too hard for his embrace to be painful. "He won't hurt me." I wholeheartedly believed that.

"Leave!" Malahki ordered in a deep, raspy voice.

Wyck tossed him a glare before moving his gaze my way again.

"If you need anything, just knock on the door," he told me before leaving.

Malahki shoved the door closed behind the *errock*. I noticed the door paneling was shredded and torn off on the inside. Had Malahki been clawing at it?

Sitting on the floor with me in his lap, he buried his face in my neck, rocking us softly. Sweet, achy tenderness swelled in my heart.

"Are you okay, baby?" I ran my hands through his hair. It was tangled, his braid undone.

"Valya," he groaned. "Don't ever leave me like that."

"I needed some time—"

He shook his head wildly.

"Yell at me. Get angry with me. Punch me if you must. But don't just walk away, without talking to me first. Please. Don't leave me alone. I've nearly gone insane, thinking you may never come back, that you may never even want to look at me again."

Compassion tightened around my chest, as firm as his hug.

"I was going to talk, Malahki. But I had to think about all of it first."

After the initial excitement at seeing Nadia well and alive, I'd had a sharp feeling of betrayal by Malahki. Disappointment and hurt came right after. I felt sorry for all the time I'd spent hiding, dreading for my life and safety, when I could've been with Nadia on my ship, all along. I'd had no idea that Nadia had been hiding, too, that they had moved to the ship only recently.

"I had to talk to Nadia and Svetlana," I said to Malahki. "I needed to hear their side of the story to get the full picture."

"I'm sorry. I'm so, so sorry," he murmured against my skin. "Please stay with me."

I threaded my fingers through the long strands of his hair, smoothing the tangled tresses.

"I'm not going anywhere, Malahki," I whispered in his ear, then kissed the corner of his mouth. "I understand the decisions you've made and appreciate what you've done for me. But you have to trust me, too."

His shoulders relaxed a little, though he still gripped on to me desperately like to a lifesaver.

"At first, I didn't know you well enough to trust you not to rush to see Nadia, risking your life," he said. "If I told you what was being done to her, I feared you might plot to help her behind my back, and I knew you wouldn't succeed. Later, I hadn't seen Nadia for a while, I thought she truly was dead. Telling you that no longer felt like a lie."

He took my face between his large hands, peering deep into my eyes.

"I'm sorry, Valya. I promise never to lie to you ever again."

I linked my hands behind his neck, breathing in his warm familiar scent.

"I missed you, Malahki," I whispered. "So, so much."

He groaned, spearing his fingers through my hair. "I can't sleep without you, Valya, can't think clearly without you. I need you." He kept kissing my neck, my face, my hair. "I've never needed anyone so much before. I didn't know if you were sad or hurting, and it drove me mad. I need to know you're happy and if not, I want to do everything to make you happy."

Basking in his affection like in sunshine, I shifted my hips a little and made him groan again. His erection was trapped between us, I realized, hard like a rock.

He jerked his pelvis back, away from me, sliding me back toward his knees.

"Does it hurt?" I murmured in his ear.

"You have no idea." There was so much longing in his raspy voice.

"Can I do something about it?"

"You are the only one who can." He glanced at me.

I lifted my hand to the closure of my suit.

"It's a good thing I'm here, then." I smiled.

His eyes flashed with heat. Sliding his hands inside my suit, he slipped it off my shoulders and down my arms. I stood up as he peeled it off me. Getting down on his knees, he unbuckled and took off my boots, leaving me completely naked for him.

My feet on each side of his thighs, I stood over him as he slid his hands up my bare legs. Grabbing my thighs, he yanked me closer and buried his face between them.

I gasped, grabbing on to the backs of the two seats behind him to keep my balance.

His long hair tickled the inside of my thighs, his tongue sliding between my heated folds. The intense need for him that had been simmering under my skin all night, exploded in desire impossible to contain.

"Yes, Malahki," I whimpered as he feasted on me. "Please..."

Pleasure rippled through me, building higher and higher. I gripped the padded seat backs, riding his face with abandon.

My knees trembled and bucked as the orgasm hit me. If he hadn't held my legs, I would've fallen. After squeezing every single shudder of pleasure out of me with his dexterous tongue, he released my thighs, letting me slide down into his lap.

"When did you learn how to do that?" I murmured into his shoulder as he glided his hands over my body in sweet, soothing caress.

"Yesterday."

"Just yesterday?" I thought back to all the amazing things he'd done to me at the farm and then in the shower.

"I kissed your sex, and you liked it," he said simply.

"I did," I confessed, gazing into his eyes. They glowed with swirls of the brightest tints of orange and red.

"I feel acutely every reaction of your body, Valya, and I learn. If you like something, I do more of it. If your body doesn't explode with pleasure when I do something else, I change that."

I didn't think there had been any time for "learning" when he ravaged me against the wall yesterday. Apparently, he'd managed to note and memorize things when I thought he'd been too desperate for a release to even think.

"I'll still need to learn a lot." He moved one of my braids behind my shoulder. "But I'm looking forward to it."

I smiled, playing with a long strand of his hair.

"How about you?" I asked. "Will you teach me what *you* like?"

He released a short laugh. It came out strained. His body grew even more rigid.

"Spirits, that'd be a short lesson, Valya! I'd like anything and everything you do to me or let me do to you."

I slid my hands down the hard planes of the muscles of his chest. The bright colorful swirls on his skin came to life under my touch, following the tips of my fingers.

"You're holding back."

"Valya," he groaned. "Lately, all I want is either to fight or to fuck. And I'm not interested in *fighting* you."

"All right." I let my hand travel down the ridges of his flat belly toward the closure of his pants. "Let's not fight, then."

He leaned back, giving me a better access to the waistband of his pants. I opened the closure then dipped my hand lower. The soft touch of the thin appendages that grew around his shaft made me smile.

"What are these?" I asked, moving my fingers among their cluster.

"Feelers." He exhaled in a gasp the moment my fingers brushed his hard length.

"What are they for?"

"To give you pleasure." He panted.

"Me?"

With a strangled groan, he nodded, then lifted his hips to yank his pants down. The tapered length of his erection sprang free, the feelers around it straining toward my hand.

"Is that all they do?" I asked.

"That is their only function." He got up, lifting me in his arms. "Their sole purpose is to caress you while I'm inside you."

My inner muscles spasmed at the idea of having the gentle sensation I'd just experienced on my fingers on my most intimate place. Yesterday morning, I hadn't fully appreciated that. It all had happened so fast and so suddenly. My first time with Malahki remained but a wild swirl of need, passion, and ecstasy in my mind.

He placed me on the padded seat that had been fully reclined into a single bed.

"Right now, giving you pleasure is the only purpose of *my* life, too," he said softly, bringing his large body over mine.

My skin tingled from anticipation.

"You're holding back," I whispered again as he hovered over me, our bodies barely touching.

"I want to savor every moment with you, even if it's the moment of tormenting need."

No one had ever looked at me with so much tenderness and adoration. My heart beat wildly as my insides melted with an enormous feeling for him that bubbled and grew in my chest.

"Oh, Malahki. I need you, too. So, so much." I raked my fingers through his black-as-night hair.

He lowered his lips to mine in a kiss as he entered me.

A gasp of pleasure escaped my lips, and he swallowed it, devouring my mouth.

I hooked my legs around his middle, anchoring him to me. The tender feelers stroked me as he began to move. They caressed me gently at first, their touch like a silky glide of flower petals. The faster Malahki thrust however, the firmer their touch became. They rubbed against me, tightly winding the coil of pleasure inside me and making it ready to explode.

I moaned wildly as the orgasm rolled through me in swells of ecstasy. Clinging to Malahki's strong shoulders, I sensed him going still for a moment before his release rushed through him, too. He pumped it into me in deep, powerful thrusts.

"Spirits take me..." he groaned, rolling to his side and taking me with him. "Stay with me, Valya." He kissed my hair, pressing me tight to his chest again. "Stay with me," he repeated like a mantra.

The warm feeling inside me expanded so much, it appeared to fill the entire capsule.

"I'm here, sweetheart." I caressed his back in long, soothing strokes. "With you is the only place I ever want to be."

Chapter 16

"Be careful, okay?" My fingers wrapped around the belt with weapons that Malahki wore around his shoulder, I couldn't bring myself to let go.

It was two days after we'd come to the ship to fight its inhabitants but found the only four friendly people on the Dark Anomaly instead. With Malahki and I joining them, the supplies in the food generators of our ship had to be stretched even thinner, now. Vrateus and Malahki were leaving to pick up the preserves that we'd hidden in the gardens and other places of the Dark Anomaly.

Malahki took my face between his hands.

"I'm not going to war, just to get some food," he said softly.

Vrateus brushed by, adjusting his weapons. "Isn't going for food just like going to war?" he asked.

"You're not helping, captain," Malahki snapped, then turned to me with a much gentler expression. "I'm better equipped to fight a war, too."

"That's not helping much, either." I shook my head with a faint smile. "I don't want you to get in any situations where there is a risk to your life or health."

He arched an eyebrow.

"We're in the wrong place for that. There's always some risk on the Dark Anomaly. Even while staying here behind locked doors, you're not as safe as I'd like you to be. I hate parting with you." He gave me a long kiss.

"We won't be long," Vrateus assured me when Malahki finally released me from his arms. "Wyck is staying with you, just in case."

Malahki glared at the *errock*, who met his glare with an equally reproachful stare. There obviously was no love lost between these two. Malahki had a lingering hostility toward the entire group of the *errocks* of the Dark Anomaly. And Wyck couldn't forget my *damirian's* recent punches and blows. The dark bruises on Wyck's clay-red skin would still take some time to disappear completely, especially since being the proud man that he was, Wyck refused to use the medical capsule to speed up the healing.

"Be careful," I said again as Malahki and Vrateus stepped out into the corridor. Each carried an empty bag over his shoulder to collect the food containers. Both of them wore oxygen masks around their necks connected to tubes linking them to the air tanks on their backs.

"We won't be long." Malahki waved to me before Wyck rolled the thick metal block on rails, closing the entrance to the ship. Nadia helped him lock all the chains and deadbolts.

Despite immediately missing Malahki, I felt the safest I'd ever been since our landing on the Dark Anomaly. For once, I didn't need to listen carefully to every noise around me or get ready to bolt and hide at the first sign of danger. It felt comforting to have friends in this hostile place.

"Val." Svetlana touched my shoulder. "Malahki undid some of the repairs we've done on the capsule door—"

"Oh, I know I'm so sorry." I rubbed my eyes. "I'll fix it."

"Can you look at it now, please?" She gestured in the capsule's direction. The subtle urgency in her expression made me pause for a moment.

"Sure." I followed her as she took her tablet off the table and headed for the capsule.

We climbed in.

"Svetlana," I started apologizing again. "I'm really sorry about the damage. *Damirian* men—"

She closed the door behind us quickly, then turned to me.

"It's not about the door," she said hurriedly. "I mean, we do have to fix it eventually, and I know you will do a much better job than we did, since you know so much more about this spacecraft. But I need to talk to you about something else."

"Okay." I sat in one of the chairs. "What is it all about."

She rubbed her eyes, and I realized how tired she looked.

"Did you sleep well?" I asked.

She shook her head with a faint smile.

"I haven't slept for a few nights now. I've been thinking..." she let her voice trail off, as if unsure how to proceed, then lifted her dark-brown eyes to mine. "Can you give me some numbers in terms of speed, range, and engine power of both your ship and the escape capsule? I may need their weight capacity, fuel consumption... And a few other things, like how do you think the spacecraft would perform under certain conditions."

"Why do you need all this information?" I asked.

She hesitated, but understanding slowly dawned on me.

"Are you planning to travel some place?" I asked tentatively, afraid to voice my guess out loud.

"Maybe," she replied, just as cautiously.

My mind had been so consumed with survival that I hadn't thought about escape at all lately, not after Malahki had convincingly proven to me, using charts and graphs, that it wasn't possible.

Was he wrong? And if so, was it deliberate?

A doubt about my man slithered inside me. I hated it, hated to think he might've lied to me about that, too.

I cleared my throat.

"Malahki says leaving is impossible," I said, with a hollow feeling in my stomach.

"He's right." She nodded confidently.

Despite it being disappointing news, something inside me lifted at her words. Knowing that Malahki hadn't lied this time.

The problem with someone having lied to you once was that even if the lie was forgiven, trust didn't come automatically anymore. It would take some time for me to stop doubting Malahki.

"If you can't leave here, where do you want to go, then?" I asked Svetlana.

She inhaled slowly, leaning against the mutilated door.

"I'd love for you to look carefully at the door repair we've done. It's conveniently exposed now that Malahki ripped all the siding and insulation off it." She pursed her lips in an amused accusation.

"He was just trying to get to me." I felt the need to defend him.

"Talk about going lust-crazy," she wiggled her eyebrows. "I hope he made it worth it for you afterwards."

"Oh yes, he did," I said with a soft giggle, and she smiled broadly at me.

"Thankfully, a few of the males of the Dark Anomaly make it worth landing in this place, don't they?" She laughed, and I joined her, happy that after everything she'd gone through here, Svetlana could still laugh the way she did, cheerfully and carefree.

"Okay," I said, still with a smile lingering on my lips. "I can do it right now. I'll just need to get the tools back at the ship. Are you planning to disconnect the capsule from the ship at some point?"

"Yes." She lowered her voice as if afraid that Wyck or Nadia would hear us from behind the door. "Nadia told me she tried to take off in it, right after your landing, but she got an error message. Though she doesn't believe there was a malfunction with the system, she says she doesn't have enough knowledge to accurately diagnose it if it was. Can you look at it?"

I nodded. Part of my training for the mission was studying in detail both the ship and the capsule. Unlike the onboard engineers, I wouldn't be able to perform many major repairs on either, but I knew their systems explicitly and could identify and troubleshoot a long list of malfunctions if needed.

"I can run the diagnostics, but what good would it do? Even if both craft are in perfect shape, it's impossible to leave here, isn't it?"

Svetlana sat down in the seat opposite of mine. Her fingers drummed a nervous rhythm on the surface of the tablet in her lap.

"I wonder if we've tried everything yet," she said, her eyes focused right ahead of her.

"What do you mean?" I shifted closer to her. "Are you saying there is a way to get the fuck out of here?" My heart raced as my mind reeled at the idea.

"Listen." She placed her hand on mine. "I don't want anyone to know anything about this conversation, do you hear me? Vrateus would freak if he knew. I tried to escape here once, and I'd be long dead if he hadn't stopped me. I don't want Wyck or Nadia to have any false hopes, either."

"But do you really think there's a way?" I stared at her imploringly. Hope flickered in my heart, refusing to leave now.

"No, that's not what I said." Svetlana shook her head. "But there is one possibility I haven't fully explored yet. I need those numbers for more accurate calculations on my theory. That doesn't mean the calculations would end up giving us any viable results. It could end up being just another discarded theory. I have at least a hundred of those by now. So..."

"I see." I heaved a long sigh.

My hope was crushed before it even had a chance to take root, but it was still painful to let it go. I understood why Svetlana wanted to spare the others this disappointment.

"Okay, tell me exactly what you need, and I'll see if I can get it." I moved to the seat in front of the control panel and brought it to life.

Screens with familiar displays lit up. Everything looked in perfect order, deceivingly convincing me that all I had to do would be to take off and fly free wherever I wished.

"Okay, so..." Svetlana sat into the co-pilot's seat and turned on her tablet. "First give me the numbers, please. Then, I'll give you the parameters of the conditions, and you explain to me exactly what your spacecraft is capable of."

"Which craft are we talking about? The main ship or the escape capsule?"

"Both. They each have their strengths and weaknesses, I presume?"

"Yes, the capsule is more powerful and agile, while the ship is more suitable for interstellar travel."

"I'll look at both," she concluded with a nod.

"From what I see right now, though, neither of them would combat the gravity of this place," I exhaled heavily, scrolling through rows of data on the main screen. "The latest numbers come from the system analysis of our landing, and it says here—"

"No." Svetlana shook her head with a confident smile. "*I* have the latest analysis and the most complete data. No one knows the anomaly GR-A8502 as well as I do—no one in the world. I've been studying it very closely for months now. In and out."

A FEW DAYS LATER, SVETLANA and I sat in the pilots' seats of the capsule again. This time, we were about to take the craft for a ride—a test drive of sorts.

"Well, so far so good." I glanced back at the door while disconnecting the capsule from the main ship.

All the preliminary testing I'd done on it after the latest repair told me the door was solid. The instrument displays on the control panel said that it held fine, too. But the visual confirmation of seeing the door closed gave me the most satisfaction.

"You did a great job on it," Svetlana agreed.

"Thanks. Am I going straight from here?" I asked, turning to face forward again.

Though Svetlana and I had planned and mapped the route beforehand, I felt apprehensive. I didn't need the confirmation as much as just hearing someone's voice to reassure me.

"Yes." Svetlana sounded a bit too cheerful herself, nervously so.

Or maybe she was just excited to go on a "road trip." It wasn't every day that we got to go outside of the habitable sector of the Dark Anomaly. For me, this was the very first time ever since coming here.

I drove the capsule away from the ship manually, along the uneven surface of the disk's edge. With the transparent front of the capsule, the lights of the Dark Anomaly surrounded us.

"It's beautiful," I couldn't hold back my appreciation for the visual spectacle all around us.

"Absolutely gorgeous," Svetlana agreed with a short laugh. "I would love the lights if I didn't hate them so much."

I'd spent less time here than Svetlana, most of it in the gardens, with no windows, but I shared her feelings toward the lights. To me, the Dark Anomaly appeared like a cruel trick, a trap—mesmerizingly beautiful on the outside and deadly on the inside.

"Well, let's see if we can leave here, one day," I muttered under my breath.

Svetlana shot me a glance.

We had an unspoken rule. After our very first conversation, we didn't speak about the final purpose of all the work the two of us had done in the past several days. As Svetlana had said, there was no reason to give hope to the others. By avoiding talking about it ourselves, we also tried not to let our own hope grow. At the back of my mind, however, I knew the ultimate purpose of all of this was to leave this God-cursed place. Despite my best intentions, the hope remained in my heart.

"Do you want me to take it over the edge onto the surface, now?" I asked Svetlana to confirm the next point of our travel plan.

"Yes, please." She gripped the armrests, her gaze firmly ahead.

I steered the capsule to the left, maneuvering it from the edge onto the rim of the disk's surface.

"Just make sure to stay within the zone." Svetlana pointed at the yellow-lit area on the screen of the control panel.

"Sure." I adjusted the controls, staying on the route we'd worked out before.

"It looks great," Svetlana said hesitantly, as if needing my confirmation, too.

The escape capsule's systems performed without an issue. I'd expected that after running the tests and diagnostics on them. Still, it was a relief to see the engines in action.

"So far so good," I agreed quietly, afraid to jinx it.

When our expedition was planned, people on Earth had just discovered that the Dark Anomaly had a hard disk at its center. No one would've thought about driving on it, though. Despite Svetlana's thorough calculations, things always could go wrong.

"Is she okay, then?" Svetlana tipped her chin at the control panel where the screens and dials of the instruments displayed the continuous analysis of the spacecraft's systems.

I nodded silently, concentrating on keeping the capsule on course on the uneven surface.

"Let's take her in?" she suggested.

"Okay." I bit my lip, steering the capsule more to the left. The map on the control panel shifted into the orange area now, several hundred feet closer to the center of the Dark Anomaly's disk.

Svetlana's knuckles turned white as she gripped the armrests tighter.

"Do you feel it? The pull?" She gasped.

According to Svetlana, the gravity of the Dark Anomaly was stronger at its center. It pulled objects from its rim along its surface.

"Yes." I sharply adjusted the steering to stay on route.

"Do you think the engines would handle one more increase?" she asked, her voice breathy.

I didn't reply, just shifted the controls to take the capsule slightly left again, another three hundred feet closer to the center. Our path remained parallel to the rim of the disk but shifted closer to the center as I entered the red zone.

The pull was even stronger here. I flexed my arms to keep a firm grip on the controls.

"This isn't normal." Perspiration misted my forehead from effort and concentration.

Nothing was "normal" about this godforsaken place.

Svetlana quickly punched in her tablet, periodically glancing at my control panel.

"Actually, this is very much within the range I expected," she said.

My arms ached, and my hands started to cramp from clamping onto the controls so hard. Svetlana might have expected this, but the readings on my screens shifted very much outside of the range I preferred them to be.

"Listen, I need to get out of here." Even my lips hurt because I'd been biting them so hard.

Svetlana nodded quickly. "Okay. I'm good. I have enough data to work with, now."

I swerved back into the orange and then into the yellow zone, relieved to be away from the power that had tried to wrestle the controls from me. Maneuvering the capsule from the rim to the edge of the disk again, I glanced Svetlana's way as she furiously punched in the numbers and scrolled through calculations on her tablet.

"So, what do you think?" I asked her softly. Despite striving not to hope, I did anyway. I desperately hoped her theory would work.

"Well." She placed the tablet into her lap and folded her hands over it. "I guess it's time to share this with the others."

Chapter 17

"Fuck, yes!" Malahki exclaimed so loudly that Nadia jumped in her seat, and Lesh woke up from his nap, hissing in warning. "I volunteer!"

"Honey." I took his hand in mine and placed it in my lap.

All six of us sat around the table laden with tablet inserts. Svetlana had very carefully mentioned her plan for escaping the Dark Anomaly, which got Malahki so excited. The other two men seemed just as agitated. Nadia had a huge smile on her face.

"It's not that easy." Svetlana lifted her hand. "The risk is...well, huge."

"Send me first," Malahki insisted. "I'll test it for you."

"That's not how it works," Svetlana explained patiently. "It's not possible to do it one by one. We'll all go, or no one does."

Malahki shifted his gaze to me. Concern replaced his enthusiastic expression. As eager as he'd been to put his own life on the line, he obviously wasn't as willing to risk mine.

"What exactly are our chances for success?" he asked Svetlana, not taking his eyes off me.

She rubbed her face, placing her elbows on the table. I knew she hadn't been sleeping well. I had trouble sleeping myself lately. After the first night spent in my old bed, I'd moved with Malahki into the escape capsule. We had the back two seats converted into a bed. With him next to me, I'd been able to fall asleep easier, but I woke up often through the night.

Whenever I would go back to the ship to get a cup of tea when I couldn't sleep, Svetlana would be sitting at the table, surrounded by tablet inserts and going over her calculations again and again.

"I can't tell you the exact chance of success," she replied to Malahki. "It's impossible to calculate that precisely because the power field of the Dark Anomaly fluctuates so sporadically. I've been working with ranges, not exact numbers, and even that is not guaranteed, of course. Look here."

She grabbed a data slate and slid it into her tablet frame.

"That's the visual of the energy field of the Dark Anomaly."

We lowered our heads over the screen with the 3D model of the Anomaly's disk slowly rotating on it.

"The main part of the Dark Anomaly is the field of energy that spins through space not unlike a whirlpool of water," Svetlana started. "It drags in objects as it travels, pulling them into the center of the field where the hard core of the crashed spaceships has formed over a long period of time. Just like a whirlpool, the energy spins around the edge of the disk, its pull growing stronger and faster the closer to the centre it gets. The power compresses the ships, with the pressure getting exponentially stronger the closer to the center they move."

She slid her finger along the radius of the disk toward the bulging center.

"All this energy needs to be released at some point. Similar to a whirlpool, it blasts out from the very center of the disk." She traced the thin dotted lines that came out from the bulging centre of the disk on her diagram. "Unlike a whirlpool, however, where the water is dragged down, forming a funnel, the centre of the Anomaly's disk is raised on both sides. Its disk actually has the shape of a flat, wide spinning top toy, with the rays of energy blasting out from both sides, the top and the bottom. The power of the blasts is strong enough to propel the energy out for long distances."

Vrateus scrubbed his chin.

"The same energy that dragged us all in here is blasting out into the space from the centre?"

Svetlana nodded. "Yes."

"So, all we have to do is make it to the centre of the Dark Anomaly then let the force field shoot us out?" Wyck asked, sceptically.

Svetlana swallowed hard, rubbing her throat.

"Technically, yes," she said. "In reality, there are some serious challenges."

"Like what?" Nadia shifted closer.

"The energy travels in a loop. The trajectory of the field is similar to that of an electromagnet. Most of what's released from the center curves, spreading like a fountain or a flower, then comes back to the edge of the disk."

Svetlana moved her finger in an arch from the center of the disk down to the outer edge of it.

"It sweeps through space in a curve, grabbing whatever objects happen to be in its path, then carries them back to the edge of the disk."

"That's how we all ended up here," Malahki concluded.

"That's how," Svetlana echoed. "I'm still not entirely clear on why it takes some objects and leaves the others, but I suspect it has something to do with energy waves. That's why the Dark Anomaly sucks in powered spaceships and probes, but doesn't touch asteroids and other celestial bodies."

"Fascinating." Vrateus shook his head, staring at her. It wasn't entirely clear what fascinated him the most, the discoveries Svetlana had shared or the woman herself.

Malahki kept his gaze on the tablet screen. "That means that even if we manage to catch a ride with the energy stream emitting from the center of the Dark Anomaly, we'll risk being dragged back where we started."

Svetlana heaved a long breath.

"Yes, but I believe a portion of the energy at the very center is blasted with enough power to separate from the field. The trick is for us to get to that precise location."

"Because if we're in any way off, we're dead," Malahki said what Svetlana wouldn't.

"And that is the biggest risk," she concluded, adding, "With a number of other risks too, like losing control and crashing into the center on the way to it or getting lost in space after we leave."

"How are we getting to the center?" Nadia asked. "Walking?" She touched her still perfectly flat belly.

"No, it's way too far to walk," Svetlana replied, adding with a small shrug, "and perilous. This ship is not designed to travel along a surface. We'd have to drive the escape capsule to the center."

Vrateus stared at his hands folded on the table in front of him. "If we succeed, what will happen next? After we're blasted into space?"

"The capsule is not designed for long-distance travel," I explained, thinking about all the perils we would have to face every step of the way. Would all of them think it was worth it? To risk everything for the slim chance of getting out of here?

"Our original plan was to send a distress signal once we'd left here," Nadia chimed in. "A ship was supposed to pick us up to take us back to Earth."

We all looked at Svetlana, since she was the one with the plan, now.

"That would still be our best...our *only* option. Except that no one will be waiting for us out there. Once we're clear of the Dark Anomaly's force field, we'd lay a course for the closest traffic route." She heaved a sigh. "Then, we'll turn our locator signals on and wait for someone to find us and pick us up. Otherwise..." Her voice trailed off.

It was clear what she meant without her voicing it.

"Otherwise, we'd be drifting through space in a craft the size of a bus until the oxygen ran out or one of the other life-support systems failed."

Silence hung over the table, as everyone was absorbing the words she had said and those she mercifully hadn't.

"It's been at least several decades since either one of us traveled through space." Nadia spoke first. "I hope traffic has increased since then, and someone will be out there to pick us up, eventually."

"Omphi is the closest planet. In my time, there was a human exploration station orbiting it," Svetlana said.

I searched my brain for the information on the water world Omphi among so many things I'd learned in preparation for our mission.

"There were several small floating settlements on Omphi, the year of our expedition," I said. "Most of them were from Earth, but in partnership with other species, too."

"They might've grown in the...how long has it been, now?" Nadia turned to me. "How much time would've passed on Earth since we've been gone? Sixty? Seventy years?"

I stared at her in silence. The enormity of the time warp rushed over me anew. I counted every day spent on the Dark Anomaly, yet the cruelty of it was to fully comprehend what it meant in terms of human lives. My brother and his wife would be dead by now. My baby nieces would be more than twice my age. They would've gone through a lifetime worth of experiences by now, all without me...

Malahki took my hand, squeezing it firmly.

"Yes, between sixty and seventy years," he replied to Nadia for me.

I swallowed around the tightness in my throat, composing myself. It'd been a millennium and a half since Malahki left his world. No one he ever knew would be alive anymore. If our escape worked, for him, it'd be like visiting a completely new world.

"I'll calculate the flight path that will take us to the closest most-traveled route," I offered. No one knew exactly how things would've changed out there while we'd been stuck in here. Like Svetlana, I hoped the space traffic had increased, but it could have very well gone the other way, too. Since our disappearance, the Federation might've imposed travel restrictions on this area. Omphi's exploration could have ended. So many things could've changed.

We all sat in silence again. None of us had ever had this possibility before—to leave here.

Finally, Svetlana cleared her throat.

"We need to consider the alternative," she said softly. "The risk of going through with this is great, every step of the way. Not all of us may make it, or none of us will…"

She swallowed hard, moving her gaze around the table, from one face to another.

"What is the alternative?" Nadia asked in a subdued voice.

"Staying here," Vrateus replied, raking his fingers through the wide stripe of long fur on his head.

"Staying? When we can leave?" Nadia narrowed her eyes at him. "The Dark Anomaly is worse than a prison. What do we have going for us here?"

"Well, the crew is less of a threat, now," Svetlana pointed out.

That was true. Most of the crew had died by now, either by exterminating each other or as a result of the chemical leak into the air-supply system. A few handfuls might be surviving on the different shipwrecks, but taking into account their propensity to self-destruction, they wouldn't last long. With the six of us coming together, we were stronger than ever as a group, capable of fighting and surviving.

Hers was the voice of reason, but getting even a sliver of hope for true freedom, my brain refused to listen. My mind clung to that one chance to be free.

I gazed at the faces of the others.

The reflection of my hope was clearly displayed on Malahki's face. Nadia bit her lip. Svetlana kept her expression neutral. But the expressions of both Vrateus and Wyck struck me the most.

Having lived on the Dark Anomaly all of their adult lives, I'd expected them to be most reluctant to leave. But there was so much light, hope, and excitement on their faces, it left no doubt they longed to break free from this place, too.

Svetlana must've seen it, too. She stroked Vrateus's hand on the table.

"You don't want me to risk my life," she said, "and I'd so much rather stay here with you than risk yours. I'm happy wherever you are, even here, as long as we're together. I don't mind staying."

Nadia glanced at Wyck, who remained silent, even as his face said it all.

"I do," she said quickly. "I do mind staying if there is even the slightest chance to leave. I'd risk it all, for the baby." She crossed her both arms over her belly as if trying to protect the tiny being inside.

"Wherever you go, I'll go." Wyck wrapped his arm around her shoulders, and she stroked the hard, dark ridges of his knuckles.

Even if her pregnancy progressed and ended well. I understood the added horror of their situation if we all stayed here. With all of us eventually aging and dying, Wyck and Nadia's son would be destined to live the rest of his days as the Dark Anomaly's sole survivor. He'd live and die completely alone—a future no parent would wish for their child.

The alternative of course carried the risk of all of us dying while trying to escape the clutches of the Dark Anomaly.

"Staying here carries challenges, too," Malahki commented. "The support systems are deteriorating. The six of us could never maintain them at the same level as before. We'd need to significantly reduce the habitable sector in size."

"We're running out of food," Wyck added.

Svetlana inclined her head, not meeting their eyes. "We can clean out and maintain a smaller section of the habitable sector. We can revive the gardens for food supply."

"Wyck needs meat to survive," Nadia argued. "His species require a large amount of it in their diets. He can't live on plants alone."

I suspected that would be an issue for Malahki as well. In his male form, he had developed a new craving for meat, when he'd abhorred even the smell of it before. With the *vasai* farm destroyed and the wild *vasai* possibly all exterminated due to the lack of oxygen, chemical leak, and overhunting, there was no source of meat on the Dark Anomaly at all.

Wyck gazed at Nadia warmly.

"With the baby coming," he said, "we'll need doctors. Even your machine here," he tipped his chin in the direction of the medical capsule, "is confused about what to do with the human-*errock* baby. It doesn't have enough information even to monitor your pregnancy properly."

The system was definitely not programmed with detailed information on interspecies pregnancies. Something like that had not been planned as a possibility during this expedition.

Vrateus placed his hand on top of Svetlana's.

"You were ready to give up your life to leave here," he said softly, referring to Svetlana's failed escape attempt months ago when he stopped her from leaving, saving her life.

She lifted her eyes to his with a sad smile.

"Yes. I'll give up my life in a heartbeat if it leads to people learning something new. But I'm not ready to risk yours." She shook her head.

"Svetlana is right," Malahki said, unexpectedly. "We need to carefully consider the alternative, what we'd be giving up. Here, we have a relatively safe place, which we could possibly make habitable enough to survive for decades if not longer. That is something to think about before launching ourselves out there, to possibly face immediate death."

I stroked his hand with my fingers, making the multi-colored swirls come to life on his skin. The mesmerising colors easily rivaled the beauty of the Dark Anomaly's lights, in my opinion.

"Are you talking caution, my vicious *damirian* warrior?" I murmured, trying to lighten the heavy atmosphere hanging over the table. The choices we had to make weren't easy.

"I'm with Svetlana on this one," he said, the stern expression in his vivid eyes softening as he gazed at me. "If it were just me, I wouldn't think twice, but as far as you're concerned, I can't bring myself to endanger your life in any way."

"You'd rather I stayed here?"

He kept his gaze on me for a moment longer, then faced Svetlana.

"Are you sure it's not possible for one of us to go out there, take all the risks, then bring help to get the rest out of here, safely?"

I opened my mouth to protest, guessing Malahki wanted to be the one to do what he'd just said.

Svetlana beat me to it.

"How can anyone from the outside help us?" she asked. "If they come here, they'd end up stranded here with us. Then, we'd just have more people to worry about." She sighed deeply. "Like I said, it has to be all of us, together, or none at all."

On one hand, we had decades of survival on the Dark Anomaly, isolated from the rest of the world.

On the other, we faced the risk of immediate death in exchange for the chance at a better life.

Indeed, it was a difficult choice to make.

Chapter 18

He adjusted his grip on his makeshift spear. Vrateus had offered him an entire arsenal of guns to choose from, but the solid weight of the metal bar in his hand felt most reassuring.

Wyck clicked on the camera that Nadia had clipped to the belt on his shoulder. He often wore it for her, recording the conditions of the Dark Anomaly outside of the ship. The *errock* then rolled open the massive door.

"I'll go first." Malahki stepped out into the corridor.

Outside of the clean environment of the ship, he placed the oxygen mask over his mouth and nose and opened the supply valve. According to the recent readings of the air analysis, the conditions in the habitable sector of the Dark Anomaly remained acceptable, but it had been decided between the six of them not to leave the ship without the oxygen masks anymore. None of them trusted the deteriorating air supply system. It hadn't been maintained at all lately, and could fail any time.

Vrateus joined him, his trusted guns firmly in his hands. Wyck rolled the door closed. The three of them waited until the clanking sounds came, confirming that the women engaged the locks from the inside.

Once satisfied that the women were now safe, the captain gestured for him to start on their way.

Malahki's heart gave a loud thud as the three of them passed by the white doors to the gardens. The lighting behind the doors appeared much dimmer than it should be this time of the day for the plants to thrive.

He was glad the purpose of today's trip did not require them to enter. Seeing the gardens in their current state would break his heart. The controlled destruction he'd done when Valya and he still lived there was hard enough—he had to let some plants die, making others grow out of control. Now, he suspected everything inside would be gone, dead, and rotten.

Coaxing plants to life in the challenging conditions of the Dark Anomaly had been one of the hardest tasks he'd accomplished in his life. It'd been one of the most rewarding, too. He loved watching the seedlings grow, transforming the dead world of metal and plastic into a green space. It had brought him peace and even an enjoyment among all the cruelties and devastation of this place.

He'd been proud of the hard work he'd done in the gardens. Seeing it all ruined now would be crushing.

Thankfully, they didn't need to enter the gardens today. Their destination was the spacesuit storage room on the opposite end of the main corridor of the habitable sector. Svetlana insisted all of them have functioning spacesuits for their journey to the center of the Dark Anomaly.

The day after she'd first informed them about the escape plan, the six of them had put it to a vote. Personally, he would've loved to take all the risk on himself, sparing the worst for Valya and the others, but there was no option like that. Like Svetlana had said, they had to be in it together.

"Watch out!" Wyck shouted behind him, yanking Malahki out of his thoughts.

A male he didn't recognize jumped at them from a side corridor, attacking from behind. Malahki swung his spear, whacking the male flat across his jaw with it. The blow didn't kill but stunned the attacker, tossing him against the wall.

A *raimoid*, Malahki finally recognized his species.

"I thought it was an animal." Wyck took a closer look at his former crew mate. The *errock's* mouth behind the clear material of the oxygen mask twitched in disgust.

Malahki was especially grateful for his own oxygen mask as he studied the male spread on the floor. The *raimoid* looked so filthy, he probably stunk unbearably.

"Leephron." Vrateus lowered himself to his knees next to the male.

Malahki knew the name the captain had said. It belonged to one of the very few *raimoids* on the Dark Anomaly. Leephron had come to the gardens with Urkril once. But the male was simply unrecognizable.

His normally purple skin had paled to light gray now, the typical for *raimoids'* bright blotches of color had completely disappeared. With not a shred of clothing covering his body, it was apparent how malnourished Leephron was—his skin stretched tightly over his skeleton with no fat and hardly any muscle tissue left. His two legs and four arms were almost as thin as the metal rod in Malahki's hands.

"He's starving," he said softly.

"Leephron." Vrateus touched the *raimoid's* face.

Snapping to awareness, the male jerked. His gray eyes bulged out of their sockets. Void of any emotion, they seemed muddy and unseeing.

With a feral growl, he launched on Vrateus, sinking his teeth into the captain's arm.

"Fuck!" Wyck punched the *raimoid* in the head the same moment as Malahki speared the male with the metal rod, pinning him to the floor.

Vrateus's chest rose and fell quickly as he ripped the bottom of his voluminous sleeve and tied it tightly over the fresh bite.

"We'll need to treat it when we get back," Malahki said. Even if the *raimoid* didn't carry any contagious diseases, his bite couldn't be clean.

The captain nodded silently, his gaze on the dead body at their feet.

"I didn't get a chance to talk to him," Vrateus said with regret.

Malahki lowered his hand on the captain's shoulder.

"I don't think he *could* talk," he said, remembering the unhinged expression on the *raimoid's* face. His bulging eyes appeared dead even before he died. No wonder Wyck had mistaken him for an animal, there was not a shred of intelligence or even self-awareness in the male.

"They can't be rescued anymore," he said, understanding the struggle Vrateus must be going through. "There is nothing we can do for them."

Frankly, most of the crew weren't redeemable even before the air supply malfunction or the chemical leak. But he understood the captain's desire to protect those he'd been responsible for. For more than seven years, Vrateus had protected the crew, often even against their wishes. Seeing them in this state must have felt in part like a personal failure to him.

Wyck frowned, heaving a long sigh.

Malahki yanked his spear from the dead body. If there was anyone still left alive around here, the body wouldn't be lying here for long. Overall, the corridor looked less disgusting than the last time he had walked here. The rotten remains were mostly gone now, only bones remained, cleaned of every shred of meat.

"They've made poor choices, captain, long before the air system malfunctioned. And even long before they got to the Dark Anomaly," he said to Vrateus.

Most of the crew came from questionable backgrounds. Smugglers, slave traders, and pirates, they travelled too close to the Dark

Anomaly to avoid being caught and persecuted, ending up being sucked in here instead.

The bones crunched under his boots as he headed down the corridor, followed by Vrateus and Wyck.

The strings of lights had been torn in some sections. Wyck took out a flashlight from the tool belt across his chest and turned it on, allowing them to keep moving ahead.

In the bluish ray of the flashlight, the space looked even more wretched and desolate. The panelling had been stripped from most of the walls, baring scratched metal and torn cables. There was so much dirt and litter on the ground, the floors were impossible to see. Bones and pieces of chitin snapped and crunched under their feet, in every section of the corridor.

Worry racked him when he thought about all the challenges they would face when trying to escape this place. But watching the deterioration of life on the Dark Anomaly made staying here not just depressing but emotionally impossible. Even if he were never to see the sun of a planet again, any chance of getting out of here was worth taking.

"Here." Vrateus stopped shortly after they had passed the airlock.

The captain shoved the door to the storage room open, and Malahki braced himself for the sight of the dead *akuks* that Valya and he saw the last time they'd been here. However, the bodies were gone, now, and he decided not to dwell on what might've happened to them—eaten most likely, since the door didn't close properly.

"Well, this doesn't look as decimated as the rest," Wyck observed, taking in the storage room.

Someone had ransacked it after Malahki's last visit. It looked even messier than before, with most things that weren't attached to the walls now littering the floor. Wyck was right, however, the room's contents were misplaced but not taken. The crew, apparently, had little interest in what could not be eaten or used for a weapon.

Vrateus got to work.

"Check the spacesuits," he said, lifting one from the floor. "We need three functioning ones, with built-in locators. And be mindful of the size." He slid an assessing gaze down Malahki's large body, muttering, "You may want to try one on to make sure it fits."

The spacesuits that the humans had on their ship had proven too tight for either one of the three of them.

"We need *four* suits," Wyck corrected him. "Lesh is coming, too."

Vrateus turned to him.

"You're not planning to stuff the *mahdi* into a spacesuit, are you?"

"I'm not leaving him here." Wyck crossed his massive arms over his equally enormous chest, taking a wide stance.

Vrateus blew out a frustrated breath, shaking his head. "I don't want to leave him either, but it's not going to work."

"Why not?"

"Are you kidding me? For one, he has three heads and four legs."

"So?"

"We don't have the suit to accommodate that. How is he going to move?"

"I'll carry him," Wyck replied, unfazed. "I just need a suit wide enough to have him comfortable inside. It can be short, but it needs to be wide, with a large helmet."

Their arguing shifted Malahki's thoughts to their escape plan. Svetlana counted on the force of the Dark Anomaly's energy field to blast them into space. But what if they could aid the field in getting them out of here?

Stepping over the suits, he searched for power cells collected from the crashed spaceships over the years. The older ones had less energy stored in them than the newer ones. Their combined effect, however, would be substantial if set off at once.

"The spacesuits are just for a backup," Wyck stubbornly contin-ued to argue with the captain. "We're taking the capsule, aren't we?"

"There is no seat in the capsule for him, either. It only has six." Vrateus clearly hated the argument. He had a soft spot for Lesh, all of them did. As the captain, he had to be the voice of reason, but Malahki already knew he was fighting a losing battle. Wyck wouldn't leave without Lesh.

"I'll put him in my lap," the *errock* kept going.

"How? He's almost the size of Nadia!" the captain exclaimed, whipping his long fluffy tail around his boots in irritation.

"And I have a big lap!" Wyck slapped his muscular thighs, the size of tree-trunks. "Nadia fits here perfectly."

Malahki headed for the exit, leaving the two of them to it.

"I'll get a cart from the waste processing room," he told them be-fore exiting the room. "We'll need something to transport all of this back to the ship."

When he came back with the cart, Wyck had two suits set aside. Malahki guessed he'd won the argument and Lesh was coming with them. He knew Vrateus would concede eventually. Lesh had become a part of their small crew long before even Valya and Malahki had joined. Though, he still had no idea how Wyck would accomplish getting the suit on the *mahdi* if it came down to it.

After trying a few suits, Malahki finally found one that fit him more or less comfortably. It was an older model, but it seemed to function just fine. He'd need to test it more when he was back on the ship with Valya.

His thoughts drifted back to her. The desire to be near her itched deep under his skin. Being away gave him an anxious feeling he se-verely disliked.

"Are we all set?" Vrateus asked after they had loaded the suits in-to the cart. The captain obviously had no desire to linger here for too long, either.

"I want to take the power cells, too." Malahki lifted one shaped like a cylinder off the floor.

"What for?"

"I have an idea I'll have to run by Svetlana first, but we may as well take them now. It'd spare us another trip to get them later."

Vrateus regarded him carefully.

"How many do you need?"

"All of them."

Chapter 19

The night before our planned take-off, I turned to Malahki the moment we entered the capsule which had served as our bedroom for the past few weeks.

I needed to be close to him, as close as possible. Because tomorrow... So many things could go wrong tomorrow. If I thought about any of them for another minute, I'd lose my mind.

He understood perfectly. Without saying a word, he cupped my face, kissing me deeply.

My hands trembling, I fervently opened my suit then let him slide it off me. The glide of his large, rough palms along my skin felt invigorating, making each nerve in my body stand on end.

He got down to his knees, taking off my boots, and I raked my fingers through his long, dark-as-night hair. He'd been wearing it in one braid, lately. With all the preparations for our departure, there hadn't been much time for the elaborate braiding he'd done before.

Leaning over him, I took his braid and tugged at the end of the tie. The braid unravelled as he got up to his feet. When he kissed me again, the fragrant curtain of his hair draped around our faces, adding to the intimacy.

Suddenly, we were completely alone in the entire Universe. Just the two of us. And at that moment, I needed no one else in the world.

"I love you," I whispered against his lips. "I love you, Malahki, all of you. I love the person you've always been and the man you have become."

He inhaled sharply, breathing my words in.

"Spirits, I love you too, Valya." He pressed his forehead to mine, holding my face between his hands. "So, so much," he groaned.

I had to tell him how I felt because this might be the only chance I'd get, because tomorrow might be the last day of our lives or the last day of us being together or...

I grabbed his shoulders, finding his mouth with mine. I kissed him with the desperation of a drowning woman grasping for a life raft. He was my escape from the terror and despair that had been the past three months.

"I love you, I love you," I chanted like a mantra as I opened the closure of his pants and found his erection. "I love you," I repeated as he propped me against the back of one of the seats and gently slid inside me.

The feelers around his shaft caressed me tenderly, as if welcoming our connection. Their gentle rubbing grew more intense as his thrusts got stronger and more desperate.

"Valya..." he groaned my name, setting off the explosion of pleasure inside me.

Blinded by pure ecstasy, I gripped his shoulders. The orgasm was still rocking through my body as he pumped his release into me.

His hands wrapped around me tightly, he buried his nose in the dip between my neck and my shoulder.

"Hold me," I panted. "Don't ever let me go."

"Never," he said firmly, making the word sound like a vow. "You're my life, Valya. Whatever happens, we'll stay together."

Chapter 20

I flipped the front section of my transparent helmet back and clipped the gloves up, freeing my hands for a better grip on the controls. We'd decided to wear our spacesuits inside the capsule to be prepared for the unexpected.

Today was the day we were finally trying to say goodbye to the Dark Anomaly, and it felt surreal.

"Ready?" Svetlana asked from the co-pilot's seat of our escape capsule.

"No!" I wanted to scream.

I didn't feel ready. Not ready to die or potentially lose any one of our small team with whom I had connected so closely over the past weeks. Not ready to risk parting from Malahki.

But I nodded anyway, as calmly as I could manage.

Nadia was sitting behind Svetlana. Malahki was in the seat behind me, I couldn't see him unless I turned around, which I might not be able to do once we started moving. I turned to him now, while I still could.

"I'm ready," he said softly, giving me an encouraging smile. I smiled in return, grateful to hear his voice.

Vrateus was in the last seat behind Malahki. Wyck sat behind Nadia, with Lesh in his lap. He had managed to coax the *mahdi* into the spacesuit with only minimal protests from the animal. All three of Lesh's heads now were inside the wide, round glass bowl of the suit's helmet. Two appeared to have dozed off, while the middle one looked around, watching its surroundings intently.

At the very back, the power cells and batteries of all possible shapes and sizes were piled up. Tied together with cords, they were supposed to be set off when we reached the center of the disk.

Malahki's idea was to increase our speed by giving us a boost through an explosion. After a series of fervent calculations, Svetlana had agreed to it, saying that an explosion wouldn't hurt.

Svetlana joined me in surveying the cabin of the capsule.

"Well…" She straightened in her seat. "Let's go. Take us away, Val."

The air inside the capsule was charged with high energy from everyone present. I sensed their anxiety, their fear of what was to come, and their hope.

I chose to focus on the hope.

"Let's go," I echoed Svetlana, starting the engines.

We disconnected from the spaceship that had been our safe haven on the Dark Anomaly. Just like during our test drive with Svetlana, I took the capsule along the edge first. It ran rather smoothly despite the uneven surface of the dented hulls of the smashed ships.

"Going into the yellow zone now," I called out, shifting the controls to stir the craft from the edge onto the rim of the disk.

Far in the distance to my left, the black, bulging core of the Dark Anomaly glimmered under the colourful lights. That was our target, except that I had to approach it at an angle.

"Orange zone," I said, inching our craft more to the left and closer to the core, which looked even more menacing as it remained largely unknown.

Both Svetlana and Vrateus speculated that the core was soft, either gelatinous or completely liquid. Of course, no one had gone there to verify that. We were the first ones ever.

"Red zone." I kept getting closer, gripping the controls harder.

The pull of the core got stronger. To avoid being dragged to the centre too quickly and possibly crash or sink on impact, I had to move the capsule along an invisible spiral, like a needle moved along the surface of a music record in the old play-back devices. Starting from the edge, we circled the center in the tightening curve.

"Going in," I gritted through my teeth, holding on to the controls with all my strength.

We'd given no name and assigned no color to this zone. This close, it was all pure danger.

I bit my lip, forcing the capsule to proceed on the pre-planned course as Svetlana monitored the systems. Using the data from our test drive, I'd planned for the corrections to counterbalance the pull of the core. The brakes I had to engage and the reverse trust I had to apply on the engines were hard on the system, consuming a lot of power.

"Doing good, Val," Svetlana's strained voice reached me. She made an obvious effort to sound encouraging, but tension was evident in her tone.

"How far are we?" I asked, keeping my eyes on the trajectory line on the screen. Maintaining the course proved too difficult for me to even glance elsewhere.

Svetlana read the numbers to me out loud.

I nodded.

"Getting closer," she announced.

From the corner of my eye I saw the core rising to my left like a smooth, glossy mountain.

With another shift in its direction, something snapped. I still held the controls in my hands, but the capsule skidded and swerved, sharply turning toward the core.

"It's too fast!" Svetlana warned as the speed accelerated, propelling us forward.

The capsule completely abandoned our carefully planned route, heading straight into the core.

I reversed the engines, killing the forward trust completely and diverting all power into backward motion. Yet we kept speeding ahead, the dark mass of the core rapidly growing bigger.

"Turn it off!" Svetlana yelled over the sound of my thundering heart that echoed in my ears. "Kill all power completely."

Without the reverse trust, the core would only suck us in faster. I hesitated.

"Do it!" she shouted louder, more urgently. "The field reacts to energy waves."

My hands moved before my brain had fully comprehended her words. I shut the engines off, immediately turning off the back-up battery and the axillary power as well.

Everything went dark inside the cabin, illuminated only by the swirling lights of the Dark Anomaly outside. Every sound stopped too, except for our hard breathing.

The capsule skidded and rolled ahead, but without the pull of the Dark Anomaly's field, we no longer accelerated. In fact, the traction of the wheels on the bumpy surface slightly slowed us down.

"It worked..." Svetlana exhaled, slumping back against her seat.

"You weren't sure it would?" I asked, without taking my eyes off the approaching bulge of the core straight ahead.

"Well, you know, that was largely just a theory that the Dark Anomaly reacts to energy waves." I heard a smile in her voice.

Most of our plan was based on Svetlana's theories. Many were now being tested for the first time ever.

The capsule tilted, climbing the steep incline of the rising core toward the summit in the center. Our momentum slowed down significantly.

I clicked on the camera built into the underbelly of the capsule. The image of the wheels rolling along the smooth surface of the core came into view. Up close, the surface didn't look smooth at all, however. Wide ripples ran along it. As if someone poured thick caramel out of a bowl.

"The core *is* soft," Svetlana confirmed yet another theory of hers. And if so, the hard caramel would turn into syrup the closer we got.

"We'll sink." I placed my hands on the controls again, ready to restart the engines. "I have to take off!"

Svetlana frowned. "Val, we're on the core, now. That's where the energy stream starts lifting off. We need to stay on the surface or as close to it as possible. Instead of fighting moving forward, we'll be fighting to stay down. You understand?" She stared at me intently.

"I do." I nodded, gripping the controls harder.

"We'd better close the helmets, now," Svetlana said softly.

"Secure your suits!" Vrateus ordered, his voice booming through the capsule for everyone to hear.

I inhaled deeply, going over the sequence of the steps I had to take to start the engines then to prevent the energy field from sweeping us up and smashing us against the edge of the disk. I had to be quick.

From the back seat, Malahki placed his hand on my shoulder.

"I'll see you on the other side, my love," he said softly, before sliding the front of my helmet down for me and clipping it in place. The sound of his beloved voice and the tenderness in his words made my heart melt and brought tears to my eyes.

What could "the other side" mean in our case? Freedom? Or death?

I couldn't allow myself to dwell on that. So much depended on me keeping my head cool and my thinking straight.

I put my gloves on, sealing them with the cuffs of my suit and lifted my right thumb up, signaling everyone I was ready.

We had one chance at it.

The wheels of the capsule's landing gear had completely submerged into the thinning material of the core, effectively stopping any progress toward the summit, now.

I took a long breath, positioning my hands over the control panel.

"One...Two...Three..." I counted in my head then let my fingers do the rest. Quick and practiced, they flew through the sequence with lightning speed. The engines vibrated to life, and I shifted the controls, forcing the capsule down against the stream of the Dark Anomaly's force field.

The capsule jerked up, out of my control. The wheels of the gear snapped off, stuck in the material of the core, the Dark Anomaly refusing to give up anything it had claimed.

Using whatever power the capsule had left, I set the engines full thrust forward. Our craft sprang ahead, jerking me back against my seat.

The next moment, a bright red dot flashed in the middle of the control panel. We were right above the center of the Dark Anomaly.

Svetlana grabbed my arm, urging me to act.

I yanked at the controls, sharply turning the capsule up. Instead of fighting the force field, I let it carry us up, now, away from the surface.

The vibrations of the engines reverberated through the capsule. I felt them with my hands, too, through the controls. The sensation halted suddenly. When it resumed, its rhythm was broken. The engines struggled.

The warning message on the control panel flashed red. Then the vibrations stopped completely, bringing our ascent to a sudden stop.

Svetlana glanced at me with a silent question in her deep-brown eyes. I met her gaze, but couldn't hold it. I couldn't give her anything good here—we were out of power. Completely.

The engines had been pushed to the limit to get us to the centre, exhausting the capsule's resources. Without the waves generated by the engines, the Dark Anomaly's force field wouldn't react to the capsule. For it, we were no different than an asteroid, now.

For a moment, we just hovered uselessly right over the gaping mouth of the crater of the Dark Anomaly's center. Then, the dreaded slide downwards began.

The Dark Anomaly's gravity was pulling us straight down into the gaping mouth of its crater, filled with the liquified bodies of the ships that crashed here millennia ago.

We needed some kind of energy waves for the force field to hold us. I turned off the engines then frantically tried to restart them. All in vain. Svetlana put her hand on mine, stopping me from trying again. Instead, she gestured at her back and at the built-in power pack of her suit.

Each of our suits was a mini-spacesuit, equipped with a power battery. We had the comm devices and locators there, too, to generate enough energy waves for the force field to carry us along. We just needed to get out of the capsule, first. The craft had become nothing but a dead weight. The speed of its descent was increasing exponentially, leaving us little time.

The black mouth of the center was closing in. I could already see the liquid inside it rising up in spikes and peaks with the release of the stream of energy in the center—the stream that could still take us to freedom if we just could make ourselves a part of it to hitch the ride.

I unclipped my seatbelt, and opened the front of the capsule, making the large glass portion of it slide back.

Svetlana had already gotten Nadia out of her seat. Together, they helped Wyck advance forward. Holding Lesh in a bulky suit, he moved awkwardly. Vrateus and Nadia held him from each side, as the three of them climbed over the control panel and out on the hull of the capsule.

Malahki grabbed my hand, tugging me to follow them and Svetlana.

The capsule now plummeted toward the bubbling crater at astonishing speed. Scrambling into a circle in the front, we turned on the power packs of our suits. The force field grabbed us immediately, helping the engines to propel us up as the capsule plunged down.

Svetlana frantically gestured for us to come closer, obviously worried someone might fly away from the center and into a weaker stream of energy that would end up curving under the gravity of the Dark Anomaly and drag them back to the edge of the disk.

Malahki yanked me closer, wrapping his arm around me. I grabbed on to Wyck, who held Lesh with one arm, having another one hooked with Nadia's. Vrateus had his arms around both Nadia's and Svetlana's shoulders on each side of him. And Svetlana closed our tight circle by linking her arm with Malahki's.

As we ascended higher and higher, away from the Dark Anomaly, we put our heads together, watching it move away from us.

The abandoned capsule plunged into the crater of the center, quickly absorbed by its black-as-night liquid. From what I knew about the Dark Anomaly, there was enough pressure to crush it into a pancake right away. The metal and plastic of the capsule would be liquified and assimilated into the body of the disk, eventually released in the form of energy with the bright, multi-colored light effects.

Suddenly, the liquid in the crater bubbled up higher, rising above the rim. A bright light tore through the bubble, ripping it into pieces that blasted up after us.

The core of the Dark Anomaly had crushed the power cells left on the capsule, setting off the explosion Malahki had set up.

The black pieces of the Dark Anomaly's matter rushed after us, catching up and passing by. Some were as small as a drop, others were huge like icebergs. Some seemed liquid like water. Others had the rounded shapes of blobs or ragged edges of solid material.

Our circle grew tighter as we flexed our arms, getting closer. No matter how hard I tried to hold on to them, however, I felt some invisible force trying to pry me away from them. The streams of energy shot out from the center of the disk. I remembered the 3D graphic on Svetlana's tablet, the rays then dispersed, opening up like a flower. Our tight circle in the middle was being forced to break up with the streams as well.

"No!" I yelled, even as no one would hear me.

I flexed my arms tighter, trying to hold on to both men on each side of me. My grip slipped off Wyck first. Thrown aside, Lesh was torn out of his arms, too. I saw Wyck try to go after the *mahdi*, but the energy field was now in charge, allowing no control over our own spacesuits.

Lesh didn't stop moving, however, and didn't go down like the capsule did, which told me that Wyck must've at least turned on the locator on the animal suit's before the *mahdi* had been ripped away from him.

The locator beacons on the rest of our suits went on the moment the power packs did. It reminded me of other systems we could use, too, now. I turned on the comm.

"Malahki?"

"Valya," his deep voice came through.

The sound of it resonated through my chest. Hope grew stronger.

"Stay with me," I begged, trying hard to hold on to him with both hands.

It was like fighting a centrifugal force, with no way to lessen the effect of it. My fingers kept sliding off his arm, no matter how hard I tried to cling to him.

"Wyck! No!" Nadia's panicky screams broke through the comm.

A large blob of the black material bumped into Wyck, sending him forward, far ahead of us. Nadia flailed her arms and legs, in a futile attempt to follow him. The energy stream kept her on course, making her slowly drift away from us, even as all of us flew further from the Dark Anomaly's disk.

"Hold me!" I screamed in panic, feeling Malahki being torn from me, too.

"Always," I remembered his reply from last night.

But he couldn't keep his promise this time. The invisible force ripped him out of my grip, our hands disconnected, the fingers pried open.

"No!" The agony of losing him lanced through me.

"I love you," he said as the comm crackled.

"No!" I cried. "Malahki, please. Stay with me..."

"Valya, I'll see you on the other side..." His voice broke off as he drifted out of range.

Through the fog of tears, I watched in horror as he floated farther and farther away from me. A large piece of matter from the core rushed between us, shielding Malahki from view.

I glared back at the disk of the Dark Anomaly as it steadily grew smaller and smaller. It was no longer perfectly round, however. Deep cracks formed from the center all the way to the edge, crumpling its smooth, even form.

The explosion had disturbed the balanced flow of the energy the Dark Anomaly absorbed and released. The entire thing was imploding now.

The material bulged up along the cracks, thicker closer to the center. The edge crumbled up and broke, the distorted disk getting smaller as the Dark Anomaly consumed itself, shooting the pieces of its body out from its center, into the space after us.

Another piece rushed by me. The impact of yet another one sent me into a spin. I had to engage my stabilizers to get myself out of it. By the time the spinning stopped, and I got back on course, there was nothing but open space around me, with pieces of debris floating by.

"Malahki!" I screamed his name through the comm, but there was no answer.

There was no one around me, none of the five people who, like me, had risked it all for the tiniest chance of freedom.

Far in the distance, the remnants of the despicable place called the Dark Anomaly crumbled to pieces, leaving nothing left.

I turned my suit engine off. It had hardly any power left to keep it going, and it was useless now, anyway. The momentum would keep me moving through space, roughly in the direction of the travel routes that used to be in use over seventy years ago, back before I fell into the clutches of the Dark Anomaly.

Maybe, someone would stumble on the signal of my locator beacon. Maybe I'd run out of oxygen before then. Or maybe the suit's life-support system would fail first. There was nothing more I could do for my survival.

I'd done all I could.

Drifting through the dark open space, I felt more alone than ever. If this was my fate to die here alone, I just had one wish before I went. I wanted to see *his* face one last time.

I closed my eyes, recalling his beloved features in my mind. Every familiar line and curve of the face that had changed so much lately, yet always remained the face of the man I loved.

During all the dramatic physical changes that Malahki had gone through, the love and affection in his eyes always grew steadily. The warmth of it kept my heart and my soul alive in a place where everything wholesome and beautiful died.

"I'll see you on the other side, my love..."

Chapter 21

VAL

I'd thought our choice was either the life trapped on the Dark Anomaly or the risk of an immediate death while trying to escape it.

I'd been wrong.

An immediate death would've been too easy. Apparently, I was destined to die slowly while agonizing over every single choice I'd made in my life and mourning all the people I'd lost.

Breathing was growing harder. I panted in short, shallow breaths. As the oxygen level dropped, I inhaled slowly and deeply, trying to draw whatever was left into my air-starved lungs.

Eternal chill had set so deep into my bones, my body stopped shivering, giving up and growing numb instead.

I was no longer sure whether my eyes were open or closed—darkness was everywhere, with erratic light flashes slashing through it, either from space or from my vision shutting down.

It wouldn't be long before I crossed over to... Where? Would it be to "the other side" that Malahki had been talking about. Would he be there to greet me? Would I get to see him again?

A tear separated from my frosty eyelid, slowly crystalizing as it floated in front of my face.

A scraping vibration ran through my suit. I had no idea what it was. But my eyes must have been open because I saw a pattern across the glass of my helmet—black, thin lines that formed squares.

It took me another moment to place the image—a net. A net had been dragged around me, scraping against my suit. I couldn't move my arms or legs. It could be because I was trapped in the net. Or maybe because my body went numb. Somehow, it didn't really matter either way.

Nothing mattered anymore...

—⧓⧓—

"VALENTINA, IT'S TIME to wake up."

Valentina...

No one I truly held dear used that name.

My friends called me Val. My family called me Valya.

Valentina was reserved solely for people who hardly knew me.

"Valentina," the female voice insisted. "Please, open your eyes."

He had called me Valya, too.

Malahki... The man who had become closer than family to me.

"You can wake up, now," the woman kept coaxing.

Wake up? Was I still alive then?

I tried to lift my eyelids. They felt so heavy as if laden with lead.

"Very good," the woman cooed approvingly at my efforts. "Can you see me?"

A middle-aged woman with dark skin and black hair that had been generously touched with silver gazed down at me. The expression in her golden-brown eyes was kind, and I managed a smile.

"Excellent." She gave me a wide, toothy grin in return. "Now, how are you feeling?"

A clear oblong shape hovered high above me—the cover of a medical capsule, I recognized. I lay on a padded surface with the woman leaning over at my side.

"I'm Doctor Kimathi," she said. "Can you move your legs for me, please?"

I glanced down my body. I was naked, save for two wide, glossy strips of material, one over my breasts, another one over my pelvis area. Pressing my elbows into the padded surface under me, I tried to get up. The white strips turned out to be not just to protect my modesty, they held me in place, gently but firmly.

"It's too early to get up yet." Doctor Kimathi stopped me by placing a hand on my shoulder. "Just try to move your limbs first."

The feeling returned to my body, though it felt not entirely my own, like a new suit that hadn't been broken in yet. I lifted a hand in the air, then the other one, followed by the right leg then the left. My limbs seemed to listen to me well enough.

"I'm good..." I croaked, my throat painfully dry. "Can I... Water, please?"

"Of course." The doctor nodded but didn't leave my side. Someone else handed me a glass of water. There were more people in the room.

I took a long drink of water. Not just my mouth and throat, all my insides felt like they had shriveled and dried from thirst.

"Where am I?" I asked the doctor. It'd just registered with me that she was human. A moment later, I remembered I was a human, too.

"On a passenger ship from Earth," she said. "We're currently orbiting the planet Omphi."

"Where is Malahki?" I asked. The sound of his name tugged at my heart with ache, pleasure, and longing—all at once.

"Who?" Doctor Kimathi blinked at me.

"Malahki. He is a *damirian*, from planet Ak'ae. He was with me..." My voice broke off, and my heart dropped into the hollow of my stomach. I already knew from her expression she had no idea who I was talking about.

"Valentina." Another woman came forward. She was younger, blonde, and dressed in a uniform I didn't immediately recognize. "My name is Sylvia Kraus. I'm with the Earth's Space Coalition, and I need to ask you a few questions—"

Doctor Kimathi stopped her by lifting a hand in the air. "She's still too weak for long conversations."

"It won't take long," Sylvia Kraus insisted.

I winced at a headache that started pounding inside my skull from their voices.

"Can I...sit up?"

"Sure." The doctor moved away, and two other women covered me with a sheet then removed the white bands, allowing me to sit upright.

I dropped my feet from the medical capsule bed, clutching the sheet to my chest.

"I'll answer any questions you have," I addressed both the doctor and the Coalition rep. "But only if you answer mine first. Who else has been found?"

They both just stared at me.

"Nadia? Vrateus? Wyck? Svetlana? How about Lesh, the *mahdi*? Anyone?" I felt like a piece of me died every time I said a name and found no recognition in their eyes.

"We only found you," Sylvia said slowly.

I pressed my hands so tight to my chest, it hurt, then realized the pain was actually inside me.

"Just me, then?" I said softly, dropping my head between my shoulders. Here, surrounded by people, my people, I felt more alone than ever.

"This ship was en route during its scheduled trip from Earth to Omphi when they caught the signal from the locator of your space-suit," Sylvia hurriedly explained. "You were in poor condition when they brought you on board two weeks ago. They placed you in the medical capsule. Luckily, Doctor Kimathi also happened to be on board as one of the passengers. She kindly volunteered to oversee your recovery."

I nodded, blankly staring at one of the floor tiles in front of me.

Sylvia continued, "I represent the Earth's Space Coalition in Crystal Wave, the capital city of the planet Omphi. Once your identity was confirmed, it raised a lot of questions."

"I bet it did," I said flatly.

"Your expedition was thought lost without a trace. With your...um, re-appearance..." She drew in a long breath. "Well, we're wondering if you could provide an explanation on what happened to your ship and the crew as well as how did you suddenly re-appear seventy-three years after going missing, physically almost unchanged."

Physically? Maybe. Emotionally? It felt like much longer than seventy-three years had passed.

"Did you say it's been two weeks since you found me?" It finally registered with me.

"Yes." Silvia nodded. "It'll be exactly two weeks in Universal time tomorrow."

"The condition you were found in required some time to heal." Doctor Kimathi stepped in again. "We kept you under for the duration of the flight, letting your body recover. The damaged tissue needed to regenerate. But your muscle tone has been maintained artificially, so you can try to walk soon."

"And maybe answer some questions?" Sylvia clicked something on the wide bangle around her wrist.

I fought the overwhelming flood of darkness that threatened to suffocate me.

"I'll explain what I can," I said, staring imploringly at her. "I'll answer all your questions. But please, there were five more people with me. Please, please keep searching the area."

"THE PASSENGER SHIP is leaving for Earth in four weeks," Sylvia told me.

Our shuttle landed in Crystal Wave, the capital city on Omphi. There used to be several floating research facilities here the year Nadia and I joined our ill-fated expedition. By now, they'd built three real cities on this water world planet.

The huge buildings were constructed like icebergs, with their largest parts submerged under water for stability. They were connected by flexible bridges and underwater passages, creating a grid that floated in the endless ocean of the planet Omphi.

We walked through a passage from the office of the Omphi Government where my identity had once again been confirmed, this time for immigration purposes. The underground passage was a wide, clear, flexible tube with a rigid walkway inside it.

The light of the Omphi's sun pierced through the surface above, illuminating the horizontal platforms suspended under water outside of the tube. A variety of plants of different shapes and colors grew on the platforms, making the waterscape outside a true feast for the eye.

"These are the Crystal Wave's famous underwater gardens." Sylvia tipped her head at the gorgeous plant life outside. "The people here take a special pride in the aesthetic. Not to mention that the gardens provide close to ninety percent of the city's food supply."

"They are gorgeous," I said softly, admiring the clever way the plants had been arranged on the platform to showcase their colors and forms in the best light possible.

"Malahki would've loved to see this..."

The thought speared through my heart with so much pain, I staggered, nearly tripping over my feet. The long flowy dress I wore suddenly felt too tight in the chest area.

"Are you okay?" Sylvia grabbed my elbow.

Would I ever be okay?

I nodded quickly, closing my eyes for a moment and forcing the thick, heavy darkness out of my chest so I could breathe again.

Sylvia gave me a moment to compose myself then took me up an elevator to a room on one of the upper floors.

"Your request to contact your family had been sent," she said, using a wide armband on her left wrist to unlock the door.

My brother and his wife would be gone by now, but I hoped to locate my two nieces. They were so small the year I left, they'd be women in their seventies, now. They probably wouldn't even know me anymore, but they were the only family I had left.

"The Earth's Space Coalition will pay for your accommodation on Omphi for the next four weeks and for your ticket back to Earth with the passenger ship that brought you here."

"Why would they do that?" I stood awkwardly in the threshold of the spacious room. "I have little to do with the coalition. They weren't in charge of my expedition."

Sylvia turned around, waiting for me to follow her in.

"We know your expedition was organized privately, Valentina. But the company responsible for it is no longer in business. You will be needing some help with integration back into society, and we'll be happy to be there for you."

"In exchange for what?" I clasped my hands together so tightly my knuckles ached.

"We would like your cooperation in our investigation. We recovered some data from your spacesuit and would love for you to help with its analysis."

They needed Svetlana for that, not me. The amount of information that woman stored in her head was larger than any system could collect. She'd process, organize, and explain anything to them.

I thought about Nadia and the videos she'd made of our life on the Dark Anomaly. She'd taken all of them with her when we left. Her suit would've been much more valuable than mine. It had built-in cameras, too, as she'd wanted to film our escape as well.

My insides tightened again, twisting with pain and survivor's guilt. Why me? Why did I have to make it, and they didn't? Every single one of them was so much more worthy of life than me.

Sylvia came closer and placed her hand on my shoulder.

"Valentina, if you need anything, please let us know. I'll talk to you again tomorrow, and your therapy sessions will be starting tonight. Doctor Kimathi came to Omphi for work. She's staying in Crystal Wave and will be happy to talk with you as well, whenever you feel like you need it."

I just nodded again then struggled to keep it together as she showed me around the room, pointing out all its amenities and explaining how to use the latest models of the bathroom fixtures and the built-in food replicator.

After she left, I stood on the small balcony, looking out into the ocean beyond the floating buildings of the city, and watched the sunset.

The vivid colors of Omphi's sun sinking beyond the horizon brought to mind the shades of red, purple, and gold that lit up Malahki's skin when he made love to me. The color combination was different when he felt angry or ready to fight. When he took me, his skin came to life with a unique pallet of colors that only I got to see.

Memories flooded my mind, burning my eyes with tears, and I let them flow, unable to hold back the grief and sorrow I'd been struggling to contain all day.

My knees buckled, and I slid to the floor of the glass balcony as I cried.

It'd been two weeks since we escaped the Dark Anomaly and blew it the fuck up. I hoped against all odds the Anomaly hadn't managed to exact its revenge on us even while dying.

Logically, I understood that after two weeks, none of the space-suits would've made it. By now, all their life-support systems would've long failed. The suits were not meant for long-term travel.

In my heart, the stubborn hope refused to die. Many other ships traveled along the route where I'd been found. Other races and nations had regular transportation going through there. Even in today's age of instantaneous communication, the information could get lost for a little while. More of our group could've been rescued around the same time I was or even earlier. Those who'd found them just wouldn't think about searching for me to inform me.

Our team was a mismatched group of people of different races from different planets, separated by distance and time we'd come from. It would take a while for anyone to establish a connection between us.

The hope refused to leave me, giving me strength to go on.

But even if I lost everyone I held dear for the chance to come back to this life, I couldn't give up now. If I survived while they didn't, I couldn't throw it away.

I had to try to go on.

Chapter 22

For four days I tried. I tried to go on as I'd vowed to myself I would. I'd started therapy. I'd met with Doctor Kimathi for lunch. I'd chatted with Sylvia about my employment opportunities. In the afternoon, I went for walks around the Crystal Wave, exploring all the amazing things this city had to offer.

But at night, I couldn't fight the darkness. I cried. Every time I closed my eyes, I saw *his* face and felt his touch on my skin. And every time I opened them, not finding him beside me, I died inside, over and over again.

Sylvia had given me a personal communication device. It wrapped around my left arm like a wide, flat bangle. Its surface on the top of my forearm was a curved screen.

The morning of my fifth day on Omphi, the device vibrated and the screen lit up with a call.

I was having breakfast—a cup of coffee and dry toast from the food replicator. I could've chosen anything from the long list of breakfast foods available from the replicator. I could've ordered anything fresh to be delivered, too. But day after day, I kept having the same breakfast I'd had on the Dark Anomaly—coffee and toast.

"Yes?" I picked up the call, but left the video off, not ready to face anyone yet.

"Valentina?" A male voice sounded.

"Yes."

"Another survivor of your group was delivered to the medical center earlier this morning." The male sounded irritated, as if complaining.

The toast fell out of my weakened fingers. I jumped to my feet, shoving back the chair I'd been sitting in.

Another survivor! I was not the only one.

My heart pounded so hard in my chest, the sound of blood rushing through my veins echoed in my ears.

"Where?" I asked, dashing for the door.

"He has violated the rules of quarantine, so he had to start over."

He.

"His name?" I croaked, fumbling with the door lock and the handle.

"Malahki."

I froze, my forehead pressed to the cool surface of the door.

"Thank you, thank you, thank you," pulsed through my brain as a prayer to every god of every planet out there.

I swallowed hard, trying to regain my ability to speak.

"Is he well?" I asked, finally opening the damn lock and hurrying down the corridor.

"Yes, but he's rather irritated," the man replied, the annoyance growing stronger in his voice. "Unruly and uncontrollable. Our tranquilizers have proven ineffective, so we can't even sedate him for long enough. He's been asking for you, and we were wondering if you could come down here to see him. Otherwise, we would need to take measures to physically restrain him."

"Don't." I ran into the elevator then found the location of the medical center on the electronic map on the wall and selected the floor it was on. "Please don't hurt him. I'm on my way. Tell him I'll be there."

"He's not cooperating," the man replied sulkily as the elevator, moving torturously slow, took me down to the floor with the passage to the medical center. "He is extremely *difficult* to communicate with, which is a major characteristic of all *damirian* males, really," he added with a frustrated sigh.

"I'm almost there," I panted into the communication device, running through the underwater passageway toward the building with the medical center. "Where exactly is he? What part of the building?"

He gave me the room number of the room, and I located it on the map on the screen of my device.

"I'm here." I stopped in front of a wide door with a narrow glass insert. Behind it was a small empty room with another door opposite of this one. "How do I open it?" I shook the handle of the locked door.

"You're at the emergency exit of the quarantine room, Valentina, with the decontamination chamber in front of it. But you'll have to go to the visitors' area just around the corner to your right," the male instructed. "There will be a glass wall with a microphone and a speaker on each side so you and the patient can see each other and talk. Since he is in quarantine, no physical contact will be allowed, of course."

Of course...

Disappointed, I was about to turn in the direction the man had told me to go to the visitor's area, when a large hand splayed on the glass of the door on the other side of the decontamination chamber. Then the face I'd only seen in my dreams for the past four days came into view.

"Malahki," I whispered, pressing my forehead to the glass.

His eyes met mine across the decontamination chamber and the two doors separating us. There was everything in his gaze—my hope, my dreams, and my entire life.

Shoving away from the door, he stepped back.

"*Stay with me,*" I mouthed.

Not taking his eyes off me even for a moment, he charged the door, kicking it in. Alarms blared. A red light flashed over the last door that still separated us.

"Valentina!" the man's voice exclaimed in panic from my device. "You *must* go to the visitors' area. The patient is quarantined. You can only see him from the other side of the glass."

The other side?

"No." I said softly, as my man was breaking through doors and walls on his way to me. "We need to be together. He and I. On the *same* side. Always…"

From the decontamination chamber, Malahki gestured for me to step aside before crashing through the remaining door and into the corridor to me.

Air left my lungs as he crushed me to his chest. And with the air, a huge portion of the darkness left me. My next breath was filled with light, hope, and so many more wonderful things.

"Hold me," I begged as tears rushed down my face, happy tears, for once.

"Always," he murmured, holding me so tight, I couldn't move a muscle, and I loved it that way. "Valya, Valya, Valya…" he chanted, rocking side to side with me in his arms. "Don't ever leave me again, do you hear me? I won't survive watching you drift away from me ever again."

"Ma'am! Please step back into the patient's room immediately!" People in protective gear rushed down the corridor to us.

The alarms kept blaring, coloring the lifeless walls of the corridor with streaks of bright red light.

"Valentina!" the man on the call sounded outright furious, now. "I regret to inform you that due to the physical contact with the patient, you will have to be quarantined with him for the next two weeks."

I just smiled at that as Malahki showered my face with kisses.

"That's absolutely fine with me," I murmured, sunshine flooding my veins with each kiss Malahki placed on my skin. "I'm planning to spend much longer than two weeks with this man."

"The rest of my life," Malahki demanded between the nibbles and kisses he peppered down my neck. "I'm not letting you go for the rest of my life."

WE TRIED TO STAY AT the medical center for quarantine, but it didn't go well. My presence soothed Malahki, but he took it upon himself to dote on me. If he believed I experienced the slightest discomfort at any time, he flew into a fit of rage against the staff.

His overreacting was deemed to be amplified by our forced confinement. After everything we'd gone through to regain our freedom, we ended up being locked up again. It was hard to take for him. I knew he tried to control his emotions, but it proved too much.

After some intense negotiations, the authorities granted us the permission to quarantine in my room, instead. I suspected they'd just gotten tired of dealing with Malahki's temper flare-ups.

Once they moved us to my room, things started improving. Technically, we were still locked up, unable to leave the room, but it was a much more comfortable environment than the medical center. We had more privacy here, less supervision, and a balcony—a window into the outside world, which made this feel less like a prison and more like a holiday.

When we first got to my room from the medical center, Malaki stopped in front of the closed glass doors to the balcony.

"I never thought I'd see a sunset ever again," he said in awe, staring at the setting sun.

"Did you get to breathe the ocean air yet?" I asked.

He shook his head, not taking his eyes from the horizon.

"Come." I gently took his hand in mine, leading him out to the balcony.

The neighboring buildings flanked ours, but our room was high enough to have an open view of the sunset.

Tall, massive spikes floated upright in the ocean in the distance. They were a part of the system that controlled the winds and broke up the ocean waves, preventing the massive turbulent storms that used to be a norm on Omphi. Thanks to the system, the storms never reached disastrous levels here anymore.

Today, the weather was lovely. A warm breeze gently blew from the open water, stroking my skin and playing with the long ends of Malaki's unbound hair.

Tilting his head back, he drew in a deep breath, his wide chest rising.

"I forgot how fragrant the air can be," he murmured, closing his eyes.

I had only been gone for seventy-three years, but the world had moved on so much in that time. I had to re-learn some things and learn anew so many others.

It would take time and work for me to hopefully stop jumping at every loud noise—one day. To stop working out an escape route the moment I walked into a room. To stop calculating the distance to the nearest exit in case there was a sudden attack and I had to run for my life.

It had been fifteen centuries since Malahki had left his world. I realized that everything I felt he must be feeling so much more profoundly. The issues I was dealing with must be multiplied by a thousand for him.

There were and still would be so many issues for both of us to overcome. But there were pleasures waiting for us, too.

The scent of the ocean mist. The view of the sunset. The caress of the wind. The simple things that people often took for granted held special meaning to us, now. Even more so for Malahki, because he had been deprived of it for so long.

"It's beautiful, isn't it?" I leaned my head against his arm.

He moved me in front of him, my back to his front. Wrapping his arms around my shoulders, he rested his chin on top of my head.

"I don't think I'll ever get used to seeing this every day," he said softly.

I thought the same about having his arms around me. Every hug, every kiss of his felt special. I didn't think I would ever get used to that or would ever take his attention for granted.

Having to stay in the room for two weeks, we finally had the time to enjoy each other in peace, without the fear of danger constantly looming over our heads.

We talked, learning more about each other. We made love whenever we felt like, which happened to be often.

One evening, as we sat on the balcony, watching the sunset again, Malahki told me about how he was rescued.

A small *dimo* ship had picked him up, apparently even before I'd been found.

"When I saw the *dimos* hauling me on board, I punched the first one before they even got me out of my suit. It was almost a reflex." He shrugged apologetically, and I understood what he meant. The only *dimos* he'd seen in the past five years were the ones who hurt and taunted him.

"That didn't leave a good first impression of course," he continued with a sad smile. "The four of them managed to maneuver me into a storage room where they locked me up until they arrived at their research station on the asteroid a few days away from here. They contacted the government of Ak'ae, asking them to come and get me. I stormed and raged all that time, knowing they had left you behind. I demanded they go back, but at that point no one really listened to me anymore, thinking me deranged."

I placed my hand on his, and he grabbed it like a lifeline.

"Ak'ae couldn't confirm my identity, because I'd been officially declared dead centuries ago. For a while, I was stuck in limbo. But the *dimos* really wanted to get rid of me. So, one of them finally requested information on the human expedition that disappeared seventy-three years ago, like I kept telling them. They contacted the Federation, and from them learned that someone from the expedition had been found and sent to Omphi." He stopped abruptly, swallowing hard.

Reaching over, he scooped me out of my chair and placed me in his lap. I leaned against his chest and wrapped my arms tightly around him. Even the smallest distance between us sometimes felt unbearable.

I understood the reasons for the *damirian* custom of self-isolation of all newly matched couples at the beginning of their sexual relationship. The explosion of emotions that came with the gender transformation needed some time for each person to sort through. The couple found comfort in each other's bodies, slowly processing their physical and emotional changes.

Malahki had barely had that time with me. Most of the time he knew me, we'd been fighting for survival. For the first time ever, we got a chance to slow down and connect while feeling absolutely safe.

During the days of our quarantine, Malahki was gaining more control over his body and his emotions. His behaviour was getting more stable, his confidence more solid.

"They brought me here, but wouldn't let me see you," he said softly. Taking apart my ponytail, he started spreading my hair strand by strand along my naked back. Neither of us wore any clothes. It made little sense to bother getting dressed with only the two of us being here. "They kept talking about another quarantine."

"Why did you have to do another one? Didn't the *dimos* keep you isolated already?"

"Not long enough. I tried to escape the research station on the asteroid, twice. I wanted to steal their ship and come back to search for you. Once they brought me here, they concluded that I had to be isolated again."

He slid his hand down my back to cup my backside.

"Little did they know," a smile filtered into his voice, "that I'd never agree to be isolated from you."

I thought about the damages sustained by the doors that had dared stand between us.

"My uncontainable." Smiling, I lifted my face to his, catching his kiss on my lips, and he shifted me in his lap, closer to his growing erection.

Straddling his hips, I rocked my pelvis against his hard length, the tantalising caress of the gentle feelers igniting my blood with desire. I lifted my hips, letting him slide inside me.

Growling, he covered my face and chest with hungry, biting kisses as I rode him hard, until both of us moaned with pleasure.

One part we still couldn't talk about was the moment we'd been ripped away from each other by the force field of the Dark Anomaly. That part would haunt both of us in our nightmares for some time still. Even while dying, the Dark Anomaly had found a way to exact its revenge on us by tossing all of us away from each other, to float in space completely alone.

Could anyone else have survived?

Malahki and I were researching the names and home planets of each transportation company that used the nearby routes. Through Sylvia, we sent out messages with the names and the detailed description of the four people still missing. Against Sylvia's advice not to divert the focus from people to the animal, I also insisted on finding Lesh. The *madhi* had become an important part of our team, too. He'd escaped with us, and he deserved every effort to be found.

Less than a week since our confinement began, another call with amazing news came.

"Nadia!" I rushed to Malahki as he exited the bathroom after taking a shower. "They found her!"

His eyes flew wide open with surprise and excitement.

"Where is she?"

"On a research ship from Earth, on her way to Omphi!" I pressed my hands to my chest, afraid it'd explode with relief and excitement filling me.

"How is she?" he asked, his brows moving into a concerned frown.

"They said she's well. The baby, too..." My voice shook and my lips trembled as tears of joy prickled behind my eyelids.

"Come here." Malahki took me in his arms, kissing my hair.

"Oh God..." I pressed my face into his chest, letting my tears mix with the shower water droplets on his skin. "I'm so, so happy," I sobbed. "I've never cried so much in my life."

He laughed, rocking with me in his arms.

"Let's hope this is just the beginning."

He was right. More happy news quickly followed. Wyck and Vrateus had been found together, by an *errock* cargo ship. Both had delayed the ship for over two weeks, making the crew search the area for more of us, but they'd only found Lesh. The ship was on its way to Hexol, the *errocks'* planet, when one of my messages reached them. The three of them then had to board another ship via a shuttle and were headed for Omphi.

Svetlana had actually been found before any of us. Her suit had been damaged from the collision with the debris of the Dark Anomaly. She was unconscious when the crew of a transport shuttle found her on their way to work at the station orbiting a small unpopulated planet nearby.

When she got better and was woken up from the medically induced coma they had put her under, it took them a while to confirm her identity and then find a transportation here, to all of us.

All of them were supposed to be on Omphi by the time Malahki and I had finished our quarantine. Everyone was alive.

The Dark Anomaly no longer had a hold on us. We'd escaped. So many possibilities awaited us now. We had our lives to leave any way we pleased.

We won.

Epilogue

VAL

"Ready?" Malahki leaned against the door frame of the bathroom, folding his arms across his chest.

The crisp white shirt stretched tightly over his shoulders. The short sleeves would've burst at the seams, struggling to contain his bulging biceps, if there were any seams at all. The latest human fashions weren't sewn, they were molded from one piece of material.

I'd never seen him wear a shirt before. Come to think of it, I barely remembered him in clothes at all. We'd spent the past two weeks not wearing anything.

Today, our quarantine was over.

I stood in front of the mirror.

"How do I look?" I smoothed my hands down my outfit—a loose, blush-pink blouse with a high collar and a long, ivory skirt. The light, flowing material felt like nothing against my skin.

"Gorgeous." He smiled, his intense gaze roving over my body. "Absolutely perfect."

My face heated, my cheeks taking the same shade as my blouse.

He tossed his long braid back over his shoulder, sauntering to me.

I twisted the end of one of my braids around my finger, taking a step back. It didn't take much more than that smoldering look in his gorgeous multi-colored eyes to make my heart race and my skin buzz with awareness.

"We'll have to go soon," I reminded him as he came closer, sliding his large hands up my bare arms. The same hands that so deftly braided my hair just a little while earlier. The weave of the five braids I wore reminded me of intricate macramé. This hairstyle must be severely outdated, even on Ak'ae, but I loved it so much. "We can't make them wait."

Wyck, Nadia, Vrateus, and Svetlana waited for us in the restaurant one building over. Today was the first day Malahki and I were free to leave our room after the quarantine, and we were about to finally meet everyone in person for the first time since our escape from the Dark Anomaly.

"Just one kiss," Malahki murmured, lifting my face to his with a finger under my chin.

"*Just one* doesn't happen with you," I smiled against his lips.

He placed a second kiss in the corner of my mouth, proving me right, then trailed more kisses down my neck.

"You're going to get hard," I warned with a giggle.

"Mm," he agreed, but kept kissing.

"And your feelers will start squirming," I added.

He leaned back a little, lifting an eyebrow.

"Squirming?"

"Like this." I wiggled the fingers of my both hands in the air.

He laughed. "I can't help it. Like me, they get excited. And like me, they love making you come."

Warm tingles trickled through my chest to my lower belly at the thought of having him between my legs again. We had no time for that, though.

"We can't do it, honey," I gently stroked his cheek. "We need to head out now, and you have to calm them down. Otherwise, they will be squirming in your pants, which are pretty tight by the way. So, everyone will see all that squirming."

He blew out a disappointed breath.

"I hate wearing pants."

I smiled, taking a step back and giving him a once-over.

"I do prefer you naked, but you look rather dashing in pants, my love."

He heaved another heavy breath, the pretty pink swirls on his skin fading away as he reined his desire under control.

"Fine. Me and my *squirmy* feelers will have to wait until tonight, then."

I laughed, heading for the door.

"Don't tell me you're not looking forward to seeing everyone again."

A huge smile spread on his face.

"I can't wait," he admitted.

I took his hand as we left our room for the first time in fourteen days. As we walked down the corridors then along the walkway, the space looked suspiciously deserted. The moment we stepped into the restaurant, I realized why.

The people at the tables turned our way the moment we entered. The patio was filled with photographers, a flock of reporter-drones hovering over their heads.

"What is all of this?" I muttered under my breath, stopping at the entrance and wondering if we should maybe do this some other time.

"We're celebrities, remember?" Malahki said softly. His voice sounded calm enough, but his hand tightened on mine.

Right. The news of our rescue had gone out. Sylvia had said something about a lot of interview demands. She knew about our plans for lunch and must've arranged for the hallways to be cleared. But this...

"Should we leave?" I fought the immediate desire to flee.

A person rushed to us. A *kreer*.

I sucked in a breath, gripping Malahki's hand tighter.

"Come with me, please." The *kreer* stretched his lipless mouth, displaying the sharp teeth. It took me a moment to realize he was smiling. The word *"Manager"* glowed on the lapel of his uniform.

I breathed slowly, trying to calm my racing heart. One day, I would be able to face a *kreer* or an *ognat* or the people of some other species without a jolt of panic or fear of an attack.

One day...

The manager took us upstairs, explaining over his shoulder, "We'll be serving you in our private room. Enjoy your lunch." He opened a door into a round space with a large table in the middle.

The four people I'd feared were dead just a few days ago were sitting around the table.

I forgot all about my apprehension or about the reporters outside. Pure happiness filled my heart, momentarily banishing every other feeling.

"Val!" Nadia shoved her chair back, jumping up, then rushed to me for a hug.

Svetlana and the two men got up too, coming closer.

The happiness inside me bubbled up to the surface. Tears of joy trickled down my cheeks. I opened my arms to them, and they all joined us in the hug.

Svetlana, Vrateus, Wyck, and Malahki put their arms around Nadia and me, making an even tighter circle than we'd formed when the stream of energy whisked us away from the Dark Anomaly and toward the unknown.

The six of us had been united forever by the place that now only existed in our nightmares.

When each of them first got to Omphi, I'd spoken to them over the communication device. I'd seen their faces on the screen. But having them all here in person, safe and sound, overwhelmed me with joy so much, I was crying and laughing at the same time.

"I can't believe this. I can't…" I wiped my tears with my shoulder, only for more of them to rush out.

"We're alive." Nadia laughed, gazing at me through her own tears. "It worked. We won!"

I caught Svetlana's eye.

"Thank you," I said to the woman who made it all possible. My heart filled with so much gratitude I thought it would burst in my chest.

Svetlana quickly brushed away a tear from her eye, too, shaking her head.

"We *all* did it," she said. "I couldn't have done anything without all of you."

We loosened the hug, eventually moving back to the table. I spotted Lesh hiding under Wyck's chair. I crouched next to him, gently petting his side.

"Hi buddy," I said to him softly.

Lesh's middle head flicked its long tongue out, tentatively giving my hand a sniff. He then pressed his nose to my palm, letting me know he recognized me.

"I'm so happy to see you here." I scratched the side of the middle head.

"He is a little overwhelmed by all of this," Nadia said, taking her seat next to Wyck's.

"Aren't we all?" Wyck laughed with a nervous edge in his voice.

Wyck was wearing dark sunglasses, even though we were inside. Both he and Vrateus avoided looking at the floor-to-ceiling windows surrounding us.

Neither of the two remembered the outside world. The Dark Anomaly, with its artificial lighting inside and the permanent darkness outside broken only by the lights of its energy field were all they had ever known, until now.

"How do you find it here?" I asked them both.

"Too much light," Wyck confessed with a wince.

"And space," Vrateus added with an uncharacteristically unsure smile. "I haven't been outside yet, but even what I can see through the windows is too much."

"We're working on it." Svetlana gave him an adoring look, taking his hand in hers. "There're amazing therapists here in Crystal Wave. They also managed to connect us with someone from Nofoi, Vrateus's home world."

Nadia gently rubbed Wyck's thigh. "It's getting better. The first day, Wyck refused to leave our room. But now, he likes going for walks in the underwater gardens."

"Oh, I need to take you there, too," I turned to Malahki. He'd seen the gardens on the screen of the entertainment unit in our room, but I couldn't wait for him to see them in person.

"Maybe we can go together after lunch?" Wyck suggested.

I smiled brightly. It felt amazing to be able to freely move around again.

A drone took our lunch orders then a robotized cart brought our food to the table. It was such a normal thing to do getting together for lunch with a group of friends. Yet I still couldn't wrap my mind around the simple fact we were now free and alive. We had reclaimed our lives to do with them as we pleased.

"What are you planning to do, now?" Svetlana asked, taking a sip of her sparkling water when we finished eating.

I glanced at Malahki. We'd spoken a little about the future while being locked in our room.

"We're considering staying here for a while," I said. "I could get a job as a space shuttle pilot. The Earth's Space Coalition has offered to help with my re-training."

Malahki took a long drink from his cup of the sweet tea imported from Ak'ae.

"I'm interested to see the underwater gardens," he said. "I've read a little about the technique they use to grow them here, and I wouldn't mind learning more about it. I may apply to work there."

"No joining the *damirian* army for you?" Vrateus smiled.

Malahki laughed, shaking his head.

"The army has never been my thing, either before or after my gender transformation. Though, I'll need to look into the local sports clubs," he added, rolling his massive shoulders back. "These muscles need to be worked out, and I'd rather punch a bag than people if I have a choice."

"Well..." Nadia cleared her throat, looking like she had something important to say. She took a brief pause, waiting until all attention was on her. "You certainly can have jobs if you want to, but it looks like neither of us may have to work for a living anymore."

"What do you mean?" I blinked at her.

All of us stared at her in question. Except for Wyck, who had a knowing smile playing on his full lips.

She clasped her hands on the table.

"I've been going through the videos I brought with me. There's some really good footage there, of all of us and our life on the Dark Anomaly. I want to put it all into a film, a documentary of sorts." She scanned our faces, tentatively, as if trying to gauge our reaction.

"You'll get to do your movie after all!" I felt my face stretch into a wide smile as excitement for her spread through my chest.

"I'm thinking about it." Nadia nodded. "But it would have a personal feel rather than scientific. Sort of a look at our entire adventure from the point of view of someone being there. Traveling to the Dark Anomaly, landing, surviving on it, and finally escaping it."

"It'd be neat to see it now that we're safely out of there," Svetlana mused.

"Well, a lot of people would like to see it, actually. The public interest is there." Nadia gestured downstairs, to the crowds of reporters we thankfully couldn't see from here. "So much interest, that I already have several huge companies wanting to buy the rights. They're offering a lot of money."

"Wow. This is amazing, Nadia." I gasped.

She shook her head.

"The most important thing for me is to have all of the people—those who passed and those still living—represented properly and with respect. I will be obtaining the permission of the families of our deceased crew. Also, if any one of you is uncomfortable with the idea of making this public, I'm not going to do it."

Nadia was not a stranger. As someone who'd lived through the experiences she wanted to depict in the movie, she was the one I trusted to tell the truth without sensationalizing it or exploiting her subjects.

"You have my permission," I said. "I trust you."

"Thank you," she replied. "We'll talk about all of it in more detail of course. I'll show the footage to all of you, too, whenever you think you may be ready to watch it."

"Are you planning to stay here on Omphi, too?" Malahki asked.

"Well..." She glanced at Wyck. "We may do a trip to Hexol, first. To see Wyck's home world."

"The crew of the *errock* ship that found Vrateus and me invited me to Hexol," Wyck explained. "I'd love to see the world I came from."

"We'll just have to decide whether we'll do it before or after the baby is born," Nadia added.

"How is the baby doing?" I asked.

"Oh, he's great!" She leaned over the table, showing me a 3D picture on her communication device. "Just look at his cute little face," she cooed.

"He is adorable," I agreed, admiring the tiny being, still shaped very much like a bean, with skinny legs and arms. The baby looked so defenceless and vulnerable, his survival appeared a true miracle after everything his mother had gone through.

"He is so big," Nadia gushed excitedly. "The doctor already told me to get ready for a C-section. There's no way I'd be able to deliver him any other way."

"It will be fine." Wyck kissed her face.

"I know." She beamed at him.

The dark worry I'd seen in her eyes before was gone. Now, there was just hope and pure happiness.

"How about you?" she asked Vrateus and Svetlana. "What are your plans?"

"In terms of babies, you mean?" Svetlana smiled, shooting a glance at Vrateus. "We've enquired about it, and apparently interspecies pregnancies are now much more common than ever before. There have been a number of children born to *themul*-human couples. I've heard *damirian*-human babies have happened, too." She winked at me.

Malahki squeezed my hand, and I smiled. We hadn't talked about starting a family yet, but it was wonderful to have that possibility in the future—now, that we had a future.

"We want to do something else first, though," Svetlana continued. "We've been able to find the exact location that's marked here."

Lifting her hand, she gently traced the tattoos above Vrateus's pointy ear. Strings of numbers and symbols decorated the skin on his scalp below the wide stripe of long fur in the middle of his head.

"The captain's tattoos?" Wyck lifted both of his eyebrow ridges with the question.

Vrateus took Svetlana's hand and placed a kiss on it.

"My tattoos are the names of the home port and the ship of my family," he explained to us. "The location of the town I hail from."

"Do you want to find your relatives? The descendants of your family?" Malahki asked.

"No, that wouldn't be possible. Thousands of years ago, *themul* lived and travelled in clans. My entire family was on the ship when it crashed. They were merchants, but..." Vrateus frowned. "Like many others who ended up on the Dark Anomaly, they weren't always on the right side of the law. My family were smugglers."

"So," Svetlana blurted out excitedly. "We want to find some of what they smuggled."

"How?" Nadia asked.

"Ooh." I gasped. "You're going treasure hunting?"

Svetlana beamed, and Vrateus gazed at her adoringly.

With a glance over her shoulder, as if concerned about being overheard by anyone outside of our circle, she leaned over the table, bringing all of us closer, too.

"I did some research into this while being transported to Omphi," she said.

"Of course you did!" I laughed. "It wouldn't be like you to just relax and do nothing."

The busy brain of this woman wouldn't rest, even for a day.

She shrugged apologetically.

"I tend to always be thinking about something," she admitted. "Anyway. Vrateus's clan was fairly well known in their time. However, not much information remained about them. Vrateus has read everything he managed to recover from their ship. We're going to follow some of their routes and revisit the stops they'd made, starting from their home port." She glanced at Vrateus's tattoos again.

"It sounds so exciting." Nadia gushed, her eyes lit up.

"A real adventure," Wyck agreed.

"What will you do if you find something?" Malahki asked.

"It depends on what it is," Vrateus replied. "By the law of the Federation, the finders are entitled to keep any treasure if it was lost or stolen longer than a thousand years ago."

"So, we'll keep it!" Svetlana announced. "Unless it happens to have some historical significance, then we'll donate it of course."

My device bracelet vibrated with an incoming message. While Vrateus and Svetlana continued to discuss their plans with the others and answer their questions, I quickly scrolled through the message.

"What is it, my love?" Malahki asked me, no doubt noticing that my expression had changed.

"My family..." I inhaled a shuddered breath, pressing my hand to my mouth as tears started to gather in my eyes again.

The conversation around us stopped, and I realized everyone's eyes were on me.

"Here," I said, pressing the audio button. I didn't trust my voice to read it out loud. "Just...listen."

"Dear Valya," the mechanical voice read in Universal. *"I've never met you, but I've heard a lot about you from my parents and my sisters. As children, we often watched videos of you playing with them, and I always wished I was born before you left, so I could be in those videos, too.*

"The hope of seeing you again one day always lived in our family. I wish our parents were still alive when we got the amazing news that you had been found, alive and well.

"Mom and Dad lived long and happy lives. They got to meet their eight grandchildren and six of their great grandchildren. We are a large but close-knit family, and you will always be a part of us, Valya, no matter where you are.

"My sisters agreed to let me write to you first because I never had the chance to meet you in person. Well, now I have the real hope that I will get to meet you one day.

"Sincerely,

"Your niece Valentina."

"She has your name," Nadia whispered in the silence that followed.

I nodded, unable to speak through the tightness in my throat. My brother and I weren't close. Learning that he'd missed me, enough to name his third daughter after me, wracked me with regret. I wished I'd tried to be closer with my only sibling. I couldn't even remember if I'd told him I loved him the day I left Earth. I didn't recall when was the last time he'd told me he loved me, either.

At the same time, I was happy he lived the life he wanted. And I felt grateful he remembered me and kept the memory of me alive in his children. One day, I would share the memories of him with my children, too.

Malahki brushed away the tears from my face, bringing me out of my thoughts.

"I guess we're going to Earth for a visit, now?" He grinned.

"Really?" I blinked at him, smiling through tears. "You would do it? You would go to Earth to visit my family with me?"

He drew me closer for a quick kiss. "Of course, my love. Where you go, I go, remember? For the rest of my life."

Svetlana straightened in her seat with a deep breath.

"Wherever life will take us, please let's stay in touch," she said, her gaze sweeping over all of us at the table.

"We need to make it a regular thing," Nadia suggested, linking her hands with Wyck on one side and with Vrateus on the other. "Let's get together for lunch, every year. No matter where we are, let's make it happen."

Holding Malahki's hand in one of mine, I took Wyck's in the other. Svetlana gripped the hands of the men on either side of her—Vrateus's and Malahki's—closing the circle.

"No matter where we are," she said.

"No matter where we are," the rest of us echoed in unison, sealing the vow.

The Dark Anomaly might no longer be there, its disk gone, its field dying a slow death by dissipating into space, but the bond we'd formed by surviving it was stronger than ever.

Nothing was going to make us drift apart anymore. No matter where we were.

Thank you

Thank you for staying with me through the darkness of the Dark
Anomaly trilogy and for trusting me to lead you all the way to the
happy ending.
I hope you enjoyed the journey.
Your reviews are always deeply appreciated.

EXPERIMENT

"Isabella Bruno." The man in a dark suit wasn't asking. Staring at me from the other side of the front entrance as I held the door open, he stated my name confidently, as if he already knew it was me.

"How can I help you?" I asked cautiously, glancing at the two others behind him. The large, black vehicles parked at the curb in front of our house did not put my mind at ease either.

"Michael Trevin." He offered me his hand. "May we come in?"

"Trevin?" I stared at him in shock, ignoring his hand. "The Michael Trevin?" I asked, dumbfounded, even as I had already recognized the face of one of the three North American representatives in the coalition of Earth Governments. "You're here? In Deer Rock?"

The fact that someone so high up in the government personally visited our small town—far up North on the territory that used to be Canada before the three countries of the continent had been merged into one—should be a huge event.

Had his visit been made public? How had I missed the news? And why was he at my house?

"Can we come in?" he asked more persistently, moving forward, which forced me to step back.

"Um, sure," I mumbled, as if my permission meant anything at that point—all three had entered our small hallway.

I smoothed my hair quickly and brushed my palms down my t-shirt, feeling painfully underdressed in my pajama pants. It was mid-morning on a weekday, but I had an evening shift at the store today and hadn't changed yet. Luckily, I had at least put a bra on.

"Who is it, Bella?" Mom came out of the kitchen, bouncing Lily, one of my sister's twins, on her hip. "Mister Trevin . . ." She stared at the representative, her eyes opened wide, her mouth agape. "In my house?"

"Mrs Bruno." He shook her hand energetically. "Where would be the best place for us to have a quick talk?" Without waiting for an answer, he shoved past her and into our kitchen. His escort followed.

"Um . . . About what?" Mom hurried after them. "Would you like anything? Tea? Water?"

"We don't have much time." Trevin pulled a chair from the table and sat down. "Secretary Carter. Agent Miller." He gestured at the two men accompanying him as they took seats at the table too.

"What is it all about?" Mom moved her gaze from one man to another. Both her and I remained standing.

"We are here to collect Isabella Bruno," Miller blurted out, earning a stern glare from Trevin.

"Me?" I stepped into the kitchen from the entrance where I had been standing.

Surely this was some kind of misunderstanding.

"What did she do?" Mom sent me a questioning stare.

"Before I explain," Trevin raised a hand in a calming gesture, "allow me to remind you that although our coalition is the main human governing body on the planet, it has been under the jurisdiction of the planet Keala for the past nine years. The extraterrestrials have left us to administer our population, but the Kealan laws take precedence over ours."

The aliens had come to Earth suddenly one day. Several giant flying saucers had hovered over a few major cities, and it didn't take long for them to make it clear they did not come in peace.

All military attempts by the coalition to attack the spaceships resulted in the immediate annihilation of our aircraft and missiles.

Then they attacked us. Entire populations of several towns and small cities around the world were eradicated within minutes when bright rays of light had descended from the ships. All structures, machines, and animals were left intact. However, the people in those places were turned to dust in seconds—white ash all that remained.

Human capitulation came right after the aliens threatened to annihilate the entire population of Earth in the same fashion if we didn't surrender.

As Trevin pointed out, the Kealans left the coalition in charge of Earth's administration, not getting involved much in our politics or our way of life. They built two facilities, one on each of Earth's poles, and implemented mandatory annual medical evaluations for all humans aged eighteen to sixty.

Other than that, it was easy to forget with time that Earth had been conquered at all.

"Please take a seat, Isabella." Trevin's stare carried a power I found myself unable to disobey. I sat at the table across from him, folding my hands over the large red strawberries printed on the plastic tablecloth. "About a week ago, the coalition received a request from the Kealans. They demanded you be handed over to them."

"Me?" I repeated, stunned, a fog of confusion and denial settled over my brain. "There must be some mistake . . ."

"No mistake. They want you," Miller bit off.

Trevin leaned in, resting his hands on the table. "We were able to negotiate some time to discuss the situation last week. However, this morning, their request was made urgent—" A sudden thought appeared to flash through his mind. "When was your last medical examination?"

"Yesterday," I replied, clutching my hands tight. "What do they want with me?"

The exams were done by the local doctor, for free and with no known health consequences observed. Alien robot-drones delivered the test kits and collected the data obtained. After nine years, the global medical exams had become the norm. By now, hardly anyone questioned it, begrudgingly accepting having to go see the doctor once a year as something that had to be done—kind of like renewing one's driver's licence, or filing taxes.

"You had one done yesterday?" Trevin exchanged a knowing look with the other men at the table. "That may explain the urgency."

"How?" Even more perplexed, I moved my gaze from one face to another. "What do they want?" I asked again, since no one had answered me the first time.

"Well." Trevin leaned against the back of his chair, stretching his neck and obviously stalling his answer.

"Your current physical state may be of some importance to them," Carter joined in.

"What do you mean? When will I be able to come home?"

Carter glanced at Trevin. Something in the expressions of the two sent a chill of trepidation down my spine.

"I will come back, won't I?" I insisted, louder.

"The extraterrestrials offered you Kealan citizenship. Through marriage." Trevin shifted in his chair, making it squeak. "To that extent, they also agreed to honour our traditions and have a proper wedding ceremony—"

"What wedding?" both Mom and I said at once.

Rolling his eyes to the ceiling, Miller leaned back in his chair and crossed his arms over his chest. "Yours," he explained, with a dramatic sigh of exasperation. "The aliens want one of them to marry you."

"Which is a good thing when you think about it," Carter rushed in. "It could be presented as a gesture of good will—"

"Presented to whom?" I jumped from my seat. All of it stopped making any sense whatsoever. "What are you all talking about? I'm not going anywhere. I'm perfectly fine where I am. Why would the aliens want me anyway? I've never met them and don't want to."

I'd watched the news broadcast of the few official visits of the Kealans with the coalition. The images of their tall figures, draped in black cloaks, hoods drawn low over their faces, left an unpleasant impression on me, bringing the Grim Reaper to mind.

"And . . . a wedding? Really?" I wrung my hands, pacing in front of the table, as if moving could help me wrap my mind around all of this.

"Miss Bruno . . ." Carter jumped out of his seat, too.

"This is just stupid!" Skipping down the stairs, my sister, Mary, barged into the room, her son Luca under her arm. "His diaper is changed." She handed Luca to my mom, who put him on her other hip, opposite to his twin. "Honestly, guys." Hands propped on the tabletop, Mary stared down Trevin and his escort. Less than two years younger than me, she had always been the more assertive and outspoken one. "Just listen to you! An alien wedding? What the hell are you talking about? Is this some kind of a joke for reality TV or something?"

"It will be televised," Carter announced, brightly. "The preparations for the event have been in full swing since the initial demand was received."

"Even before I was notified?" I muttered, wishing I could just wake up and stop this nightmare.

"And who are you?" Mary threw at Carter sarcastically, one corner of her mouth lifting up. "The wedding planner?"

"Ma'am." Miller rose from the table and moved on to my sister. "It's imperative we deliver Isabella Bruno—"

"What do you mean by 'deliver?'" Mary scoffed. "Bella is a free woman, she has rights—"

"Exactly," Mom stepped in, balancing the twins on each hip. "You can't just come in here and take her—"

"You're forgetting that none of us are free, miss." Trevin got up, shoving the chair back with a screeching noise, his jaw muscles flexed. "Not since the capitulation to the Kealans nine years ago."

"We have orders to take your sister." Miller crossed his arms over his chest. "Your permission is not required."

"I don't want to go." Dread slithered up my spine, cold and sticky. "My home is here. My job. I have a life . . . I—"

"Isabella." Trevin took a step my way.

"No." I glared at him.

"She is not going anywhere," Mary insisted stubbornly.

"This is all definitely way too fast." Moving her gaze across the room, Mom appeared completely lost. "Why all this rush? Who is this man . . . um, this alien, who wants to marry her? Why? Does he like her? They've never met . . ."

"Like?" Miller grimaced. "What does that have to do with anything?"

The front door opened with a knock.

"Bell? Are you home?" I heard the familiar voice of Johnny, my boyfriend of four years.

Mom bounced on her heels to calm the twins who started fussing. "What I'm saying is that this is not a proper way to ask someone to marry you," she argued with Miller.

Trevin pinched the bridge of his nose. "You're missing the point, ma'am. We are not the ones who make demands here."

"Who is getting married?" Johnny walked in, tossing back his shoulder-length blond hair, some of which perpetually hung over his face.

"The freaking aliens are planning a wedding with Bella!" Mary blurted out, gesturing at Miller and Trevin, as if they were the aliens in question.

"Mary . . ." I exhaled, feeling like my knees were about to give out, a pounding headache threatened to set in.

Johnny moved a confused glance from her to Miller then finally to me. "Is that true?"

"We don't have much time." Trevin ignored him. "The flight to Capital City will take at least two hours. With the ceremony scheduled for tonight, the team will have to start getting you ready soon."

Ready . . .

Ready for what? The wedding?

Tonight?

My heart skipped at the realization that all of this was real after all. Fear settled heavily in my chest, threatening to turn into panic.

"How will you ever get anyone ready to marry some alien dude?" Mary yelled at the three. "No matter how much time you have. Who the hell is he anyway?"

"We have not been given the groom's identity," Trevin replied coolly.

"Mary is right, though." Mom shook her head. "This is insane."

"Your family will be well compensated, of course," Carter started.

"This is not about money!" Mary snapped.

"Her dad is in the hospital," my mom muttered softly, shifting her pleading gaze from one of the men to another. "At the very least, you need to let her say goodbye . . . Why this rush?" she groaned.

"Johnny . . ." I grabbed my boyfriend by the arm and shoved him into the hallway, desperate to get away from it all, to shut the noise out, to get some time to do something . . . Anything.

"Is it true what they're saying, Bell?" Johnny asked as I dragged him around the corner and out of everyone's sight. "Are those SUV's outside theirs? And is that Michael Trevin, for real?"

"Miss Bruno!" Miller's voice thundered behind me.

"A minute, please. Give me one freaking minute!" I yelled back. "Johnny." I whispered quickly, panic vibrating through me. "This can't be happening . . ."

"Do they really want you to marry an alien?"

"Apparently, it's the aliens who want this. Johnny." Gripping his shoulders, I gave him a shake. "Please, help me. Let's run."

There was no way I was going to return to that kitchen where they all waited for me.

Until this morning, I'd been a regular small-town girl, working in a convenience store since I graduated high school eight years ago. With my oldest brother in and out of jail for the past several years and my father in and out of hospitals with his ailing heart and lungs, I had been helping my mom with my four younger brothers who were still in grade school and more recently, with Mary's ten-month-old twins.

My plans for the future had mostly included marrying Johnny—whenever he saved up enough money to buy me a ring and asked me to be his wife—and eventually starting a family.

It was not a glorious life, but it was my life, and I was content, living right here in Deer Rock, where I knew everybody and everyone knew me from the day I was born.

This whole thing now felt surreal and terrifying.

"Get me out of here, please," I whispered, not sure myself how that could be accomplished or where I could run to. I just needed to be far away from here. "I'm not going with them. I need to hide."

"Bell." His hesitant expression broke my heart. "You know their drones can find you by your DNA?"

I knew—that was how the Kealans traced those who tried to evade the medical testing—but I couldn't think rationally at that point.

"We'll hide in a cave, somewhere, where the drones can't fly?" My voice dropped, however, as did the hope in my heart. "I can't do this, Johnny . . ."

"Maybe just for a little while?" he suggested.

"What?" I stared at him in disbelief. "You actually want me to go with them?"

"Tony should be out next month," he spoke quickly. "I'm sure your brother will think of something."

Tony—my oldest brother and Johnny's idol since we were little—always came up with something. I wished he were here. Unfortunately, Tony's ingenuity had been wasted on raiding gas stations and convenience stores, which had put him in jail for the second time in his twenty-nine years.

"Together, we will find a way to get you out later," Johnny promised.

"It means I'll have to go with them now," I whispered, every fibre of my being refusing to accept the idea of that.

"Listen," he said soothingly, stroking my arms, but his gaze flickered to the wall behind me as he refused to meet my eyes. "If they want you . . ."

"Then you don't?" I snapped.

"No, it's not that. Just, you know, they always get their way . . ."

"Johnny. Are you afraid of them, too?" I stepped back, not wanting to believe the obvious, but feeling completely alone already. "Are you breaking up with me?"

"There is going to be a wedding, Bell," he sounded apologetic. "I don't want you to end up feeling guilty over what may come afterwards."

"Are you kidding me?" My throat tightened painfully, and I brought my hand to it.

"I just want to make it easier for you," he continued in a rush. "No matter what, I won't see it as cheating on your part. Okay?"

"I can't believe it!" With a sob, I shrunk further away from him, feeling both ashamed and disgusted.

He reached for me. "You know we don't have a choice—"

"Isabella, it's time." Trevin walked out of the kitchen, his voice firm.

Breathing hard, I backed away from both of them, moving to the front door.

"Miss Bruno . . ." Miller came from around Trevin, but I was no longer listening to whatever either of them had to say.

Twisting around, I dashed for the exit.

"You go, sis!" Mary cheered from the kitchen just as one of the twins started crying.

Shoving at the front door with my shoulder, I ran outside, without having any idea where I was going. Panic overtook me, propelling me to sprint as far away from this place as possible, away from the men in suits.

"Miss Bruno!" The doors of one of the black vehicles in front of our house flew open, and two men in black uniforms leaped out. They cut me off and tackled me to the ground in our front yard.

"Quickly, in the van with her," Miller bit out the command, catching up with us.

"Let me go!" I screamed, fighting against the hands lifting me off the ground. "I don't want this! I'm not going!"

The last I saw before they shoved me in and shut the doors were the pale faces of my family standing in the doorway of the house where I grew up.

My sister, comforting Lily in her arms. My mom, her hand over her mouth, Luca crawling at her feet. The thought of Tony and my dad flashed through my brain. The images of my little brothers who would come home from school that afternoon and find me gone.

I never got a chance to say a proper goodbye to any of them.

AVAILABLE NOW

More by Marina Simcoe

PARANORMAL ROMANCE

Madame Tan's Freakshow (The World of River of Mists)
Call of Water
Madness of the Moon
Power of Rage

Demons Series (Complete)
Demon Mine
The Forgotten
Grand Master
The Last Unforgiven - Cursed
The Last Unforgiven - Freed

Stand Alone Novels Set in Demons World
The Real Thing
To Love A Monster

Midnight Coven Author Group
Wicked Warlock (Cursed Coven)

SCIENCE-FICTION ROMANCE

Dark Anomaly Trilogy (Complete)
Gravity
Power
Explosion

My Holiday Tails
Married To Krampus
My Tiny Giant

Standalone Novels
Experiment
Enduring (Valos Of Sonhadra)

About the Author

MARINA SIMCOE LIKES to write love stories with characters, who may or may not be entirely human, because she firmly believes that our contemporary world could always use a little bit of the extraordinary.

She has lots of fun exploring how her out-of-this-world characters with their own beliefs, values, and aspirations fit into our everyday life.

She lives in Canada with her very own captain, their three little offspring, and a cat, who is definitely out of this world.

For more illustrations of all of her books please visit Marina Simcoe Author page on Facebook or www.marinasimcoe.com.

Please Stay in Touch

Newsletter signup:

Facebook Readers' Group: Marina's Reading Cave
www.instagram.com/marinasimcoeauthor
www.marinasimcoe.com
www.facebook.com/MarinaSimcoeAuthor/
www.amazon.com/author/marinasimcoe
www.bookbub.com/profile/marina-simcoe
www.goodreads.com/MarinaSimcoe
TikTok: Marina.Simcoe